I0671792

# The Last American Housewife

*pieces of a marriage*

**Eleanore Hill**

A BETA BOOK

The Last American Housewife © copyright 2014
Beta Books Eleanore Hill
ISBN 978-0-930012-20-5

www.eleanorehill.com

The Marty Trilogy by Eleanore Hill

*The Family Secret: A Personal Account of Incest*
*The Last American Housewife*
*Period Pieces*

also
*How to Cook for Your Dog*

Beta Books is an imprint of Mudborn Press
www.betabooks.us

## *Eachother*

Happy families are all alike; every unhappy
family is unhappy in its own way
—*Leo Tolstoy*

This story of two decades of a marriage documents a catalog of
changes accepted and changes refused, between two people who
grew up in the Forties and Fifties. By the Seventies, the world had
changed and so had they. And so had the marriage.

The uncommon word *eachother* is the main topic of this book—
the relationship of two people in which every action or thought,
whether expressed or not, affects the partner. *Eachother* is precious
when it works, treacherous when both feel trapped with the other.

# Contents

## TEN YEARS

# *Introduction*

Marty and Alex are no Romeo and Juliet, though they both come from very different family backgrounds, both dysfunctional. As author Eleanore Hill weaves their story over a fifteen year period, they are more like Taylor and Burton, loving and hating each other with equal passion and vehemence. Early on in the book, Alex says, "We were meant to be, without joy, 'like a man sentenced to the rope.' " He is from a privileged, abusive background, while she is from the other side of the tracks, self-sacrificing to his demands, but not without penalty and a bitter mouth. They do "ordinary things," like have breakfast together, make passionate love, go on errands, have dinner, have babies, raise them, and in between all of life's dailyness they spar like duelists from another century, or as Hill says, "like two mad dogs, and then get on with life." Theirs could be many a marriage in the turbulent 60's, when the Women's Liberation Movement was heating up, but Marty doesn't like to see him unhappy. She gives in. "I cannot rise above my role as wife," she confesses. Thus, the book title.

Hill's novel moves at a frantic, page-turning pace, capturing the tension and push pull of their relationship, organized in three sections like a play: The Beginning, Ten Years, and Fifteen Years. Each division is developed in several small scenes, all titled as poems might be, signposts for the action and trouble ahead. Hill is a master storyteller, making fifteen years pass in a flash, like it does when any of us look back. Also outstanding is how we feel trapped with them, her ability to climb inside her characters with such detail and intimacy, it feels like you are watching a film until she finally succeeds at what she plans all along, her escape from Alex's cruelties and her inability to think of herself as "real," a woman unto herself deserving of moving on with her life.

—*Perie Longo*

# The Attachment

I look out the windows and see Alex, or the impression of Alex, blue shirt, blond hair, brown janitor pants, and he is twisting some bolt on his giant pipe submarine trailer. I want to laugh at his belief in himself and at the same time I want to cringe from his strength, or weakness, or whatever it is that allows him to plow forward and make headway no matter what.

Sometimes he sits where he can't see me, on the other side of the fireplace, to put on his shoes, to keep the distance and silence going. If I peek I can see his lips moving as he escapes the present with a conversation with himself. And I am always lonely when I have made him that angry. When he refuses hotcakes and goes out alone to town saying he'll eat out. And he goes while I stand behind the curtain in disbelief because he used to be bigger than I was.

I watch him drive away and know that in his head, the blond head I see through the windshield is a kind of leadership I miss when he withdraws it. And the vacuum is in his ego. Because he fixed it. And I'm afraid to turn around and prepare the house for his return by vacuuming for fear of breaking his handiwork and being subject to his version of why I break things.

His absence shows me the resentment he feels for me when I make him the structure in which I can perform. He senses and I have told him, "Just stay in place, don't rock your position as provider." And once he wept. One night. One or two tears for the dead friendship. Not because he wanted to embrace it and have it, but because it was the way it was and that was sad.

Instead of vacuuming in preparation for his return, I go to the mirror and brush my hair and I see that I am caught with a hair style and a whole life style that is based on Alex's support. And all the while I had believed that I had remained prepared to live without him. That we were living side by side independently. Now I see that I have a happy hair style that needs time to groom, that needs curlers that he can buy for me. And in his absence I want to pull back long serious hair into a bun and mourn.

I think of getting hurt and of him coming to me. And I remember my grandmother, forty years divorced from my grandfather remarking that when he died, she heard rumors that he whispered her name on his death bed. And I am ashamed that I have not risen above the same fantasy.

Somewhere up ahead in my future, I see myself abandoned and looking out for myself and never recovering from the drudgery of it. I look at the two new scars on the back of my hand and know they will be with me as brown spots in my old age. While I am looking at my hands in the quietness of the empty house, I find all the jagged minute pieces of cuticle and proceed to bite them off, but I give up after awhile and do not look because I cannot get them down to nothing.

I listen and wait for the sound of his car and realize I have been left with nothing. Not even any more summers because the sun has already harmed me in the past. Only the sound of "ma'am" echoing in my ears.

The wind begins to blow and because I know what it could do to me if I did not have a home, a wall to hide behind, I stay inside my kitchen and begin to put on pots of water for stew and coffee and to mix up bowls of dough for cookies and bread. I begin to create *home* even more, reassuring myself.

My right arm serves me, hardening perpetually for beating dough, and softening for dialing the phone. I am thankful and conscious of my right arm being under my command, obedient, efficient, accurate, as if it is a servant. And I want to pray for it.

After awhile, I lay down on the couch and above me is the one-ton beam which has separated me from Alex because in his mind he is *hero* for putting it in place all by himself and I have not done anything equivalent to that to neutralize his heroism and make us equal again, even though he used me as ballast to erect the beam. I hung from one end to steady it as he hoisted it in place with his A-frame winch.

---

*Matriarchal Advice*

*Mama said:*

*"Go to bed when your husband goes to bed. Don't let him go to bed alone or he might look for another woman. He needs you."*

*One grandmother said:*

*"Never put pepper in food you cook for your husband; it irritates the stomach lining, and he is the only machine you have. Don't break your man."*

---

# The Equalizer

He was due home early in the evening, so she kept creating scenes for him to walk in to. One was at the table with the kids. When he didn't come and that passed, she got behind the ironing board and looked busy. That one passed too, and still he didn't come.

Marty didn't want to be caught on the floor doing her exercises, "playing with the flesh," as he called it, but the evening was passing and it looked as if he would be late, so she took off her slacks, kneeled on the floor and began doing pushups. Alex opened the door and saw her there in her underpants and t-shirt.

A tugging began inside of her as soon as he stepped inside. Alex threw his coat over the couch. She wanted everything from him. He put his hat beside his coat and said, "Well, what's new?" She could think of nothing. She wanted to tell him too much. He went into the kitchen and got a drink of water, came out, lit a cigarette and sank into his soft chair and said again, "Well, what's new. Anything?" His eyes were on the television screen. The sound was turned down and the ten PM newscaster spoke without being heard. "Turn it up," he said, leaning forward to hear it. She crawled on her knees over to it and turned it up. Her body without clothes or with them meant nothing to him with the news on. She lay flat on her back and did eighty leg raises. He sucked down the first cigarette, crushed its filter and let another and began sucking that one down.

Perspiration burst out on her nose and lip. She wiped it off with the tail of her t-shirt. She wanted to run to him and leap into his lap and hug him. Smoke drifted over to her and she sucked it into her lungs as her breathing deepened. She stood up and ran five hundred steps in place, counting on one leg. She had rushed to him before and hugged him. About a week ago. And he had kissed her. But it was no big thing. They could hug and kiss or stay apart. It was all the same. They had gone for days apart and then spent each hour of many days together, and it was all the same. There prevailed a presence between them, a third thing that the two of them were by merely existing together.

The news went off, and when the commercial came on loudly, he asked above it, "Nothing new, huh?"

She turned the TV sound down again and stood on her head against the door, which he had just entered, to balance herself. Her face filled with blood and she said, "There must be something. Oh yes, Miss Lear called about the new music lessons starting Friday. She was chatty and talked about her classes." Marty's lip began to go numb with pressure. She counted by a series of movements of her tongue, but did not know which number she was on. She could tell by the feel of her body and her tongue if it was getting close to two hundred. She liked the way her legs looked upside-down. The thigh muscle looked lean, hanging back the wrong way and her blue shin veins did not bulge. She kicked down and turned red-faced to him. "Let me see. There was something else, too. Oh, I know. Pat and June want to know if we can come over for drinks Tuesday night. I hope we can?"

She had broken her silence, the silence she goes into when he's not around. She sat before him on the floor and willingly breathed his smoke and told him everything she could think of. Relaxation came to her chest and her stomach and she gained momentum, entertained by her own speech. With him she could put in all the extra things, her feelings, because he was Alex, her husband, the man who belonged to her.

She said, "And it's true, June said she didn't have a grass-roots background, but was brought up in the tinkly glass set."

Alex raised his eyebrows.

"Tinkly glass? Now what does that mean?"

"She didn't use that word. June said 'glamorous' or something like that, but I like 'tinkly glass'."

He pretended to consider other words to himself. "Now

what would be the proper word to describe that set of people? Sophisticated, perhaps? An ache like ice went down from her chest into her belly and drew her away from him.

She said, "Sophisticated's too common. It can mean too many things. When I say tinkly glass, I mean, you know, the kind of people who stand around with little glasses of liqueur and bend their wrists, chattering and tinkling their glasses."

"Tinkling," he repeated and looked upward. "Humm." He was stabbing her and he knew it. His mother had switched his bare legs with a willow branch when he was young. "Tinkly," he laughed; but it was not a laugh. In order to protect herself, she saw them as two mated water buffalo. There was the male, braying loudest in order to intimidate his female and keep her down.

Marty went on, "Glasses *do* tinkle. Sophisticated can mean all kinds of things that have nothing to do with June."

"You know, it's not that you won't try to find better words; it's that you do this. Just this. What you're doing now, resisting any assistance to improve your speech." She felt the willow switch cutting in deeper. she turned her back on him and rocked twenty times on her stomach, grabbing her ankles from behind.

"Well, anyway, that's about all the news there is." A knot in her throat cut off her voice. She turned up the TV sound and his pale blue eyes snapped to the screen and followed the cowboys around. She bit the inside of her lip and raised up off the floor into a back-bend. She asked, "Well, how was work today?"

He did not answer for a while because the shooting was going on. When the station break came, he said, "Oh, I had lunch with a guy who was a real bug for gliders."

"Bug? Now, what is a better word for 'bug'?"

"Mmmm," he tipped his head and raised his hand as if pulling words from the air and said, "Votary, devotee…" She repeated the words, but showed that she did not recognize them. He said, "Go to your dictionary."

"Go to yours," she said. She wiped the sweat from her forehead and went to the kitchen and exhaled to rid herself of his smoke. *Dear Ann Landers*, she said, *What can I do? I'm a nonsmoker, but I have to breathe smoke anyway. What can I do?* She put water on for tea, and while she waited for it to boil, she lay her head on the sinkboard and cried. She wanted to break the toaster and the percolator and the mixer and the potted plants and to bash in the window of her oven. But it wouldn't make any difference if she did or if she didn't. She had flung a pan of scrambled eggs on the floor once, ten years ago in her new anger over him. And he had flung another pot of something on the floor saying, "Oh, you want to play this game, huh?" And then she had to clean it all up.

It was like hugging and kissing. Breaking or not breaking. It was all the same thing. To do it or not to do it left them exactly where they were when they began.

She came out sipping her cup of hot tea. She said, "I saw Bob."

"What?" he asked, narrowing his eyes at her. She did not answer because she was sipping her tea. He waited.

"When?" he asked. She kept the cup to her lips and balanced her elbows on her bare knees and kept her eyes downcast.

"I just might believe you sometime. You'd better be careful," he said and did not take his eyes from her. "Did you really?" he asked. The cowboys were yelling in the background. But he was studying her.

"What do you think?" she asked, returning his concentrated gaze.

He looked away at the TV. He began to sniff the way he sniffed when he was trying to get balance back in his mind. Strength grew in her chest and stomach. The power flowed warmly. He sniffed intermittently until his program went off, and then he said, "Well, I'm going to bed," and he left her there alone.

She thought about Bob. If she had really seen him, Alex could not have made her cry.

# An Effort at Being

At Moby Dick's, Alex is fighting for aloofness. He is regarding me with hesitant blue eyes that do not want to see what I am. Across the table from himself he sees sourness and a mouth that is only pleasant when it is smiling and it is not smiling.

He says evasive things like, "It's a beautiful day."

We look blankly at the currents riding the water and the seagulls dipping and disappearing.

I say, "A year or so ago we were here and you were talking about buying a truck; Now you got the truck."

He says, "I've had that truck over two years...." and does not look at me. He is warding off whatever I am getting at.

I say, "Why are you defensive? What do you think I'm saying?"

"I don't know," he says, not budging, remaining alone on his pinnacle and eager to avoid slipping down to where I am because he believes it is down. He's taller. If I were six feet tall and had moods, he'd look up to me, believing they were elevated thoughts.

I say, "You're missing the point. I'm saying that here we are again, not any happier and you have the truck. What next? What can you buy next to make us happy? Something bigger and better? And next year and the next? Will we be returning and sitting here wanting to buy something else thinking that'll do it for us?"

"I've used that truck," he says with ice in his voice. "It helped build the house. I couldn't have built the house without it." He glances hungrily out the window at the beauty of the ocean and sky and hills and harbor and the whole world where there is no woman across the table from him, asking a question, presenting a sentence he cannot answer because there are no answers for her. Because she wants what she can't

16

have, to be at peace with herself and for him to give it to her as the waitress can give her a plate of eggs and hash brown potatoes.

"You missed the point," I say. "I'm glad you got the truck. I'm not complaining. I'm just saying that it didn't do it for us. The truck didn't make any difference. Here we are. Nothing is changed except that we used to enjoy having coffee together. That's the only change."

"Ah," he says, yawning and stretching or mimicking a stretch and glancing behind him with his side vision to see if there are people within hearing; And then he tries to change the subject by speaking about a program on television the night before. But I interrupt by finishing his sentence my way and claiming that the program proved all that I ever stood for.

He avoids my face and looks nowhere, turning his head toward the window, and then smoking and concentrating on the act of inhaling and flicking the ash. And even though he is my husband, I want him to look at me and like me. And because I am unlikable and cannot even like myself, I want to be liked by him even more.

"Ready?" he asks cheerfully, determined to stay out of it.

I have always jumped up when he says that, but this time I say no and go on drinking coffee, feeling guilty that he wants to go. I know he wants to go because I am unpleasant, not because he is ready to leave.

He is restless, but controlling it. We sit there awhile longer in silence and he appears to be thinking hard about us, but I know the look. He has to go to the bathroom. The hot stimulant is like clockwork.

"Well, I'll be back," he says and goes off to the bathroom.

I exchange eyes with a younger woman. She has looked at me from a booth three tables away and is leaning against her boyfriend's arm. She looks at me to see if I am looking at her. I look to see if she thinks I am worth looking at, and she looks away believing I think she is worth looking at because I looked; we want attention from eachother but do not want to give it back. To give another woman that much.

When Alex returns, we leave immediately and drive to Harbor Boat Sales.

Alex parks the truck in front of Harbor Boat Sales.

He slams the door. It is a violent sound that violates me.

I have been parked in front of boat stores before while men go in and talk about boats and motors and all the possibilities of putting a boat on water and floating around in it.

And I have waited, as men wait in front of the women's restroom, for her to get through with what a woman must do. I wait, not thinking of what he is doing in the boat store, but for him to get through with what a man must do because he's made that way.

Finally I get out and go into the boat store and look around, but I cannot see anything because I do not know what any of it means. I see colors and shapes. The merchandise is only design to me. Nothing registers, and I know that other wives would be beside their husbands, knowing what he is doing every minute. They would itemize his purchases at the boat store.

I stand beside Alex and look at the conglomeration of things he has put on the check stand. I lean against his arm and the salesman asks if we are together. And I wonder where to begin to try to understand what is going on.

# *The Switch*

We were watching an old George Raft movie. Not really watching it, it had come on and we hadn't changed the station. Alex was sipping whiskey and flipping the ash from his cigarette on the floor behind him because he had forgotten that the ash tray was on the floor near the couch.

We were sitting there naked and talking about the people we knew and what was wrong with them. He had taken off his clothes on the way to the shower. I had not finished sewing his bathrobe. And I was on my way from the shower and had left my bathrobe in the bedroom. He came to a lull in the discussion, so I said, "Well I'm going to bed. I'm dead."

I went in to turn on the heating blanket and heard the hen making a loud noise outside the bedroom window. "Alex," I called. "The hen, hurry."

He ran to the back door. "No, the front," I yelled and dashed out the door after him into the night.

"Is it a dog?" I yelled in a whisper behind him.

"Shhh," he said. "It's the raccoon." I saw Alex fumbling and thudding in the dark, moving swiftly up the street, his nude white body thrashing around a furry form. I heard the hen's sounds and then he came back and handed her to me. We took her inside and lifted her wings to see if her chest was punctured. When we saw that she was all right, Alex grabbed his flashlight and went looking for the rooster in the tree in the backyard. He wore his bathrobe.

I laid the broom across the bathtub and set the hen to roost and then pulled on his T-shirt and went out to look for the rooster too.

We could not spot him among the branches. He said, "These damn chickens. I want you to get rid of them tomorrow."

I felt like one of the people we had been talking about

then, with something wrong with me, because I had gotten
the chickens as pets.

*When Alex can't fix something, I
grow panicky and full of disgust
for him. The pool is clogged. His
solution, "to chop the pipe in half."
I feel true hate form in my throat.
I could spit. The pool man comes.
From my chaise I hear mild chugs
and gentle drippings of water as he
unplugs the equipment, and right
away I feel unplugged, free, that I can
go on awhile, until the next clogging
(when Alex will use violent phrases as
solutions).*

# The Chair

The last part of the chair is burning and he is in bed. The light is still on in the bedroom and she knows he has fallen asleep over his electronics book. She sips the coffee. She has drunk a cup so often that the taste reminds her of herself. It is a personal taste.

It was a simple oak chair. It was strong and the only one in the house that didn't creak when she leaned back in it. He had never liked the way she leaned back in chairs. She had revealed much about her character to him the first time she leaned back in a chair in front of him.

She watches the seat of the chair lying in the fire, being eaten by the low slow flames and knowing it is because she had put her two feet up in his chest and pushed him back when he came to toy with her on the floor. He had fallen against the chair, grabbed it and raised it above his head and brought it down against the floor three times. She watched the rungs fold and each stick collapse. And then he gathered them into handfuls and placed them on the grate in the fireplace. She had said, "No, don't burn them. I can glue it back together again."

She wanted the chair to hear her, out of loyalty. It was an innocent chair, and, a moment before, had been a strong chair. She did not want to watch it burn, so she drove away into the night in her car and told herself that it hadn't been crushed. She remembered it sitting there and tried to believe it was still sitting there. And then she saw it being broken and there was a broken feeling inside of her. She said, "The poor chair," and cried because it had stood there for so long watching her as she moved about the house and passed by it and dusted its little green cushion and used its back as a hand rest when she did leg raises.

Earlier in the day they had driven into town to shop and afterward they stopped at a drive-in and he bought a chocolate malt, and she refused to have one even though she wanted one. Money, calories, or because she liked to go without things? She did not know. She only knew that chocolate malts weren't necessary.

While he drove home and drank his chocolate malt, she swallowed when he swallowed and told him about a time when she was eleven. "I rode the bus into town with my dishwashing money," she said. "My father used to pay me to clean up the kitchen because my mother could never get everything off the sink board. She had no knack for it."

She looked at him but saw herself wearing her brother's Levi's and wiping off the linoleum sinkboard and liking the job of making it neat.

"So I earned about two dollars worth of change over a period of time and rode the bus into town to spend it." She saw herself getting off the bus in town, small and a bit tacky and full of the belief that if she had everything in the stores it would make her like everyone else and she would not have to be embarrassed anymore. "I felt a little guilty having the money to spend because my mother would have liked to have it for things she needed for the family. We were that poor. Do you see it? Two dollars?" She watched him pinch the chocolate malt cup closed at the top and place it carefully upright on the floor of the car.

"I was afraid I might waste it. I was torn between getting what I knew she would buy and what I really wanted. So I bought some fruit from an open market. That's what she would have done. And then I went on to the other stores looking for the right thing to buy so I wouldn't waste the money. I walked back and forth in front of the notebooks in Woolworth's and could not leave them. I wanted all of the notebooks, all of the kinds and sizes there were. Some had lines, some were plain, thick, thin, colored paper and white. I wanted enough to stack up and shift around and thumb through the corners and fan my warm upper lip with. So I bought three of the biggest and cheapest ones and carried them home on the bus in a sack next to the sack of fruit which was seeping through the bottom by then."

She looked at his profile as they drove, watching for a sign to show her that he understood what she was saying. His own lips began to move and she knew he was in his own thoughts, and was talking to himself. "Didn't you hear anything I said?" she asked in a loud voice.

"I'm listening, go on," he said without looking over at her.

"No, you're not."

"Yes I am."

"OK, then what was the last thing I said?"

" 'The fruit was soaking through the bottom of the bag.' " She was delighted.

"There had been so many things that day. I had wanted a doll carriage and a doll for my little sister so she would be like all the other little girls who had them. And I saw furniture I wished my family could have and things like that."

He looked over at her and nodded once and then got out his cigarettes and took one out of the pack with his teeth, giving a loud sniff to rid himself of the chill from the malt.

"So, anyway," she continued, eager to package the message she didn't even know herself into words and give it to him. "When my mother looked into the bags, she slammed the notebooks on the kitchen table and yelled, 'Junk'."

"I can still see her contorted face because she needed food for the baby. And I felt ashamed of myself. I knew I had made an awful mistake. I was afraid, because I hadn't been able to spend the money on what I should have. I wondered what was wrong with me that I didn't know better than to buy notebooks."

He nodded again as she finished the story and smiled a little as if she had just told him an amusing story about her youth, something dear to her.

She waited for him to say something, and when he didn't she wished she had not told him. They drove awhile in silence and she wished he would say something about poverty. She looked at his lips to see if he was talking to himself, and if he was aware that she had stopped talking. She said, "I wish I hadn't recalled that incident because it makes me uneasy to remember how pathetic it was hanging around stores wanting things and buying the wrong thing and feeling so ashamed. Damn it."

He nodded and smiled again.

"But I guess most people on earth from the beginning of time have been poor and felt shame."

He nodded, watching the traffic.

"It's the exceptions who are rich and do not go through that, don't you agree?" He did not say anything.

It was dark by the time they drove into their driveway. The house was comfortable and he began to make a fire in the fireplace, while she went to the refrigerator to look for something that would give an answer. She wanted to do something that meant something but she did not know what, so she took two pieces of bread out and buttered them and put some lettuce in between and went out for a walk in the night and looked at the stars.

He had adjusted the television while she was out and had it on with the volume too high. The coldness of the night was on her face as she entered and the warm air of the room hit her. The loudness of the television filled her too full. She pulled off her clothes and began exercising flat on her back on the floor.

He stood before the fireplace and she wanted to say to him, *So what are you going to say about what it means to you that I was poor? That I suffered. That I'll never get over the sting of that shame. That I still shop the same way?* But she would be screaming by then.

Instead, she said, "Move over so I can do my leg kicks." She said it in the voice he hates, and he came down to ease her through her bad mood, and her feet came up automatically. When she drove away, there was no place to go.

She looks at the chair seat. It is a big piece of charcoal. The tiny fire is dying on its edges. And he sleeps with the blue paperback copy of *Electronics In Everyday Things* at his fingertips. And his fingertips lay limp and sprawled. She finishes her coffee and listens to the fireplace snapping and popping gently. And then she goes to bed. He is breathing heavy. She lays on her back without a pillow and wishes the strong simple chair still sat there. She wishes he hadn't killed it.

*In the electronics store with Alex, she looks at manuals and feels abandoned. The manuals are all about electronics. There is nothing about the electronic engineer himself, and how he feels about electronics. So she enters the speaker room, is drawn to it because there is a folk song playing and the words are about the feelings, needs and awarenesses and other things that are going on inside of the singer.*

*So she sits there and hovers in the warmth of the sound, away from the manuals, as Alex looks for certain electronic parts for the TV aerial, so he can bring facts into their home, such as are in the electronic manuals; Information so he can know himself.*

# The Cycle

"Bedspreads are only ten dollars," he said, after they were awake and contemplating shopping, eating breakfast out, and doing all those things that would take them away from the grimness of the home which required too much continuous labor.

"I don't want one of those quilted ones," she said, envisioning the bedspreads on sale for ten dollars.

"Why not get a spare?" he asked.

"I'd rather get one good one instead of two cheap ones," she said. They lay in bed together thinking about it. Side by side looking at the ceiling discussing bedspreads.

She said, "Yes, one good one."

He said, "A bedspread gets dirty. It's something you use a lot and have to clean, so it'd be practical to get something inexpensive, easy to wash; you wouldn't have to worry about it getting ruined."

"I'd rather have a good one. Expensive ones last forever and wear well. I want one that doesn't show the dirt."

They turned off their electric blanket, a button on each side, and got up.

Within twenty minutes he was spraying the back of her head and all, with the yard hose, following her right up to the front door, parting the back of her hair with a stream of water and cursing her and calling her a spoiler. A destroyer.

In the house, drying herself with a towel, crying a little, but wanting to laugh, she knew it was all exterior. Getting wet. It didn't matter. The real worry, her vital concern, was that she was getting old and even after a shower that morning, when she felt so fresh, so clean, so renewed, she saw an old, tired worn out face in the mirror. A face concerned about bedspreads, caring what was thrown over the bed, as if it mattered.

So when she had to sit in the car and wait while he tried to water the yard; in five minutes, before they left, she could not like him. She sat, knowing she was getting old even though she had sat and waited for him before, patiently over the years. It was all without reward. So she could not be patient anymore. She could not wait. There was no time for her to waste while he watered.

She had gotten out and said she had things to do, too. He said, "I'm coming, just a minute," and went by her with the hose on his way to hang it up, but he saw her face.

"I'm not going," she said, And that was when he thought she was a spoiler.

For the rest of the day they are as skitterish as two enemies in a woods. He appears from behind a piece of furniture and she dodges behind one. He startles her, coming right toward her, in her path. She looks up in fear and bewilderment, but he goes by on his way to something else.

Later, she goes out the door in his direction in the back yard, and he glances up, keyed, ready, but she veers off and goes into the garage on some duty.

All day they keep it up; they never end it. At the end of the day, he goes off to work and it has ended for them. They cannot untangle themselves from the woods, once they are in it anymore. Now they are surviving separately.

They are back in bed the next morning together. It is a new day and a new chance to go out and buy a new bedspread. Their teeth are showing in smiles again. And their diaphragms are tightening in laughter for the first time since the morning before.

She says, "I needed to wash my hair anyway." They are weary from the tension of not liking eachother for twenty-four hours.

They hug and she says, "It took us that long just to be able to like eachother again," and laughs.

He says, "What'd you mean? I didn't dislike you. I just didn't think about you at all. You may have disliked me, though."

She protests at his accusation, and they can see the woods looming within view again.

# When She Was Tired,
# She was Very, Very Tired

There is nothing she wants to eat but she opens the refrigerator and looks anyway hoping she will see something that will make her hungry. There is no one she wants to see and nothing she wants to do. She goes over it in her mind. She sees the names of their friends spelled out in her mind's eye and no craving for any of them begins. She thinks of buying a new pair of boots, learning to fly, packing a box for Alfa school, meeting someone who is like she would like to be. None of them appeal to her because she is too weary to take anything on.

She is tired of trying to hold her own with a world that wants her to know her place. She is exhausted with trying to know what it is saying and making something of it. She is tired of giving up the things she can do easily and doing with effort the things it wants her to do.

She is tired of fearing being embarrassed and of guarding herself, of being inadequate so she will not be caught making a mistake and appearing inadequate for real.

She is tired of days when they are driving in the car and he is saying, "You have sucked the life out of me until there is nothing left." It is it after she has mentioned a blonde he looked at as she passed. And he means, "Nothing left to give another woman."

She is tired of being jealous and of being bothered by these women, and of hearing him say, "That is all you can talk about, other women," of her heart leaping with adrenalin when she realizes that she has started it again, and he is going on, "And you can't even judge… these cheap blondes. God, why can't you be jealous of someone who warrants it at least. How come you're not jealous of someone of quality… like Jeannie?"

She is tired of meeting his crescendo with her own, of matching madness for madness with, "Because I'm like Jeannie. It' s the cheap flat-chested blondes with high cheekbones who look like whores whose praises you shitty men sing." She's tired of swallowing about then and getting a second wind and going on, "I know about the Jeannies. But I don't know about the women you men snap your heads off for when they pass by. The blondes, the bony-assed blondes."

She is tired of him punching his fist into the wind wing trying to get it open if it doesn't come easily. Of fearing that he'll bust it out and then blame her for making him that angry.

She is tired of fearing his larger muscles. She is tired of wanting to take Karate, and never getting around to it.

After they have settled the subject of blondes for the time being, she is tired of telling him that she is tired of hearing him blame the world for his unsuccess. Of telling him that everyone get's the same treatment and that he didn't get screwed any worse than anyone else and to cheer up.

She is tired of him yelling back that, "I'm too busy to cheer up. Too busy making the most of it to be cheerful. Too busy making up for shortcomings, too busy getting ahead and dragging you all the way."

She is tired of saying that she doesn't want to get ahead, of energizing her words with wave upon wave of anger. She is tired of discovering that she has more capacity for anger than for anything else anymore.

"You want it. *All* of it, a bigger house, more clothes, money for trips, a new car." She is tired of hearing it. Of him saying it.

"I've never asked you for any of those things. *You're* the one who wants them. I'd make do with anything. You're the leader." She is tired of feeling so basic and humble that she isn't interested in climbing.

She is tired of telling him that she doesn't push him and of listening to him explain that she insinuates it. "You keep hinting."

She is tired of trying to make her voice sound calm and rational and delve behind it all with a touch of psychology.

"Well, of course. It's just understood. It's human nature to want *the good life*, but I never tell you to do anything specific."

And of hearing him say, "You tell me specifically that the damn car won't start in the morning, that you don't like kicking around the edges of the old rug."

And of her trying to retort with, "You tell me specifically *what* to do. You give me specific things to do. The yard, the car, the truck, and every specific duty. You make lists. I never tell you specifically to do anything."

"You imply it."

She is tired of his remorse after her tears. After he has begun with her grandmother and worked up through her mother and father and each brother and sister in order to point out examples of her own blood inadequacies. Of seeing him lie on the bed and stare at nothing and eventually look at her and say, "Come here," gently and then insist. "Come here and let me tell you something."

She is tired of getting another lump in her throat when he says it that way. Of him knowing the difference between his strengths and hers. Of giving her a pat and a caress, of trying to get her to wag her tail again. She is tired of not wanting it to be that easy for him to get her back.

She is tired of leaving him there on the bed and walking into another room and trying to remember all the bad things he has said and pretending she is really neutral.

She is tired of being afraid to get too close to him again.

# *Bad Morning*

It is a bad morning, all the former conditioning I've had to get something from men by acting a certain way. The morning is bad. And it is more than getting something from men. It is getting something from life, and men are the source because I have been trained.

It is a morning of waking up beside the man who chose me. And he wasn't too sure anymore if he still wanted me. My mouth was dry and sticky. It had not been a good night. My neck hurt from bending at an angle to allow my head to rest upon the polyester stuffed pillow my mother had given me for the king-sized bed. They were king-sized pillows, and for three years they had given me a stiff neck, but I did not want to replace them, out of a feeling for my mother and for the poor pillows that couldn't help it, and because why should I spend more money on pillows when I had some already. And other reasons having to do with practicality, so that until the pillows were worn out, I would use them.

I locate his head when I open my eyes because I like to know how he feels about me and where he has put his head tells me. I see that he needs my warmth because he is close. His face lies still and closed-lidded between the two king-sized pillows on the small understuffed pillow between them. It is always a conscious face. I can never speak to it that it won't answer me, no matter where or what time it sleeps. I say, "Are you awake?"

"Ummm," it says, the blond face I am a partner to. The pale blue eyes flicker and then close and the mouth speaks. "How are you, Honey? How's everything going?…"

It is only one minute since we've both awakened and he asks me that, but I know he asks, referring to our past eleven years and all that my life means to me and how it goes on my side of the partnership.

"Okay," I say. "Nothing new...." And I am glad he has shown concern because I want to tell him everything, even though there is nothing to tell. I want to tell him what I am feeling and about what I have read, and what I just learned and what I believe *now*, after learning it in words but knowing it for thirty-four years in wordless form. I want to tell him that *I knew it already*, but confirmed it by reading.

I want to start by saying, "And it came on its own in the night..." not meaning an orgasm, but meaning an insight into the two of us and what is the matter. But I do not speak. *Yet.* One leg finds the other, knowing it works in pairs. It moves over and sees that the other one is still there. And my hands roam on their own, coming together to greet again after the night.

We have bodies and there is a *way* for them to be. An ideal way. A perfect way. And we have minds. And the same applies. So I lay there knowing that and knowing the difference. That is what is the matter, that he and I, separate or together, are not the way we know we should be. And even though it seems as simple as simply *being the way we believe we should be*, the way the ideal person *is*, we cannot do it. We are confused by what we want all the time. And especially what we want from eachother.

There is an ideal of a wife getting up at six in the morning, if not five, and making hot biscuits for the husband. My grandmother did it, and her mother did it, And sometimes my mother did it. But I cannot do it. He does not need biscuits. They are not even healthy, and I hate to get up early. But even though he doesn't eat biscuits and I don't get up early, we worry about not doing what we know would be a good thing to do. We have said to eachother for eleven years, "We should get up at six o'clock and get a regimen going. We should get an early start and then we'd feel better. It's sleeping in that gets us off to a bad start. The day's half over and we're just starting."

And I would say, "And psychologically we know and feel ill at ease because instinctively a human animal, any animal, knows about waste." I feel as qualified as Desmond Morris. I get feelings too. Of truisms.

We sleep awhile longer, dozing off but waking and knowing it is time to get up. Past time. And I want to question him and get him to make me feel settled. I want him to make me feel the way I would feel if I had already done all I am suppose to have done by this time in the morning so that I could feel good about myself.

I ask, "What time did you get in?"

"About twelve-thirty," he says, always innocent of what I'm getting at. Being straight. Answering honestly, as if that's all I want, is just an answer to my question.

"I thought you said eleven?" I say, wedging a block between us that he will have to remove so we can be together again.

"Eleven to Los Angeles," he says, lying with his eyes open now, staring straight up at the bumpity ceiling we did together with white paint and putty to save money instead of having it sprayed on by a professional. I watch his black pupils in the center of the pale blue. They are like two specks under resin. Specks jelled there, too dark. They are too harsh for the delicate blue. There should be lighter pupils for fairer eyes, I am thinking. And I see the tiny red capillary, like a tiny electrical wire reaching across the white part of his eye and almost touching the edge of the blue. And I imagine again as I have imagined dozens of times that he is an electronically controlled man. A robot.

I know he is seeing the mistakes, the flaws up there on the ceiling. They are mistakes we're unable to correct because we are human, not machines. He is not a mechanical man. There is the long crack, unfilled, thinness in areas, too thick in others. It plays on us, this imperfect ceiling that we console ourselves with by saying, "We saved at least two hundred dollars."

And then we doze some more.

# An Obstruction Over the Mouth

They want to be entertained. It is a desire to be somewhere where something important is happening, where the most current things are going on, and the most current people are doing them. They look to escape, for one evening, the daily-ness they have gotten into and to look into the faces of successful people and to see dreams that have come true.

They search their minds. Is there someplace to go. They do not know anyone who has done anything. and they haven't been invited to enter into any place where anything is being done. Everyone they know is sour and bitter and complaining that nothing is working out for them and blaming other people or things for it. Their heads are clouded with trying not to hear these complaints anymore.

They think of several places that could give them that feeling of being somewhere. One is a night spot where the music will be loud and everyone will be drunk and moving in dance motions that are not everyday motions, or talking the way they don't usually talk leaning across small tables. Or the movies. And because they are tired of drinking and moving farther away from themselves, they decide on the movies. They scan the paper, longing for a title that will strike on what they want. They choose the best-sounding title although none of them sound any good. But they want to be entertained.

It is a drive-in. She makes instant coffee in their new unbreakable thermos and grabs a bottle of sweet red wine. She empties the cookie jar, dumping the contents into a Tupperware container and snaps on the air-tight lid. She roots for sweets and finds a box of chocolate-covered cherries that have been in the refrigerator for three months. These are the foods of their entertainment. They are ready. He stands by the front door with a sleeping bag draped over one arm and two pillows, waiting for her to go out so he can lock up. He does not believe that she can lock up. He has to do it himself. They walk to their car in the driveway, carrying the things they will need while they are being entertained.

They drive along the freeway with their two heads sticking up, looking out the windows of their car, anticipating going somewhere and being there. She has brushed her hair and shined her face and has hopes of being seen when she walks past the lights of the candy stand on the way to the restrooms. He has put on the checkered dress pants that were a gift from his mother for his forty-first birthday. They are his best pants. He has never paid that much for a pair of slacks. And they feel good. He feels rich wearing them. And successful. He likes to be seen wearing them. He has worn them every time they have gone out, for three weeks now. To the hardware store, to Sambo's, to one concert, and to dinner at his mother's. They make him look like a man whose dreams have come true.

There is a line of cars at the drive-in theater because it is Friday night and they are not the only ones who are eager for something that will put them into the real life. The price of tickets for this kind of thing has gone up. Two-fifty now instead of a dollar. After paying it, they are determined to really get something out of it.

They park in their usual place, just forward of the lights of the playground and snack stand and to the right. They are late. The cartoons and previews have already shown and the credits for *Dark Star* are running by. They face forward and set their focus into the distance on the screen. The first feature begins. They are here. At the movies. Where it will happen. They settle into the seat the way the body settles when it is going to be immobile for a long time.

She reaches into the bag and finds the red wine and two plastic cups and pours the first round of their entertainment treat and hands one to him. The bag is on the floor near her feet. She always puts it there and it always is in her way. She is always irritated by it and irritated by always being the one to handle serving from it. He has not taken his eyes off the screen. He has developed the ability to concentrate over the years and she has not. She rummages around inside the bag, finding the things she has packed and bringing them out so they are accessible. She glances at the screen from time to time. Without concentration she can tell that it is a bad movie. Bad acting, bad script. Bad idea, bad everything. The wine makes their heads heavy. After awhile she is too bored and drowsy to stay awake. There is nothing to prevent her from falling asleep. There is nothing to being here in a dark car. There is no one to see her. There is no one to see. There is nothing going on after all. She does not want to stay awake. It is too cold outside to parade past the candy stand. And she does not have to go to the bathroom. She leans against his corduroy shoulder for awhile. He leans his head against the top of her head. After awhile, she crawls over the seat into the back and inside of the sleeping bag and falls into a drugged sleep to the sound of the speaker's inane dialogue. The car is on a slant upward. The incline tugs at the fluids in her body. The wine swings low in her stomach. Her feet feel heavy. He chuckles in the front seat and uses phrases that state the ridiculousness of today's films. They know without saying it that they have made a mistake in coming here. They have wasted their time and two-fifty. She is on the edge of wakefulness and sighs like a seal washed up on a beach. She turns over to get her other hip to pop a joint into another position. He clears his throat and coughs for awhile.

She says why don't they go. And he says why don't they wait to see if the next one will be any good. She says why doesn't he come back and be next to her. He climbs over the seat and they unzip the sleeping bag and spread it over the car mats. They share the pillows, and lie side by side. In the back of their station wagon fifteen miles away from their bed at home. When there is an interesting sound effect from the speaker, they both lift up their heads and stretch their necks and lean on their elbows and watch the screen. Seeking their entertainment. She tosses and turns. Sand has filtered from the car mats into their pantlegs. They tug at the sleeping bag to keep their shoulders covered, but because his shoulders are higher, he gets more and she is prevented from having it snug and firm around hers.

Finally they laugh and say, "This is entertainment." But still they do not go home. The night seems to go on forever. The first movie ends and people go for candy. She is too disheveled by now to go to be seen. He is content to turn off the speaker and sit propped up on his elbows and muse in the back compartment of his car inside their down sleeping bag.

The second movie comes on. She stretches her neck to see if it is going to be a good one. He has one arm over the back of the front seat, holding on as if there is a chance that he might begin to slide off of something. They watch the film for awhile in disbelief that it can be as bad if not worse than the first one. And then almost simultaneously they say "Let's go." One at a time they climb back over the front seat and get into their positions to drive home. Their eyes sting.

When they pull into their driveway they know they have, once again, been nowhere. And they say, "There is nowhere to go anymore. There used to be good movies. There used to be things to do. Places to go. Fun."

They used to neck in movies. She tells him now, in the front seat before they get out to go inside their house, "Kiss me." He gives her a peck. She tells him they don't kiss anymore. He says he guesses they don't. He explains that they probably don't like the idea of the other one smothering their face. She adds, "Cutting off our air." They do not know when or why they stopped kissing and started thinking of the other as an obstruction over the mouth.

*I see my male. Alex. Big hard brown shoes. Blue, blue, blue clothes. And a black pupil in the center of a blue, blue eye, focused on a serious TV program. And I feel safe. I can go off into mysterious places and he will pull me back. With his big brown shoes. And his blue, blue eyes. And his standard blue shirt and pants and conscience.*

# Dreams

She and Alex wake up knowing about death and destruction as if they have experienced it. They have had a bad night fighting pillows, eachother's bony knees and elbows, crooked blankets, contour sheets coming undone from the corners of the mattress, and all the while the sound of wind. She dreamed of Martha burning to death in her bed. Alex received her restlessness. He is picky after he gets up, wanting to point to and blame actual personified reasons why his life has gone wrong. She is foolishly amused by the ordinary necessities, cleaning up after the dog, cooking eggs, making toast, sweeping the floor. She feels snug in a place away from the dream about death. Alex turns down the burners, begins vacuuming underneath and inside the clothes dryer.

Dust is destruction. He hunts it out and destroys its presence. He sniffs the air, suspicious, She has tried to hide the information about the dog's diarrhea on the rug. But Alex is a keen creature. He knows without words but cannot accuse anyone of anything unless it is spoken. She is mute. He takes a shower, standing under hot water, letting it run on his back for forty minutes, and calls for wax paper. He curses the torn wax paper above the tile shower. Paper he tacked in place to protect the fiberboard wall. It has come loose, Water has spattered, soaked in, begun to destroy his work. It is new wallboard he is in the middle of installing. She brings him the box of waxpaper and snaps the door shut on his muttering and hissing, locking him into the small bathroom cubicle, and into his own presence and anger and fear and suspicions. Dead Martha is still there with her. The wind is with Alex. They pass the morning fighting private visions, and try not to blame the other. It is a new technique. Not to point a finger in the other's direction…

# *Not One of Those Men Who Crack*

He would say now and then, "My teeth are shifting..." and give various reasons why, each time coming up with a new speculation. At forty-one he stood in front of the mirror with his wife. She wanted to see what they looked like hugging. They had wrapped their arms around eachother and, as people do before the mirror, smiled. As they tightened their grips around the other one's body, she laughed out loud and asked, "We still look good together, don't we? After all the wear and tear? We don't look too bad, do we?"

He told her she was a pretty woman because it pleased her. He said she had pretty teeth, a nice smile. He liked her best when she was smiling. He didn't like her mouth when she was angry. It turned into an ugly thing, and she had been angry more than smiling during their marriage it seemed to him. She had a way of sneering that made her top lip thin out and curl up. She was not pretty then.

He tilted his head back so that his teeth would be more visible and said about himself, "My teeth aren't even. That's the one thing that ruins my face. I'm not bad.... I wouldn't be bad if I had straight teeth."

They stood smiling and analyzing their smile types. He told her, "Your teeth show more than mine when you smile. I don't have a very big smile." He had to lift his chin to get his mouth at an angle to show a toothy smile. "I have a tight upper lip."

"A stiff one," she laughed. "It's in your German blood." He ignored her. She had it in her mind that he was a cold, orderly, calculated German type. He had to admit, he admired the Germans and had German blood, but the way she thought was ridiculous. She thought it was cute. To call him a German. It let her get away with a lot of things. He accused her of wallowing in olive oil once in awhile to dig her ancestry.

But at the moment they were holding eachother and examining their faces. He stepped closer to the mirror, letting go of her, and let his upper lip peel back and expose the top row of his teeth and his gums.

"By God," he said, as she leaned closer, "My teeth are shifting." He tilted his head way back and saw that his left front tooth had moved out front so that his right one and left incisor could close in behind it and have more room. "That tooth didn't used to be that far out of place.... My teeth are on the move."

His wife had her opinions. She said, "As you get older, your teeth spread. The cartilage or whatever pads the bone on your jaw begins to deteriorate and your teeth get farther apart. It's better to have tight teeth like yours. They'll straighten out. If you had straight teeth now, they'd get spaces between them as you get older."

They forgot about eachother and left the mirror with his teeth in their minds, and what would become of him in old age. How bad could they get. How crooked. Or would they straighten out. Would he go into old age like some men, transforming into a fiend with snaggle teeth. Would *life* do that to him. His brow was knitted with contemplation. Wondering what fate lay in store for him. He toyed with being dealt a low blow. It gave him strength to back off and stand alone and fight. But how could he be sure if it were accidental or intended. If it were *him* or *life*.

He believed he had been "screwed" in the past by *life*. That every decision he had ever made had been bad and that had to mean only one thing, that he was marked. So many numbers have to fail. It's in the odds. Like marrying her. That cost him years of misery. Never had he thought it was possible to take so much from someone for so long. It had worn him down. And money. Every investment he had ever made lost him money. He had a talent for picking losers. Every one. And no one loses every time unless...

When he first met her he told her, "Life is just a bowl of cherries, but someone put mildew all over mine." They were sitting on the beach with the philosophy club. He was a bachelor with a trailer. "A damn nice setup." And fresh out of the Air Force. An officer. A fly boy. He had flown the big ones at night. It was a joke. She said, even back then when she had no hold on him, when he could have walked away from her, "What a stupid thing to say. What a feel-sorry-for-yourself way to think. It's dumb."

It was what got his attention, that mouth of hers. He knew she had some problem of her own to attack him like that. She was bitter too.

Later she denied it when he accused her of putting him down because she thought he was a rich boy and felt threatened, felt she couldn't have him. He still thought that was it, even though she told him that the thongs he wore and his big broad white indoor feet in outdoor sandals was what disgusted her. And she *knew* she could have him. There was no doubt. She didn't *want* him. Not with that mamsy-pamsy attitude. A grown man sitting there blubbering about mildew as if he was the only one whose cherries were ruined.

They had fought off and on over the years about it. They brought the topic out as if from a filing cabinet, and argued until she was in tears and he wanted to strike her. Neither one ever won. It was never resolved, and then in exhaustion they would file it away again until a next time when they had more strength and needed to butt heads in competition and test to see who would lead. The collapse of their marriage and the loss of their fighting partner being more of a concern than whether she thought he was stupid back then or whether it was because she felt stupid and he was a threat.

He had a choice back then, to walk away from her, but he misread the signs. He married her thinking she needed him. To take care of her. And then she wouldn't be so bitter. She would be grateful. Someone had evidently put mildew on her cherries. Together they could make it up to eachother. She would understand him. They had that in common. And he had gravitated toward her sharp hateful tongue as a fly toward stink.

Once he said, "It was inevitable. We were meant to be." He said it without joy, like a man sentenced to the rope. He added, "There was no escape," with the glumness of a man proving that if that's the way *life* is, then he can take it. He won't crack under the strain. A stiff upper lip. He's no sissy.

He went about his business for the rest of the day, but at times his teeth would surface in his mind and he would go to the nearest mirror and look at them again. Once, in the car, he turned the rear view mirror down, and examining again the front tooth that had moved out of position, he said, "Ever since I quit smoking.... That's it.... That's why they're moving.... I'm not holding my mouth the same since I quit smoking...."

She turned and looked at him and saw the wonder of discovery in his face. She said, "That is really stupid. What a dumb excuse to dream up so you can smoke again...."

He hated her. He took her and what was happening inside his mouth as the same thing. A test of endurance. And he would pass it. He was not one of those men who cracked. He did not look at his teeth again in front of her or mention them.

# Getting There Was the Fun

In red satin party pajamas and high solid-soled clogs she stumbled in the dark along the railroad track, stubbing her toes, catching herself with her hands, finally carrying her shoes and running as fast as she could in case he was behind her…. Running in the night where she had played as a child, along this same strip of land bordering the railroad track. The railroad paralleled the ocean and 101. Houses ran along it all the way up and down the California coast. As a girl she had lived in a little house right here and ran across the railroad track every day to the beach. The house was gone. In its place there was an old gas station which had been converted into a feed store. At night it was difficult to distinguish this structure from others that had been built alongside it, but almost intuitively she sensed her childhood property. Smelled the ice plant as it was crushed under her bare frantic feet, the juice of it stinging into the cuts the granite gravel between the railroad ties had made. An old palm tree whose "hair" she had cut with her mother's sewing scissors was still standing, watching her as she rushed past, the way she had rushed past years ago from out of her house which was full of anger. She ran then in fear the way she ran now. Away.

She arrived at the back of a restaurant-bar, hurried around the front, put her shoes on the pavement in the shadow of the wall, stepped into them, and then entered the carpeted room, panting but breathing deep to control the movement of her chest. There was no time to steady herself outside. He could be gaining on her. She knew the cocktail lounge, had been there under many different circumstances before over the years, so that she felt like a tramp coming in this way. A record breaker. She had hit a new inevitable low. She paraded past tables of people and went straight to the restrooms. A woman in cocktail gown was combing her hair before the mirror, and glanced up almost frightened by her violent instant appearance, so she hid inside the single toilet cubicle, to wait for the woman to leave. She slid the lock across the door with relief. Sweet safety. Privacy. Her hands shook. He would not get her in here. He would not come after her in front of all these people. He wouldn't dare. Or would he? Was his anger so great that there was no place she would be protected from it. Was he capable of snatching her from the vary arms of a policeman and strangling her before his eyes? Had she inflamed his mind so, like a mad dog, he would run right into his own destruction and welcome it as relief?

Her ears would have twisted and turned had she had the ears of a coyote she was listening so acutely for his sound. A stomp of his shoe. A turn, sharp enough to break the knob from the door, of his hand. A preparatory snort as he approached the restroom door. The feet of the woman making her leave was the only sound there was to hear so she came out. And saw herself in the mirror. Red gloss lipstick still glistening. Her lips ready for the party she would not be attending now. Not after what she did. There was no way to recover the evening. She could not turn back. Not after jumping out of the car. She had gone too far this time. She could still hear the bottle of Seagram's Seven breaking in the street as it rolled out at the stop sign with her exit. The gift they had wrapped in turquoise tissue paper and tied with a paper bow for their friends. In forty years she had not progressed. Not that she was forty but she would never progress. In fifty years or sixty. She would always be a little ragamuffin girl running along the railroad tracks to the beach or across the 101, barefoot, dirty stubbed toes, tangled hair. While other women, other wives, when angry with their husbands spent the night at a friend's, at the Biltmore, with another man, or a Motel 6. Why did she always take off on foot into the night, disheveled, scared, with nowhere to go…

Except to be standing inside a bathroom of a cocktail lounge, one block away from where she grew up, still exactly the same as then. Slamming out of the house, tearing away in anger and fear, vowing never to go back. But going back, always going back. Held by the pattern. If she did not go back, how could she run away?

It happened every year they were invited to this party. Each time, on the way they would be angry with eachother. And every year for ten years they had been able to overcome their anger except twice. Once when he slammed on the brakes, let her out back at the house, then roared away in the opposite direction from the party. And this time, when she got out of the car before he took her home. She would not go to bed in tears this time.

This time the argument started early in the day, and they fed it little bits so that by evening, as they were dressing, it became fat, full, bloated. And he was saying, "What are you going to do this year, let all the oily greasy men go around squeezing you again?"

Her face burned, remembering how she had found herself being fondled and nuzzled by old husbands. Friends they had known for years. But until that year, had been mild-mannered proper men. It was a surprise to her, how, in their older years, these men were trying to loosen up, get drunk, and hug and kiss all the wives at parties. That, now, old and grey, they had become all sweaty-palms and sloppy-mouthed. They had caught her by surprise last year and she had been embarrassed for them and found she was not able to push them away.

"And what are you going to do? Sit there like a bump on a log and say nothing like you did last year. And entice, by your silence, oddball women, other losers, to come bump their breasts against your arms and try to get you to converse?"

In the car they argued about whether he would ever learn to serve drinks like other husbands. And whether she would ever learn to stop asking people stupid questions and act like other wives. She could tell by the crescendo that they were reaching the peak of the fight. When he slowed down for a stop sign and turned to her with a pulpy red face, anger playing under the flesh, swelling it in ugly contortion, saying, "We do this every year... what is wrong that we can't break out of this... can't get control of our lives, and stop. We're caught... by God... We'll go on like this forever... What is missing in us that we can't stop this…" That's when she made a dramatic gesture for the pinch-door handle and swung the door open and jumped out and he sped up to keep her in, and she was caught for an instant by the door and leapt away from it, prepared to be knocked under the tires.

She knew his next line at this point in the fight would have been, "You… You are used to this kind of carrying on. Your family carried on this way and its all that you know, all that you've ever known…" He would have expelled every last drop of air in his lungs by now and his face would be purple as he went on without air, "And now you can't break the cycle, you'll go on and on another generation, smearing your poison until you destroy both of us…" And, as he built his case around her foulness, he would have built a need for an extension of his anger, in the form of his hand striking out at her.

She ran, believing he was right at her heels. That this time, he was determined to put a stop to their patterns, to correct their behavior right then and there before another moment passed. To set them straight and right the wrong that had been going on too long.

She could see him grabbing her by the hair and thrusting her down on the ground and pulverizing her once and for all, and then walking away dusting his hands the way it was done in cartoons.

Alone in the restroom she locked the door, put her feet, one at a time, in the basin and soothed them with warm water and soap, and dried them on paper towels. They had taken the punishment meant for her. They had carried her away beyond their capability, bare, tender, as she urged them on beyond his anger. They had brought her to safety and now lay bleeding, each one in turn, before her in the basin of water. She put them back in her shoes. They were numb, shocked by violence. Yet they continued to support her. She was proud of them.

Someone was knocking quietly on the door. Startled, she called a question, "Just a minute?"

There was silence. She quickly ran a brush through her

moist wild hair, bringing it down, calming it. The night air had curled it.

"Guilt " he had shouted at her over the years, as an accusation, "is what makes you run away from me... you want to be punished... you expect it... you provoke it... won't give up until you get it..."

"Is that what makes a rabbit run from a lion?" she shouted. "Or is it just plain old normal fear?"

"You're not afraid of me... or you wouldn't carry on like this."

"Even a worm writhes when it's being squashed... Everything protests its destruction..."

*The Gingerbread Boy* was her favorite children's story. Its rhythms. The redundancy of his running. And he always got away. And he was so proud of his ability to run fast. She had read it to children after she grew up and dramatized the parts, almost singing it, and sharing the gingerbread boy's delight in how fast he could outrun the old lady, man, horse, cow, pig, chicken, and... It was the fox that spoiled the story. She never believed a fox would really be able to talk him into climbing up onto his nose. It was absurd.

Outside, in front of the restaurant, she stood in a shadow and wondered which way she should go. Cars appeared and disappeared on Highway 101. And suddenly there he was with the car door open saying, "Get in." She edged back toward the entrance of the restaurant. He shook his head, disgusted over her fear. "Get in this car... .What are you going to do, stand there all night?" She shook her head and when he put on the emergency brake and put it in park, she hurried past some people in evening clothes and sought the shelter of the restroom.

"Guilt?" she asked herself in the mirror. Over that? She did not know if he were right or not. She only knew that she had always run, like small animals do. Her only defense. Swiftness. She had always run away from anger and confusion and found something in the flight. The run, as a child, between her house and the big night, was the whole thing. The fragment in between house and night: the run, even though it lasted only a moment, was what gave her hope.

Not the being away. Even now, the escape from him had caused her an excitement she had not felt since the last time she had run away.

Except for the time she ran across the street in front of a car because she did not want to wait for it to pass. There was something boring about standing there waiting for it to pass, and something exciting about almost getting hit. The same way it was boring to sit by his side in the car while he vented his anger. Doing nothing about it. And then the excitement of leaping and racing away from him...

He was gone the second time she came outside. So she began walking along the side of the road toward town. Her hair streaming back with the wind of each passing car. It was a good feeling. A freeness she had not felt for a long time. Since the last time she had walked along the roadside with nowhere to go into the night....

That she liked the feeling scared her a little. After all the effort she had made to be pink and white, a mother, a wife, clean, sweet, alternately in a hospital bed, on a delivery table, in a white dress, sewing curtains, and trimming dough like Snow White, coochy-cooing infants, and still it did not stabilize what had gotten into her blood as a child. Fleeing is being free, she thought, as she came to a pay phone in the corner of a gas station lot.

She passed by, walked back, circled the phone booth and then went in and looked for a dime in the coin return. It was empty. A connection back to him. And she could not make it.... Having no access to a connection back to him pleased her... Did she need an excuse to be free ...?

She walked for about an hour and then asked at another gas station if she could use the phone. His voice on the other end sounded half asleep.

"What'd you do, go to bed?" she asked in disbelief.

"What else was there to do?" His voice was low, controlled, tired.

"We could still go to the party?" she ventured.

"Do you want to?"

He picked her up in about fifteen minutes. They laughed because there was nothing else to do about it. They had to be crazy they agreed, and were slightly proud of the way they could carry on and still enter a party as if nothing had happened. They filled their cups from the punch bowl, chatted and made small talk, senseless comments for the sake of being cordial, and when he asked her to dance with him, she glided into his arms, and they leaned their cheeks together and it was funny. They really did like eachother. The people they were several hours before were different people, not the two dancing now. And she felt good. As if she had expressed herself.

*A dream: That we had to be killed if we were "english." Alex was going to let us be, but at the last minute it occurred to me that we could lie. So we did and lived....*

# A Roundabout Way
## of Getting to Sambo's

He was talking to himself in the shower. That was the first irritation. She thought if they were both home, if she were in the same house with him, if they were together, he should talk to her instead of to himself She did not like it that he preferred himself to her.

Twice during his shower she stuck her head in the door, pulled open the curtain and said, "Is that right. Really well, well..." And he glanced up, laughing at himself, saying, "That's right, I'm going fast." He meant he was finished, near the end of his sanity and of his life. Theoretically, the life that mattered, the one he had hoped for and worked for and wanted and was finding out he wasn't going to get. He had just turned forty and it had hit him hard. He chose the glory of dying instead of living a life he didn't want.

Imaginary dying. He liked to toy with the idea that his options were all over him. That "life" had wrung him dry with what it had expected of him and left him, unrewarded an empty shell. He muttered constantly, in the shower, out of the shower. Always to himself about the injustice of following the rule, doing what "everyone wants you to do", believing that it will all work out for the best ... and then ... what do you get ... nothing. He wanted to have it taken out of his hands. To sink into oblivion, insanity, to go numb and not care ... She had read up on the male menopause. Robbed him of the glory of his feelings by reading out of a book how typical it was for a man of forty to feel depressed and all the other things he was feeling. Took away his individualism and made him into a mere male phase. So he did not talk out loud. Did not give her another thing to calculate into her neat and tidy categories. She got ready to go to Sambo's as they had planned, listening to sounds of the shower. Sambo's was a sane place where everyone acted normal. They liked to go there and pretend. Finally the last stage of the shower began. She could tell by the squeak of the faucet as he turned up the cold water and turned off the hot. The tempo increased as the water drilled into his flesh, all over, like pins and needles. He thrashed around, slapping himself. Cold water. A daily torture he claimed kept him young. "You've never seen anything like this in a cradle," was their inside joke, as they bared their bodies to eachother, or as he stood in front of a mirror fresh out of the shower. She had started the saying early in their marriage after hearing the corny line in an Elvis Presley movie. It stuck in her mind. And when he began using it, it was reinforced. He rarely used phrases.

Her language was a sore point with him. He was the speaker for both of them when they were around people and had to express the finer points in a conversation. She laughed when he picked up this one line from her because he didn't even know where it came from or what it meant, even though she had explained to him years ago how "this real young blonde who wanted to make love to Elvis, put on her bikini and snuck into his bedroom at a beach house and when he told her he didn't rob cradles, she stuck out her fully developed body and said that about the cradle..." She was dressed and impatient to go to Sambo's to gulp some coffee, let him gorge on pancakes which he couldn't get enough of lately, and get back and get something done in her own life for a change. She had projects dangling everywhere. Unfinished ideas laying around waiting for her time. She didn't want to hit her menopause unprepared the way he was and try to finish them while she was having hot flashes. She wanted to get them done now. And even though it was a long time before she was that old, there was a lot to do. She needed all the time she could get. When he got out of the shower, refreshed, stark white, moist, and stood flexing in front of the mirror saying that about the cradle, she coaxed him to hurry up. He kept standing there changing positions. That was the second irritant of the morning.

"Yeah, yeah, you're gorgeous, now let's go. The whole day's gone." It was ten AM. They had slept in again. In a stupor. Not wanting ever to wake up and face the fact that they were still here and repeating the same old thing. The media hitting the same receptors in the same way and striking the same old spots in the brains. Redundancy dominate. As she fussed around feeding the same old cats, starting the same old wash, opening the same old windows, he muttered to himself in the same old manner. And she pursed her lips. Finally she hollered, her same old line, "If you'd talk to me as much as you talk to yourself we might get somewhere…"

The third irritation and the last one that morning was when she came upon him in the kitchen, after he was dressed and ready to go. He was bending over the sink, concealing a half gallon box with his back to her. She thought he was eating ice cream the way he ate it at night over the sink, out of the box, by the spoonfuls. He had a craving for sweets, as if that alone was the thing he had missed out on in his life. She said, "Ah hah!" ready to laugh at the little boy in the sugar bowl, as if it mattered that she caught him. But this time he had had enough of her intruding into his life. He barked a word he rarely said.

"Shut up!"

He turned just enough so she caught a glimpse of the box. Ortho Plant Food Pellets. That was a sore point with her. He could never leave well enough alone. He could never stay in his own life and out of hers. The plants inside the house were hers. She took care of them. "The way she took care of everything—half-assed," according to him. But they lived and thrived in spite of her. He had told her a dozen times to read up on houseplants, to learn what they needed, and to take care of them properly, consciously, orderly, in a systematic manner. But she hated How-To books. She did things by feel.

When she felt it was time she made the rounds with water and iron and B-1. She didn't want to know the names of the plants. It took something away. She liked to think of them in other ways. So he had taken it upon himself to care for the plants when she wasn't looking. Now she had caught him.

He had already killed half the plants in the yard, if not accidentally, then on purpose. He had poisoned the citrus trees with an overdose of citrus pellets. He was sick about it. As they turned yellow and dry they symbolized his whole life. All his efforts to get somewhere. She had held her tongue. Did not say, "See, I told you so." Nothing he touched except inanimate objects thrived under his applied method style. She caught him feeding her goldfish once and then knew why they were dying. When he criticized her about never feeding them, she denied it and told him in detail, even showed him, how she took the dead sow bugs out of the spider webs and fed them to the fish daily. When he grimaced, she reasoned that all fish food was dried and crumbled bugs. He argued that he never saw her feed the fish. She sneered that it didn't mean she didn't. That did he believe nothing happened around the house except what he saw? All of the fish died one by one, until she unplugged the tank and gave up.

Applying herself never worked. If he would stop sneaking around applying himself in her business she would have the old successes she had before she met him. She had always had plants and fish. They never died except of old age. He said the same thing. He had successes before she came along to bungle up everything. They agreed that they seemed to be a curse on eachother's styles. What worked before separately, met with obstacles together.

The harshness of his voice was a slap. She protested, "I thought it was ice cream," and ran away innocent, in disbelief, into the bedroom. Sambo's grew distant. And then the hurt turned to anger. Crying was humiliating, feeble, weak. She stormed out of the bedroom. "So you're killing my plants now... like you killed those trees."

"Plants can't live on water alone," he shouted back, "anybody knows that who has any sense at all."

"Then how come they're living? Even morons know that water has minerals in it." Their voices reached the pitch that he knew could be heard out in the street and next door. It was that voice of hers. She turned everything into a yelling match. Her throat. He could overlook everything else, all the dead plants and fish she left in her wake, but not that throat of hers.

She was trapped with a solid block: his idea of her as a slob. He was too cruel to see no sense in her habits. He was a boy scout. A robot. A Methodist. How could she ever make him know how wrong he was to insist that she become like him. That his life had struck a dead end and even so he was not willing to let her be different. She said, "Look at you, creeping around with a box of pellets."

"And look at you," he smirked making her feel grotesque.

"All your proper methods… and what do you have?" She continued attempting to strike at raw spots.

"A neurotic wife, because she has to resist. No one could get anywhere dealing with you…"

She ran outside to get away from him, and watered the lawn. He put away the Ortho Gro and came around to the car. "Are you ready?" he asked. Sambo's, the normal life, loomed in close again. That's the way they fought now. Quick and to the throat like dogs and then it was all over. But today she didn't want it to be over. She wanted something that the fight gave her. Action. Movement. Maybe progress. Sambo's was a diversion. A sickeningly sweet, patient, coffee-sipping way to kill time.

"Are you coming or not?" he asked one more time before getting into the car. She knew he always chose the status quo, keeping them in place so they would go on and on and on until something else would have to come along and pry their lives out of their hands before they could change.

"No," she sprayed the water rapidly at different lengths through the nozzle to show her emotion. He backed out and in disbelief she watched him drive away without her. She suddenly wanted to race after him, call and beg to be taken along and not left by herself with all of her oddball notions. Without him. And it had been so close. Sambo's.

Side by side. Coffee. Together. A nice ordinary couple doing a nice ordinary thing. She had an urgency to do something to save herself from being excluded from this little plan.

When he drove up in about five minutes, to give her another chance to come along and have all that it offered, she was sitting on the side of the bed taking off her shoes and rolling up her pant-legs getting ready to jump on the bike and hunt him down. But something drove her to walk out of their little house, jump on the bike and pedal off in the opposite direction before his eyes. She pedaled hard without looking back for a mile in third gear until her thighs quivered under the strain, and all the while there were wild plans going on in her head. She planned a whole life without him. A new life: At the library. At the beach. Everywhere. Anywhere. It would take place without a setting, without a title. Out of the house. Away. Free. Without a system. She was strong. She would pedal all over the whole world. No one could stop her. Let them try. She was an animal. She was a muscle. A mind-less muscle that had an instinct and would pump her all over territories without boundaries. Past men who muttered to themselves and fed her plants and fish. Then, just before she came to the first steep hill, she thought of him at Sambo's all alone, needing her to talk to him so he wouldn't be all alone in his own manias, talking to himself. Hissing and spewing his anguish where no one could understand. Cursing the rules he had been trained to obey. And she circled around and sped four miles in his direction, threw her bike into the bike rack in front of Sambo's, raced through the glass doors, the way heroines do in movies, to the rescue style, with her pant legs still rolled up, hair wild. She spotted him at the counter. It was a good sign. He never sat at the counter. He was transient, uncomfortable, without her. He was looking up, had seen her before she saw him.

"So did you feed yourself some sweet pellets?" she laughed.

"How was your ride Sweetheart?" he asked as if she had just been out taking a little spin. He gestured to make room for her beside him even though she would be on a different stool. She couldn't wait to share her experience with him, "I passed an old man on the bike and he smiled at me as if we were the same, as if I was riding a bike for the same reason he was…" He smiled and nodded. Her thighs pounded. His lips began to move almost imperceptibly. The waitress poured coffee. The steam rose. How nice it was to be here. A normal couple. Just ordinary people. She would be pumping up that hill instead, sweating, if she hadn't turned around.

*Alex comes into the kitchen and as he stands talking or lighting a cigarette, he straightens out the salt and pepper packets into two lines and then puts the sugar and ketchup to the side. She says, "You should be an orderly. My, how orderly you are today. It's your nesting urge...."*

*He knits his brow. Worried that he needs everything to be organized. At right angles to one another. He says, "I know... I don't know...." She waits. "It's that I have to get it all sorted out so I'll know what I have, so I'll know what I can do... Then I can move forward...."*

*They spend the rest of the day cleaning out little piles of stuff, accumulations in cupboards. For him. For his sense of who he is, based on what he's got.*

# The Props

We start out by my sharing a thought I had had the night before just before going to sleep. "It's not peace that's the highest mental state. It's discovery!" It is the first thing I have said and my head is still on the pillow beside his. I rise up on one elbow, excited by the thought.

"Who wants happiness? It's a bore. I mean I get nervous if everything is too perfect. I want to find out. It's exciting to find out and then to know. I wonder why peace and happiness and that kind of thing became so exalted. I mean, the satisfying thing that fulfills you is discovery. The answers...."

I am looking right into his face for a response. "And there are no happy answers. Are there? Death? Old age?... You know? It's understanding where you stand. That's all we've got, isn't there? I mean, what else is there?" And I lay down and wait for his voice.

The sun is bright, cutting through the branches of the winter weeping willow and entering our window in stark beams. We lay warm together, smooth as silk under the blankets, and gently stretching when we shift positions.

It has been a long night of swallowing over and over in almost conscious sleep, and then drifting and dreaming of eating an uneatable thing when the dryness wouldn't go down.

I see Alex's profile beside me and the flicker of light in his pale blue eye. He is staring straight up and when he is aware that I am finished talking he begins right away, as if I hadn't prompted him, as if he was already thinking about it.

"Women are lucky; God! I'm just becoming aware of how much I'd like to be a woman and let it all hang out." His relaxed face has suddenly become contorted. "Men have to control their lives. They have to trim themselves. And modify what they feel. They can't go full tilt."

The sunlight is blinding in certain angles on the pillow.

My new morning eyes water and I am angered by the intensity of the sun and the intensity of his reaction. "Don't categorize me as *women*, and men have to trim themselves because what they do counts. So what's your problem? It's a new day and I haven't even done anything yet to make you mad."

There is a sigh. And he says, as if pouting. "I'm forty."

I am robbed of myself as the subject. It tears at me. He continues. "It's just dawning on me that I'm forty already. And I still can't do what I want."

"You're only thirty-nine." I want to get up and leave him.

"You're free to give yourself to life and get something out of it, and I'm still just holding things together. Working with *junk*."

"So? Who isn't?" I say with a harsh tone I don't feel anymore.

"Forty," he stares ahead. "It's not the age. I don't care if I'm forty. It's not being old. It's that you know there are things you can't do anymore. That the time for certain things has passed. And you missed your chance. It's not being forty. It's knowing you missed out on things you wanted to do."

"So?" I say again because it is the most blatant thing I can say, and because tenderness is still embarrassing.

I see his anxiety as something that has nothing to do with me. I do not fit into it. There is nothing I can say to him. There are no answers. I am jealous. I cannot be the answer for him. If I were the answer, he would not even be worrying about it. He would be too busy with me to give a thought to his coming old age. It has reduced me to a pile of flesh beside him of no value other than being there so that he can talk to himself through it, and believe that he talks to someone else and not to himself.

"So, it's not that you're old, because at thirty you worried. At fifty, you'll remember back and think you were a fool to worry about forty, just as you look back at thirty and laugh now."

"I know," he says. "But life is slipping by and I haven't even gotten started. There are so many things I want to do.

And I can see it now. That women get to be what they are, and be it with a flair. They don't put on any stoppers. If she's a nag, she just lets go and nags to her heart's content. She has no second thoughts. Like you. You're exhilarated over finding out about things. I'd like to be, too. But I'm too busy. There's too much to do and not enough time. A man can't just let go. He's got to keep control of both of their lives."

"Oh, God. So what are you saying. That I'm not responsible?" I get up, threatened by his picture of my self-indulgence, and of his arms that have been flung out to introduce the theory to the air around us. "Go do what you want. Leave. Do you think I'd drop off the earth without you?... I'd get along...." I grab my robe and cover my body because it exposes me too much now and I am not sure of him anymore.

"God, if I could only believe that...." he says from the bed.

"Believe it. You want a place to belong to. That's why you stay. You apparently need to stay." He cannot go into the virtue of a sense of duty because I am closing the door on his voice.

"Your life would be affected..." I hear him say through it, so I open it a crack in order to shout back.

"Of course it would. But I could get along. That's the point. I wouldn't die...." And I leave him in the soft bed. warm and silky by himself with his long lean legs rubbing against eachothers instead of mine. And I want to run back and say, "You're a candidate for an affair with a young sweet thing." But I know he'd say, "I know, and that's the tragedy. I want other things. An affair is an illusion. It wouldn't last. I want to *do* things."

Once we sat around in the front room and he said, "I'd like to go somewhere and say I was only thirty-two," and I laughed. He sat slumped and depressed that ten years ago he was only twenty-nine.

"Go somewhere? Where? To the world? To God? and say it? I'm thirty-two?... Say it here," I said, and we sat glum thinking of ten years that had sailed by and taken too much of us and not left enough in payment.

I put water on for coffee and want to adjust the morning house so I could feel excited again, but there was nothing I could change that would make a difference. I wanted to go tell Alex anything in order to keep him in place so that I could count on things remaining the same, but I would not rush into it. I could wait until the last minute. Until he had his suitcase in his hand and then I'd break down.

He had come home the night before with eyes so weary that they creased down the sides. I had been waiting for him, opening the refrigerator, going to the mirror, getting out books, listening to his classical records. And when he came in he saw his classical records stacked on the table beside the phonograph, left out of their folders, subject to dust. He went to them and wanted to take them in his hands and raise them above his head and smash them against the floor.

"And then go buy fifteen dollars worth of new ones," he shouted, to hurt me for not taking care of them.

"Go ahead," I said, turning away, determined to die before I'd kiss him ever again when he came home from work. He stood in front of the heater and regained his composure. And I wallowed in sarcasm, free to say anything now.

"Is that the message you get from classical music?" I yell. "To be persnickety? Like an old lady?"

I go pick up the book I was trying to get to just before he came through the door. We occupy the same room, keeping space between us and weighing each thought in case it should become a word. His initial outburst slowly evaporates in the silence that lapses.

"What news?" he asks, but I read with an intense facial concentration for awhile until I finally ask him what he asked with an abstract interest, knowing he will be too irritated to repeat his question.

"OK, OK," he tries calming himself. "I should know by now that you don't get excited. I don't know why I don't learn that. Let her tear the whole house down piece by piece and don't get excited." He has reminded himself and is angered all over again. He stomps back and forth, brings a beer out of the kitchen, lights a cigarette, looks at the records and walks over to them and shouts, "Did you think about it at all? Or did you just leave them out on purpose? Don't you care? Haven't we been through this once before? Didn't you hear the scratches on them already?"

I have locked myself in a distant compartment in order to get through the evening, but can feel the reverberations. My silent hostility is cool, but I mildly reproach myself for using the power of it to punish him, and at the same time am too covetous of it to give it up and go to him and say, "OK, you have a right to be mad. I don't care about your records and I was careless." But I do not want to be equal. I want him to carry the burden of his anger alone. I want to be free to be careless with his records.

He asks, "What if I spilled my beer on your book there?"

Finally I shout, "I don't care about your records. I don't have that phobia. It is not my style to fuss around like you do. Do you want a duplicate of yourself in me?"

We sit in silence again. He sniffs and smokes and drinks beer from a can and I am saddened because my silence is based on believing that we will have the rest of our lives together. So that we have time for this—for anger. But if I knew we would be divorced someday I would not take time to sulk. There would be no time to waste. I do not see the words in the book.

I see only that we have not spread a sheet on the floor in front of the fireplace for a long time and made love like strangers. We have laid in bed like man and wife and gone through a lazy routine.

I want to break through my power of silence over him and go to the hall closet and bring out a sheet. But I cannot rise above my role as wife. I cannot comfort him as a fellow person. I do not want to know the depth of his frustration. I do not want to allow anger over records. I want to be hurt and keep him in position of monarch over me. Of Prince with power over poor maiden from the woods who needs all the help she can get. If I went to him I would have to carry half the support. I would have to restrict myself, and help protect his records.

I do not go to the hall cupboard to find a sheet. I sit in silence and hope that the silence will support the props that keep him in position for my security.

I fry an egg and make toast and later stand over the stove and eat the egg on the toast, letting the yolk run over the edges onto my fingers so I can lick it off. Because eggs are succulent and make me feel well cared for. I can make an orgy of eating one, lapping at it and all the while I think of a raccoon smacking his mouth and licking his paws as he breaks into an egg on the ground.

The bedroom door has opened and the shower has come on and the egg inside my stomach has given me strength to go to him. I open the bathroom door and peek behind the shower curtain, smiling.

"So, that's the equipment, huh?" I ask, looking at his genitals and laughing, and waiting for him to answer.

He says, " 'Fraid so," and we both laugh. And I am happy because he will remain in position for at least another day.

# To Lightning, We're Pools of Liquid

They wake up side by side and she lets her hand fall upon his warm sweet yellow hair. He feels her naked chest against his back and turns his head and like a baby with hunger and closed eyes finds her and begins to nuzzle. They are heavy with sleepiness yet and she is not alert enough to wonder about whether she is good enough for him. She used to wonder, when they were new together, if she felt better to him than anyone ever had. They drift this way for awhile and she peers at his eyelid, a thin bluish parakeet kind of eyelid, out of the slits of her own eyes. And then she speaks. They are her first words of a new day.

She says, "Natasha ruined my rocking chair that time, ran over the septic tank, did not water my flowers so that they died, and burnt up my tea kettle. They got a good deal when they stayed here to house sit, didn't they."

It is a thread from the day before. The life before. It is about injustice. They speak about injustice most of the time now. The way people have wronged them. And it ties them together. This mutual understanding of abuse. She never used to think of such things before she married him. She used to let the few slights she ever got pass and feel sorry for people who hurt others; but she learned she could communicate with Alex if she matched story for story. He was bitter and filled with stories of injustice when she met him, and attaching his political science and philosophy studies to them, but not dispassionately. He took each injustice personally, wore it like a wound, and referred to it at any time to explain away his ineffectualness in this life, longing for a rejuggling of society so he would have a chance to be on top.

In time, he says, "Don took a stack of my wood home for his party once but didn't burn it in his fireplace that night. He got away with all that wood to use for himself that I stood

64

cutting up all day and you spent time stacking into a pile. And time is money."

She says, "Mrs. Ramron wanted that twenty-dollar quilted baby blanket my mother made for only ten dollars. She caused such a fuss. And the eggs … The way she got a dollar a dozen out of me after sneaking over and telling you they were a free gift for favors you did for her."

He says, stirring now, "I've done so many favors for Ted and he didn't come through with any of the promises he made."

She says, gaining momentum, "The girl at the YMCA who interviewed me… she wanted a technician for nursery school, and when I told her I was intuitive, not theoretical with children, she didn't give me the job. And I've got a teaching credential."

He raises up on one elbow and says, "I wanted to work as a mechanic once. I needed a job then and I couldn't get one anywhere. Nobody thought I could fix a car. I looked like Little Lord Fauntleroy, not a grease monkey." He takes a breath. "Even after I got out of the Air Force, after being a cadet and flying jets, the guy at Catalina Island wouldn't let me drive a golf cart. He told Larry not to let 'the kid' drive."

She has propped her head up at a right angle and says, "I would like to paint a picture of employment. An oil abstract. There would be a line of pterodactyl-like human creatures standing in a long line, disappearing over the horizon, with the hope in their glazed prehistoric eyes gone dull with self-protective indifference, while they wait for the first guy in line to get through with the kill. He would be eating a carcass, muffing it down. That would represent the job. He'd have it."

He says, "My father gave away all his tools to the neighbor who gave them to his son when we moved. He knew I wanted them. He didn't give me anything."

She says, "My mother had a way of snickering at my notions … "

They lie there awhile longer, warm, too warm because the ten o'clock sun is beating down on them from the curtainless windows.

They are quiet, busy with their own thoughts. Eyes darting through the mental file of abuse they've stored inside their heads and hearts. And then she says, "The only person who ever appreciated me was Mary Davis. And I took it for granted, thinking I would go on to better things and more people approving of me. Now, it turns out that *that was the thing I did*. What I did with her as a fellow teacher. And hers was the only praise I got."

He mused. He lit a cigarette and smoked. She knew he was pulling away from it. From the companionship of complaining together. He tried to rise away from the web of it, away from her. So she tried thicker threads to hold him to her. It was like in *The Days of Wine and Roses*, a movie they'd seen that year. He'd taught her about the headiness of griping about people and now he acted above it all, leaving her the one looking hopelessly lost in negativity.

She says, "There's an integument holding me from breaking through. It keeps me in a private place. Where people mistake me for someone else. And I cannot get through it into a public world so I can tell them what they need to know to protect myself. It's a mesentery. This thing, and as thin as gauze. Thinner. It's invisible. Like what separates a fetus from the world. But, I feel its tightness. That is the only way I know it's there. I forget it's there and keep going into it, over and over again. And it keeps holding me back. It lets people think they can use me."

He gets out of bed and goes to the television and turns on the stock market. She gets up and goes to the aquarium and sprinkles a dash of Tropical granules over five little guppies. Later, he goes outside and does his favorite thing, turns on the hose and sprays water in dry places, and smokes. She pulls the bed together and opens all the doors and windows and makes plans in her head to produce things. Lots of plans to do lots of things. She will dry and press flowers, stuff Humpty Dumpties. And fast. She will fast until it makes a difference.

He comes into the house after awhile and kicks out the cat and gets a long drink of water, tilting his head way back for a long time. She can hear it go down his throat in clunks of

Adam's Apple bobbing. That's when she thinks they are just sacs of fluid.

Alex and her. Bags of water. If lightning strikes them, that's all they are to the cosmos, as she watches Alex go back outside to muse over life, too, standing in the yard where he stares at the air. Just wet stuff for electrical currents to circulate through.

# Avoid the Void?

Alex lies abed limp. I scurry around rigid. I avoid my corner chair. Fuss in the kitchen, sweep fall leaves outside, change the fish (a dry piece of snail expanded overnight into a three-inch-long spongy decomposing, water-polluting problem), water the birds, feed the cats, dogs, kitten, peek in at Alex, seeing that he is still limp, lying on his face, in bed, mouth open, eyes shut. I see myself being perfect: a wonderful wife, going in massaging his placid white sick body with warmed baby oil. Performing professional sex, the way I believe hospitals should. Why ignore the healing quality of sexual well-being? Puffing his pillow and then stimulating his mind by reading to him: a good story, one that takes him into other worlds, into beauty, love, glory, out of his illness. It is all theory. Even though I believe these things would make him well again, I don't do any of them. I neglect him for awhile longer. I avoid. All morning I avoid something. I do not read or write letters, or tend to Alex (except for taking him a glass of orange juice and a green hard winter pear, which he awakens for and eats immediately and ravenously and then falls into his limp, open-mouthed, shut-eyed sleep again).

Because he is out of the way I leave him until I am ashamed. Or until I run out of things to do to avoid whatever it is I'm avoiding. Then I go to him. He is my last excuse to not do whatever it is I feel I should be doing. I say, "Alex, what's wrong. Why are you sleeping so much and so hard?"

He opens his eyes, closes his mouth, mumbles, "I dunno."

I get under the covers, prop up pillows, rest a paperback on my knees. "I'm going to read to you," I say.

"Okay," he lies limp, smiles weakly.

I begin. It is by a local author who writes about our town but disguises it behind fictitious names. Alex listens, moves closer. Our bodies intermingle and share heat. As I hear my monotonous tone drone on and on, I change my mind. "Let's get up. Let's go somewhere."

Alex and I are speeding along. I am insisting he decide where we should go. What I want is hidden from me. I try to force Alex to know. He suggests we drive up into the hills and look at all the new houses being built. That seems right. To look at other people's lives. The way they do it. We find roads we never knew were there, even though we've lived in the town twenty years. Discovering these places gives me an uncomfortable feeling. Little tar-topped and nearly dirt roads. With other people's lives presented in their house fronts and yards. One man (or woman) has a dozen statues in his front yard. Another enters through a walkway off the street into a house which hangs over a cliff. Every manner of entrance, angle, paraphernalia are witnessed by us as we drive and I keep flashing to our particular peering out place. Our own front door. I stop, overlooking a perfect place. We try to guess the man's age. I say, "He's probably our age…" It is a man out in his perfect yard. Alex says, "The way he drags that rake, I'd say he's about sixty." A younger man would rake with vigor." I say, "He's got it all. Everything he's all about. See his proper woodpile, and there's his pickup truck, the BBQ, a space of brick for a patio. He keeps in proportion to his needs. Nothing outweighs anything else."

Alex is annoyed. "He has no excesses. Does that interest you?"

I say, "He's *happy*. Look at him. His life is laid out. There is nothing missing. He has seen to everything he wants."

Alex says, "He's on the back-side of the hill. He has no view. He thinks small. Has built on the *wrong* side of the landscape. He can't see the ocean."

I say, "But look at his organization. Every leaf now is being swept up."

Alex asks, "Would you like that place? Could you settle for a place like that. A man like that?"

"No," I say. And drive away, unsettled.

# A Far Cry

I never liked the lack of perspective he had about his hands. His absence of comparative analysis irritated me. *His hands* were *the hands*. He didn't know what I knew about hands. My mother had laughed over José Iturbi's short stubby fingers long ago. It was a part of me. I knew a good hand when I saw one. And short fingers were not aesthetic. My grandmother used to say, "His hands are the hands of a killer. His fingers are just long enough to fit around the handle of a gun"— about anyone. I was full of it.

But he didn't know about the way hands *should* be. He only knew about the way his hand *were*. And he believed he had "perfectly proportioned" hands, the fingers and the palms in relation to eachother, because a girlfriend had told him so years before.

She told him he had "perfect fingers," and, because he loved her, he came to me knowing things about his hands that weren't true.

And I came to him believing things about my face that he did not think were true.

Things "*Daddy*" had told me. So we set about re-educating eachother in order to slay all alliances with *past*—I about his hands and he about my face. But our efforts came to nothing because the earlier attachments were not easily replaced.

And then a friend who plays the banjo came over and wanted to teach him a chord. She laughed when his fingers were too short and wide to manipulate the string position.

After that he began to look at his hands and at hers. And at mine. And I saw doubt creeping in, along with a new consciousness. He compared his hand to the "average hand" (Like mine). And his definition of long fingers being "those long spiky, salamander things," or, "those spindly, weak, knobby, skinny, spidery things," tapered off and he stopped twirling like a fairy in the middle of the floor to demonstrate long, eerie, unearthly, floating hands, and singing, "La, la, de, la."

I see him looking at his hands now, at times, turning them and saying, "My hands *are* kind of thick, I guess." The pride is gone. And I want to give it back to him. Now that he knows better. Sometimes I say, "They're really straight. Your fingers are. And they have a nice tan."

# Friends (getting a boat day)

Side by side they drive away toward town because it is a Sunday and he has a day off. It is not a *getting a boat and sailing away* day for them, nor a *going into business and getting a storefront* day. It happens to be *putting in a swimming pool and accepting what they have* day. So, they are smiling, talking, in earnest about what a good life they really do have if they'd just take time to recognize it. They begin a verbal list of the good things: They both have their health. He still has all his hair. They both have good teeth. This is important because on those other days, when he is depressed, he gets the sensation that if he would just push hard enough with his tongue, he could push his front teeth right out. On those days he believes his gums have turned to mush. She is in pretty good shape after all her exercising. He has a pretty damn good job, considering.

"I mean. I could still be working for Trit..."

They drive around and come to the pier because it is a place that will give them freedom to be who they are. They squeeze their car between two campers because it is the only slot left, and get out and lock their car, not out of habit, but because she decides not to carry her heavy purse. And they walk along, side by side, looking down at their feet, still seeing their life together and discussing it: a pool would be nice... and they'd stay right here and just be happy with what they have. They could accept that this is it for them. And it would be pretty good. He's got his tools. She's got her interests. They go on making lists. On other days, the *getting a boat and sailing away* days, he is a different man. And she a different woman. He is bitter. He sees the city as a carnivorous animal eating him piece by piece. On these days he says, "I used to like it here, but I don't like it here anymore." His voice goes hoarse with emotion, as that strikes him as a tragedy—that he should have learned to hate a place that he once loved so much. The very place he came back to after travelling all over the world. A place he remembered wherever he went, as a beautiful city, a place he would like to settle down in and live and raise a family.

In the same voice, he will say, on these days, "I've been punished here. Taxes, laws, restrictions, fines. No doctor knows what he's doing, no lawyer worth his fee. The law is in trouble. This country's in trouble. I used to believe in this city. Now I see it's an evil place. Full of incompetence and laws to protect the crooks..."

When he talks this way, she will be looking at the sailboat races out by the mile buoy and wondering what it would be like to be sailing all day. To believe in sailing like that. And after sailing, going to the yacht club for a drink, chatting it up with happy men. Laughing and wearing her pretty yellow dress, with something sparkly on her tanned wrists and fingers and maybe at the ears. To be glamorous and happy and free of worrying about not having enough of anything. She doesn't like seeing him unhappy. She doesn't like him believing a city can destroy him. She wants him to be above taxes, traffic tickets, doctors' mistakes, and lawyers' injustice. On these days, the passing of time, seeing their lives go by, will catch in their throats and they can hardly breathe, as if the air is sucked from their lungs in fear over this thing they are caught in together...

When he wants to get a boat and sail away, she gets a ruthless, daredevil urge to egg him on until he gets one, and then force him to sail. Away. So he can see what *away* is and then he can come back and never think of it again. To her, *away* is a fantasy that siphons off his energies, so that he cannot concentrate on what his real life is.

Going away and coming back would narrow him down, take away his choices and he would be cured of that sort of thing.

For years he has vacillated between going and staying, never giving in to either side. Settling down or drifting away. He could give himself to neither and as a result she also kept one eye out for an alternative life. Just in case he took off, she wanted to be ready to sprint. And she wanted to have good teeth. She could not start out in bad shape. As he contemplated their home as a temporary situation, she jogged around the block. For years, as he perched on the edge of belonging to it and to her, or not belonging, she did forty sit-ups a night., She did not want to get caught, so she kept herself prepared, half expecting to outgrow what she had gotten herself into with him before he decided to leave.

They spent fifteen years driving around, having coffee on the pier, talking about whether their life was the real one or not, or whether another one awaited them, together, or apart, somewhere else. And all the while they talked, they stayed, side by side. And once in a while this kind of a day would come along and *staying* would come in clear, and they would want to stay so strong that they would create imaginary anchors, like *putting in a swimming pool*, which would tie them to their home and take away all their travelling money so they would *have* to stay, They would have to give in and stay and swim, and enjoy having their own pool.

After the pier they walked around the harbor and looked at the boats. But he did not see them as he saw them on other days. They were so much color and design rather than purposeful vehicles. Her eye caught people's faces and she looked to see if anyone could see what she could see. And they strolled arm in arm as if they were friends. Really strolled because they were going to *stay* and live the life they were living. It had been decided by a kind of lucidity that *sitting by their pool, eating fresh salads, quitting smoking and getting every detail of their lives under control,* came and dominated every thought.

From the harbor they drove to an old beach where they had romped years before. They spread a blanket on the grass above the sand because the wind was blowing the sand. And they fell asleep side by side, so familiar with the presence of the other. Like Siamese twins. They shared the same heart. And so connected, they felt restricted and only dreamed of separation, afraid that it would destroy them both. Side by side, they longed for freedom. From eachother, from the life they had going. They dreamed of being alone, of still pursuing a future, still searching, still having choices, still deciding what to do with themselves.

She slept hard, aware that she was sleeping too hard, lying unconscious in the middle of a park. Trying to wake up to save herself, but going down deeper. She could hear his heavy breathing next to her. Time was endless. The sun was hot. She went away into a dream about a man she used to know. She was holding him, slipping her hands inside his clothing and feeling a familiar mole. Then she began asking, with a pleading voice, why he did not take her away with him when they had the chance? Why didn't we run away then. Why?

It was a vivid dream. She saw every detail of his face and arms.

And when she awoke there were voices of young boys shouting obscene words. And the bouncing of a volleyball on a picnic tabletop. The ball flew out of their hands and came at her. She had just opened her eyes and put up her hand. The timing… The ball would have hit her sleeping face a moment before.

He awoke. They sat up and he sneezed. She sneezed. She had a tickle in her chest when she drew a breath. The *putting in a pool and staying* was beginning to subside. He said they had fooled around long enough and should go home and get something done. *Getting something done* was essential to whatever kind of a day they were having. Or they would be not one inch closer to their goal. Together they drove home, side by side.

# A Scene with Vicky, Her Sister

So much, So much. For her mind. A picnic in the park. She does not foresee herself dying of lung cancer. In her cupboard is an assortment of scents in small flasks which she can choose from daily. And as she sits back there is the memory of her sister jogging with her on the beach. Her sister's face is red and awakened to physical endurance. When they stop to talk to Dion, the sister shows hidden hostility in the expression of shy fear. She is hesitant and indifferent but persistent, as if trying to prove a point to herself and to him. The sister feels awkward. A spirit trapped in a limbed structure. A fleeting ephemeral, ethereal presence that must creep on the surface of an earth. As they continue to run along the sand again, Dion grows small and her sister is embarrassed because they are physical.

At a far point where the rocks jut out into the ocean they take off their clothes and laugh as they enter the tumultuous salt water. The sister has lost five pounds and has only soft flesh where her stomach used to protrude slightly. She, herself, feels mammoth. Without clothes. They both dip their bottoms in the ocean, squealing and pretending to dodge the impact of each wave, Holding their breath. Then they race back to their clothes. A group of young fully dressed girls and boys round the bend. They laugh and cannot find their pantlegs fast enough. Finally they are covered up, and walking back the way they came and talking earnestly of why the sister has a pain in her side from jogging.

# Sound of Rain

They wake up to the sound of rain. The loose drain pipe, the one Alex has leaned against the house because he has not had time to put it in place along the roof line, is taking the downpour off one corner of the roof near their bedroom window. Through the window a bleak, grey morning filters in. She is glad for the rain because in rainy weather you are not expected to do as much. The rain will be a nice excuse. Alex is the first one up. The sound of rain falling on his unfinished work does not allow him to lie back and relax. She listens to his frustrated sounds of trying to get dressed. The scraping of the drawers of the bureau that is taller than both of them. The drawers do not come easy.

They require that he pull them exactly right. It is this exactingness that extracts the first toll from his nerves. She covers her head, trying not to hear. The drawer sticks, and he is cursing. He curses not only the drawer, but everything. His socks have holes in them.

Every single one, and they are all single. She has given up trying to match them together in pairs. The holes are not from worn-ness, but from the puppy. Every single sock. She can hear the strength of his thrusts as he slings each sock back into the blackness of the drawer after seeing a hole. He is then on the side of the bed, wrestling with his work boots. She knows he is putting on four socks with holes that will compensate the others.

Two socks to a foot. One with holes in the toe, the other with holes in the heel.

It's the whispering that gets to her. His talking to himself in anger. His cursing under his breath. Full monologues in whisperings about fate, ugliness, hate, desperation, everything gone wrong for him. She tries to drown it out with sleep but fear will not give in to sleep. She lies there in fear for this man who cannot take anything anymore. He used to be resilient. He used to be her protector. She used to be safe next to him. He used to whistle while he put on his boots to go out to work in his shop. He used to eat peanut butter and strawberry jam for breakfast, and scrambled eggs and orange juice. He used to be happy. And have an appetite for food and work and even for her. It was just in the last few years that something happened to him. Something inside. He began cursing. He began hating his shop, his shoes, socks, the rain. Everything became destruction to him.

Eggs had cholesterol. Peanut butter was loaded with cholesterol. Jam had white sugar.

Orange juice lost an enzyme when it was processed. The heat killed an enzyme that triggered the vitamin C which could be used by the body. The whole thing was dead. The glass of orange juice he drank in the morning had nothing in it. Nothing that was good for him. But these were not the things that made him angry. It was other things. Time. The amount of time he had spent getting to where he was now. And that amount of time outweighed what he had gotten. What he had done. And there was nothing she could do for him. No equivalent of egg-substitutes in time to have time back.

She interrupted his mutterings. "It's Vicky's birthday today. She'll be thirty. Can you believe that? My baby sister so old?" Her voice was sleepy. Dreamy. She did not want to come to. And be present; but she wanted to begin intercepting in this battle with himself.

"Thirty? Is that so? What a waste. Can you believe she could waste thirty years doing nothing? Absolutely nothing. Thirty years?"

"You have a big tear in the seat of your pants," she says without wanting to say it.

A kind of loyalty because he doesn't know what he looks like from behind. He feels back there. And begins to hiss.

"Sh-IT." The *it* is loud and she cringes.

He sits hard in the corner chair. Throws himself down and begins unlacing his high ankle work boots. His face is contorted. He has been trapped inside his clothes and shoes. An animal gone wild inside a cage when it discovers it's been caught. A knot in one shoe string stops his progress of going forward to undo the mistake of choosing the wrong pair of pants. The obstacle gives way. The knot comes unloose. "Thank God," she says aloud, watching him in amazement by now. His display of frustration has her frozen on the pillow, an audience to a play called, What Happens When a Man Goes Crazy In His Bedroom Trying To Get Dressed. She feels guilty. His clothes are her job. She has not done her job. But he has not blamed her yet. He does not want to take her on yet. That will come if she attacks him for being angry. Then he will throw in all the stuff about the socks, pants, sticking drawers from being stuffed too full.

She says, "Vicky has a small notebook of poetry that she keeps going. And that carving of a porpoise. Remember how good it was? She's done some things. Those sketches of different things."

He is sitting at the sewing machine with his pants turned inside out, torn seam lined up with the needle, and jabbing his fingers, which are too large, at the tiny needle.

The thread has come loose and he is trying to rethread it. "Don't tell me," he mumbles at the meanness of the machine coming unthreaded. That it would be inoperable just exactly when he needed to quickly make a seam, to stick both sides of his pants together, to mend his entire life in that one small moment. "Why?" His cry startles her. "Why now?" he cries out to the ceiling again, with his eyes closed. "There's a conspiracy... something is blocking my every move. Look," he points to the radio clock with inflamed, insane eyes. "Thirty minutes to get dressed and here I sit naked..." She sprawls tense under the covers. Wants to crawl into a hole in the mattress and be away from his inability to take an unthreaded sewing machine.

There is a catch in the air, as if all motion is stilled as he reaches with two fingers through the tear of his work pants and rips them in half. And movement begins again.

Life can go on. He is panting from that moment, arms

wide apart, holding a pant-leg in each hand. Somehow triumphant. He has won. "There," he says marching the torn-in-half-pants to the waste basket. "There." He opens the closet and pushes at hangers until he has found another pair of pants. He examines them. She imagines from her pillow of surprising him by sewing up the ones he has just destroyed. She imagines his surprise and how pleased he would be if she restored them to usefulness. He likes expediency above everything else. He likes to use everything up, down to the last thread. It is this desire to get the last drop out of everything that is part of the problem. He has driven himself to the last drop. He is squeezing himself dry. Wringing himself out.

He puts on the pants and as he laces up his boots for the second time. She says, "Vicky has tried to live the way she believed in living…"

"She has contributed nothing to civilization," he says. "The only thing she's done is spurt out a couple of kids to go out and live off society the way she has. Her life has been a total waste." They are silent. Then he sighs, fully dressed, finally. He stands up and looks down at her without seeing her and says, "Oh, God, I've got to make a breakthrough."

They have filmed-over eyes together. Neither one can see a way out. They are as dull as two beasts in the woods, instinctively feeling their way along each day. They end up in the bathroom together trying to brush their teeth at the same time over one small basin. He opens his mouth in the mirror and breathes out hard and fast so that his palate flaps, saying "Hah!" She laughs a non-laugh and says he looks like Dracula just before sinking his teeth into a neck.

He hocks and spits and she gags and says, "Don't, I can't bear that sound." He opens his mouth again and breathes hard and watches his bright red palate in his throat. She looks too.

"I've got throat cancer," he announces, as if it is true. (Later, it will be only a repairable brain tumor he finds out.)

"No you don't," she says, as if she knows it isn't true. "You just don't have any tonsils to catch the infections. That's what your mother did for you so you wouldn't get sore throats. See, it doesn't work; you get them anyway."

"It's bleeding. My throat is bleeding," he says with some satisfaction but mostly horror. It would be the perfect ending for his life: to die of throat cancer. The only thing he has actually enjoyed in his entire life is smoking. It would be fitting that this one pleasure destroyed him... He doesn't say so, but she knows what he's thinking. That has always been his theme song for as long as she's known him. The things he chooses go bad.

"Let me know when you're ready and we'll go into town," he says and heads for his shop. She can hear the scuff of his boot on the walk and the opening of the shop door out in the back. The truck engine revs after a while and she knows he is working on it so they can take it in to pick up some building materials. Wood, iron, nails, electrical boxes.

He never has enough. He craves materials to work with. And then he works like a fiend with them, and his work never ends. He builds and builds and builds. Putting pieces of things together until he has structures. And then he walks around inside these newly built structures and sighs. Never satisfied. A new bedroom, then a whole new section onto the house, sheds, small shops and then a big shop. A great big shop built over the small shops. The small shops inside destroyed by termites. Crumbling. His early work crumbling so that he has had to build a whole new shop around it. They had laughed at his Chinese puzzle: A shop within a shop within a shop within a shop, to infinity. He had grinned about the inner chamber he would go into to get away from the world. After making his contributions to civilization.

She takes a quick shower, keeping moving so to not let the water fall too long in any one spot and imbalance her nerves. Then she dresses and feels congested with the cream she puts on her face, too tight a waist band and hooves attached to her soft feet in the form of shoes with tapered soles. She is hurrying. Getting dressed is so simple an act after watching him defeat himself at every step of it. As she runs out the door to jump into the truck that he has left idling by the side door she is thinking, *It's his mother. She's done this. She made him eat too many vegetables and save too many desserts until he has come to live this way. He cannot have any fun. Everything is a chore. That's why all the joy has gone out of his life. It's all so grave and serious to him.*

A mile down the freeway a piece of cardboard in the back of the truck blows up against the rear window. It is the cardboard off the ping-pong table she bought to bring some fun into their lives. He cannot see. "My, God, that ping-pong table will be the death of me yet," he says, swerving over to the shoulder to grab the cardboard. He refers to their earlier argument over whether or not to get the ping-pong table. He said there was no place to put it. She said, "Why not inside your huge shop." He gets out, throws a piece of pipe over the cardboard and they continue toward town.

"I've got to press forward and get somewhere in my life," has begun to be a redundancy he utters several times a day. He looks at his watch now and says it. "I've got to press forward." She repeats it under her breath and frowns. They are always in a hurry.

To get where?

Oil begins to spurt out from under the dashboard onto his shoe. It spurts like a severed artery and he looks down in disbelief. His sock and shoe are black, slick, and the oil is forming a puddle under his sole. He jumps as he remembers what's going on and clamps his big thumb on a tiny tube up under the dashboard, and at the same time swerves off onto the shoulder of the road again. "God" It is the only word he says, but the sound of it resounds off the metal interior of the truck and chills her to the bone.

"Why?" Another single word that freezes her on her side of the seat and she watches, an audience again to: What It Looks Like When A Man Goes Crazy Inside of His Truck While He's Driving Down the Freeway.

He is calling himself names for being so stupid as to leave the cap off the oil tube.

She has never before in her life seen oil squirting out from under a dashboard and is confused. Of all the old cars she has been in in her life, how can this happen inside a new truck to a man who has taken such pains for nothing to go wrong?

He recovers from his rage only because he has to. There is nothing else to do. He cannot explode and be gone. That is what he wanted to do. To disappear in a blaze of particles. She watched him grow red, to turn to puffy pulp around the head and shoulders, to compact down tight and then stretch out in a silent fit within himself. And then he sat there, weak, shaking his head. After that, he turned the truck around and headed home.

She held her thumb over the tube and felt it grow hot. She didn't know what it was she was holding and didn't ask. It was whatever his life was all about. Probably some link to a meter so he could have a quickie way to read his oil. He invented all kinds of little do-dads that turned on him sooner or later.

At home they wiped oil from their hands. He changed his socks and cleansed the shoe. He was silent the whole time because this was backing up into the past they had just driven out of. This was not pressing forward. They had had to back up in time to where they were a half hour before. It was dead time. He did not speak and she did not breathe until they had passed up the spot on the freeway where the oil tube had begun spurting.

At that point they were caught up and she said, "It's inner isometrics; that's what you're doing. Why would all these things be happening if you weren't blocking yourself?"

The medical clinic was their first stop. She went to the cafeteria counter and ordered a coffee while he went in for an examination of the throat. Thirty minutes later he appeared in the doorway of the waiting room holding a prescription.

"Can you believe this waste?" he said, as they walked back to the truck. She looked and saw what he saw. The old medical building lay in rubble next to the new building and demolition trucks sat receiving the scoops of debris, broken wood, electrical boxes, copper wiring, iron, good beams of oak, cracked and carried in the bucket of a caterpillar tractor. Or was it a bulldozer? Whatever it was, it was carrying away and depositing as trash, materials that Alex dreamed of accumulating in large piles. He shook his prescription, worth twenty dollars' worth of drugs for his throat, at the wreckage.

"And it's taken me forty years to get enough metal and wood together to build what I've built. Forty years: And look. The waste. There must be thousands of dollars worth of electrical parts being buried. Do you know how much one of those outlet boxes is worth? Just the thin square of metal there? Seventy-five cents now. And you need dozens of them if you want to build anything." On the way to the pharmacy he said, "I really thought I had throat cancer. I was ready to hear the doctor tell me that there was a big red raw ulcer in my throat. And I was ready to accept it. I'd asked for it."

"I knew it wasn't," she said. "Vicky's palate used to drag on her tongue when she got sore throats as a girl. She really got bad sore throats. So I knew your palate was okay." He was off in his world of silence again and didn't hear her. He was thinking of the unfairness: He is paying the doctor forty dollars to look at his throat, the pharmacist twenty, and these men are building their dream, a new clinic, and they won't even let him go pick up all the electrical boxes out of the rubble. They pay the bulldozer man seventy dollars an hour to cart away thousands of dollars worth of building materials he could use. She knew that look on his face. Not having throat cancer made no difference to him.

Not having building materials did. Seeing the waste.

The rain kept up all day. Alex sloshed around in the mud after they got home, poking around, sweeping rainwater off his new shop floor. He had not gotten the things under the doors yet to stop the water from coming in. Later the wind came up and he climbed up on the roof of his shop to inspect any loose edges that could be whipped up.

While he climbed up and down the ladder carrying heavy things to weigh the unfinished edges down with, a layer of plastic skylight lifted in a gust of wind and stood on end in front of him, as if to salute him and then broke in half against his body.

When he came into the house after dark, his hair was standing out all over his head in curls from the rain and wind. Curls he plastered down with water every morning.

He stood in the new wing of the house he had built and

watched the wind whip at the shop roof. The rain gutter by the bedroom window was still taking the rain in a loud torrent. He said, "The Tower of Babel. I know what that means now. I can see what that means. It must have been the same for the people back them. The technology of the age. Everyone reaching for something. Everyone speaking a different language. The man on the top not understanding the man on the bottom. Or the man in the middle. That is what's happening today. We are all reaching and we have all learned our own language, and our own way of getting there."

Suddenly there was a flash as they stood there and a glint of hope shot to his eye.

A crack of lightning followed immediately. The storm was right over them. They ran to the door and looked out. All his talk of Armageddon and The Day of Reckoning, and now the lightning was striking a block away. A telephone pole lit up, crackled and fizzled to a crisp before their eyes. All the lights of the house went out and the whole neighborhood was black. In front of the fireplace and with candles all around she could see Alex's face take hope. Lightning, fire, flood, wind. Let it come. Let it wipe the slate clean. She knew his words by heart. Let it level everyone's efforts and the race to the top would have to begin again. Then he'd have a chance. He hadn't gotten off to a good start this time. Too many people were ahead of him. He didn't have a chance. The lightning flashed and the thunder cracked and the rain got loud on the roof and later the wind blew hard. Harder than he had ever remembered it in this house. And he paced, waited, peered out at his shop, and shook his head. It would probably do the most damage to his shop. No one else had ventured into anything so foolish as building a flat roof with tar paper and plastic panels. No one in the neighborhood. They all lay sleeping in their beds. He was the only one pacing and worrying all night.

They did not go to bed. About four AM the wind stopped. He inspected his roof and saw there was no more damage. Just that one panel. They heard a chain-saw up the hill. He had seen a flash in that direction earlier. They got in their car and drove around, eyes searching out irreparable damage from the storm. They came to the chain-saw. An oak tree had blown over, just missing a boat. The guy was out cutting the tree up. They sat with their headlights on him and watched. And then they drove on, seeking out destruction. Their curiosity was never fully satisfied. They saw only how quickly debris collects in the roadways and how easy it would be to lose "civilization" if the roadways were allowed to grow over. They felt small and frail seeing how easily "nature" moves in and covers up all the efforts that "civilization" took centuries to make. In one night they had to squeeze around fallen trees and go slow over broken branches. They were forced back to their house. Back to what Alex was fighting to get beyond in his "pressing forward." And back to the bed they had gotten out of almost 24 hours before.

> *What if the girl who made Deep Throat got throat cancer? There would be a lesson for us.*

# The Pfeffernuesse Dough

The pfeffernuesse dough is in the refrigerator getting hard. Marty knows she must dash out and do the shopping while it chills and then she will come home and bake the dough in little balls, roll it in powdered sugar and serve it to all the mouths that will pass her way.

Marty is not hungry. She has not been hungry for a long time, because the threat of starving has been removed from her life. There was a time when food had been scarce, but that time has passed. Marty slips some thongs between her toes and goes out the door and gets into her car. She must bring home more food and she does not want food. There is food in all the cupboards of her kitchen. There is food in the refrigerator waiting to be eaten. There is food on the back porch for the cats and the flies that no one else wants to eat. There is food in the drain of her sink, and in her own throat, there is the feel of food which she cannot swallow and which she will never be able to swallow. Marty sees crumbs of food on the floor of her car.

Marty reaches into her purse for her car keys. She sees the remains of a teething biscuit which she has forgotten to take out and throw to the birds. And although the birds will never be able to eat it because it is too hard, she wants them to peck at it, because even though Marty does not like food anymore, she cannot bear to waste it.

Marty finds the keys and at the same time she throws the biscuit out the window. It lands in the ice plant and sinks out of sight. She backs out and hurries to the freeway, steering with one hand while the other hand reaches for a spot on the back of her head. She finds the bump she has sought. Her fingernail lifts the scab. As it comes off she feels pain. It is not the first time she has picked it and it will not be the last. At one time she kept one going for two years. Her finger dips into the moisture which she has released. The salt on her finger stings into the open wound and causes her eyes to water. Marty touches it several more times until the effect of the salt wears off and then she leaves it alone.

It is the day of the midweek sales. Alex circled the ads for her to go shop at the best bargain stores. She has read the ads the night before and made out her list. It lays beside her on the car seat: carrots, two pounds for twenty-five cents, cucumbers, a nickle apiece. Oranges, ten cents a pound. Velveta cheese, eighty-nine cents at Safeway. Liver, only forty-nine cents a pound, and potatoes, ten pounds for thirty-nine cents.

Marty has cut the curve at the overpass intersection because there are no cars coming. She steps on the gas going down the entrance ramp onto the freeway. She guns it to win out over a diesel truck and makes it out ahead of him. He changes lanes and passes her. She passes him going up Ortega Hill. They race eachother down. She stays in the left lane trying to go faster than him without going too fast. She does not want to be behind him because he is not going fast enough to keep far enough ahead of her, yet she cannot go fast enough to stay away from him. She sees a highway patrolman behind them, so she lets the diesel take the lead, falling behind and decreasing her speed to sixty-five. The patrolman passes them both and disappears, darting from right to left lanes out of sight.

Marty reaches for the radio but stops herself because it is already on. There is a lack of something. She wants to turn on another radio. One is not enough anymore. The sound has become ordinary to her ears. It is mere music, mere news. She wants a super sound to stimulate her, to carry her away with the power only music has. But there is no super sound available. She switches stations from Extra Music to KDB and Mama Cass, then over to KGUD and Johnny Cash. Then she switches it off. She wants something that sound cannot give. But she is afraid of the silence with the absence of radio. A loneliness creeps into her and she must be with only herself. She must take a look and she does not find the thing she is looking for. So she turns the radio back on.

Marty twists the rear view mirror down so that she can see herself. It is reassuring that she is still there. She is never sure. She knows the mirror is deceptive, though, that it makes her look wide-faced because it is a wide short mirror. She turns it perpendicular and looks into it and sees a long thin face. She straightens the mirror and looks away because she is passing a car and does not want the driver to think she is vain.

The Salinas exit is coming up. She takes it and maneuvers down Milpas over to the Safeway parking lot. She feels safe going to Safeway. It is a big store, extravagant. It spares no expense to serve her. There is no one who hovers around hoping she will buy something so that he can live. There is no one clasping his own hands. Affluence prevails. They do not need her business.

Marty enters the door that opens for her. The bigness of the store, the amount of air in it, disperses her. She wants the small space of the front seat of her car to keep herself together. She swings a basket out and wheels past the milk and cottage cheese. The coldness of the refrigerated bins makes the hair on her arms and legs stand out. It presses against her sleeves and pantlegs. She feels the flu at the back of her neck. She feels thin as if she is wasting away. She has not eaten anything all morning. She licks her teeth and sucks them to take the brown stain and sugar out of them from the coffee she has had earlier. The swallowing sets her stomach off. She tightens it. She is hungry but she does not want food.

Marty chooses the middle of the aisle and strides into the dry foods where it is warmer. The assistant manager is checking shelves. He looks at her and she looks at him. She knows he likes her. She swells a little passing by. They have never spoken, but he caught her once when she put her heel on a grape. About five years before. He had helped her recover her balance and she went away embarrassed and without thanking him.

She fills her basket with bags of whole wheat flour and brown rice and grapefruit. She will never buy soda pop to destroy her teeth, but she wishes to fall on the floor and bleed in order to test all the people in Safeway. She wants to prove that what she is suspicious of is true, that no one would stop and get her blood on their hands. Not even the assistant manager. He might run for a rag to clean off the floor. And he might carry her into the back room where she could die out of sight of the other customers so they would not see how bad things can get in his store.

Marty sees an old lady with one tomato in her basket and a can of corn, three carrots and two little pieces of meat behind cellophane. She wonders how life can be that simple. That small. She thinks of her own grandmother who has died this summer, but who, last summer piled her basket high with watermelon because she believed they purified her blood. Marty wants to write to her grandmother again just in case part of her is somewhere, because she should not have died. She had done everything right. She had eaten whole wheat bread and roughage for her bowels. She had toiled on her one acre and brought forth fruit from her trees and eggs from one hen. And she was not vain. She wore old clothes and seldom brushed her hair. Marty did not like to think that she died anyway. And that she could not mail a letter to her now and say flippantly, "Hope all's well with you. Love, Marty."

Marty lifts a box of oatmeal from the shelf and searches the faces that pass her for what she wants to see in people. She finds nothing. There is no man in Safeway to stimulate passion in her. There is no child to stimulate love of children and there is no mother to bring out a feeling for motherhood. There is nothing in anyone's face beneath their hairdos that have come from packages. The clothing they wear is bonded so that it will not take the contour of their bodies. It will resist the creases that their living will try to put into it. Marty sees that everyone wants to look brand new, like the latest product. Even the oatmeal box has been remodeled. The coffee jar has also taken a new shape. The juice pitchers and the can openers are new shades. Only the cabbages cannot be changed.

The people come at her along the aisles but miss her as they pass. They are all new. They are wearing long skirts and boots or striped pants. Her tongue goes to the roof of her mouth and she becomes aware that it feels the same as it has always felt. It has not been redesigned. There is no new style this year for mouth tops. It is the same old one with the original ridges on the sides where the teeth grow and with the rippled patterns farther back. Marty suddenly loves the roof of her mouth. It is something she can count on. She picks up a jar of mayonnaise.

Hunger moves inside of her. It shifts her insides, lifting and falling and she tightens her stomach muscles again to subdue the sounds. She takes a gallon of cider off the floor where it has been stacked. She puts three dozen eggs into her basket and rechecks her list. It has been completed. Alex counts on her to be frugal with "his" money. She wheels her cart into the line and waits to be checked. The cashier gets to her at last and rings up seventeen thirty-seven and a young boy puts it all into three double bags.

Marty pushes her cart out to the car and unloads it. While she is backing out of the parking lot she bites the cellophane bag that holds the carrots and tears it open with her teeth. She waits for the red light to change and then takes out a carrot and begins to chew it up.

Marty takes the on-ramp leading to her house where the pfeffernuesse dough should be ready to roll into balls by now. And after she has done that, she will begin on the potato salad because they are going over to the Longs for dinner. Marty does not want to make a potato salad. She wants to lie down with Guy Long and make love instead. But she knows that her family will go over and eat their charcoal broiled hamburgers and that the Longs will eat her potato salad and Guy will glance at her from time to time and dare not think what he's thinking because, even though he's for ecology and other subjects of the day, he does not know himself. There are too many interesting numbers and initials in the air today to fill his mind with instead.

Guy will tell her how many seals are left on Anacapa Island and how many pelican eggs hatched this year and how many should have if it hadn't been for the DDT, but he cannot tell her about his own father and what it was like growing up. She has asked him already and he has already laughed and said, "Do you really want to talk about that sort of thing?" And then he tried to and could not remember much about his father.

Marty wants to drink a cup of coffee at a restaurant where there are strangers. She does not want to go home. She leaves the freeway on a Montecito exit and heads for a coffee shop at which she has stopped before. She gets out and locks the car so no one can take the food which she does not want. She goes in and sits on an orange stool at the counter next to a woman who is talking loudly to a waitress. The waitress is smiling and asks the woman a question, but before she can answer the waitress has stepped over and stood before Marty, raising her eyebrows for the order. Marty orders coffee and hunches over the counter and gazes around. It is a brooding position. Everyone at the counter is in the same posture. The steam of their coffee rises under their noses and their eyes are on their own thoughts. The waitress has turned around where the coffee pots sit and pours a cup for Marty and places it carefully in front of her. Then she pulls her pad out of her apron and in one stroke writes twenty cents and a C with a circle around it.

Marty watches the lady from her peripheral vision. She is small next to the woman. The woman is eating a piece of chocolate cream pie with a scoop of ice cream next to it. She is a large woman. She is ample as she hunches over the counter. The stool is buried under her. Her elbow is on Marty's part of the counter because it is too big to fit in the space allowed by the width of her stool. Marty fits on her stool and her own elbows fit in their proper area of counter, but she does not move her arm away from the woman. There is a warmth radiating from the oversized body. Marty wishes to lean against her as a dog leans against a person. There is a comfort in being next to the woman. She has a friendly voice. Marty wishes she could eat pie recklessly as the woman is eating her pie even though it must be harmful for the woman to do so. She wants to climb up into the woman's lap and be cuddled. She wants the woman to cradle her in her great endless arms and to give her the courage to eat such pie and become fat. To be ample.

Marty listens to the husky voice. It is the sound she was not able to find on the radio. The woman is sure of what she is saying. She is sure of what she knows whether it is right or not, whether the waitress believes her or not.

The coffee is gone from Marty's cup. Marty wishes the cup had been bottomless. She wishes the drinking could have been infinite so that she could have a warm flow coming into her mouth forever. The waitress makes a motion to refill but Marty declines. She must go home. The pfeffernuesse dough will be waiting. Marty leaves a quarter and a dime by her cup and pushes through the glass door. She gets into her car and the smell of all the food greets her. She drives home.

# One Morning

The morning she had flu swimming through her body, she sat drinking coffee on the pier. Across a table from her husband. The sick blood made insights come to her. She thought the people here were a perpetual thud. While people who had money and good looks were like a perpetual zing. And were somewhere else. She told her husband that.

He merely looked at her with those things on his face which she had never seen the beginnings of. Little acne scars he acquired when he had been chemically another person. And making all the conquests. It was just her again. Wanting love and the zing to come her way. Now. After he was all through.

A pay phone stood next to the door they had entered. In the car she told him she wanted to call their friend and tell him he was the greatest speaker on TV. In the interview about aging. The husband discouraged her over-exaggeration. He told her to exaggerate if she must but not to overdo it. And their friend wasn't that great, he said. So she did not phone at all. She did not try to invigorate their life. She subdued it along with him, instead, to be in good taste. He could teach her how to not show anything until she had nothing more to show.

When they parked their VW sedan, he told her not to slam the car door like that again. Because he noticed the gas reserve stick had been kicked over and did not know when. She had driven it last. He said it was a juvenile reaction most people who are intelligent leave behind them as they grow up. To slam things. She said she would be a juvenile then. But felt the gravity on her cheeks which had lost their puff and it made her feel foolish.

She warmed her foggy cold hands around the hot cup. And liked the steam under her nose. To feel the living warmth of it. She thought about a man she had sex with once.

It made her warm to know she had felt alive. Then. And had enjoyed what another person was once. What she was had taken on meaning. She had begun to feel attractive. So that now it allowed her to sit here with her husband and her crooked nose and the creasing down eyes and accept it. That she looked like everyone else here in the nook they had chosen. Where the down-trodden huddle together to see one another. Because she had felt attractive then.

She had learned to like herself through him. And he did not even have what some others had had. That thing she previously valued through hearing talk. He had a small penis. But on an ample strong body that gave her strength to be next to it. She felt a sense of protection in it. He made no judgments of her. He did not criticize her. And because of the silence, his absence of care, there was an acceptance of her in it. She was able to give him a lot of a part of herself. Although he didn't particularly want the self. She had put it away and presented her body as a waitress does food. It had been for the time being. A song came to her head when she thought of the back of his Ford pickup. And the two of them in it. With the horse in the corral nearby smelling their smells. And when he stood up and shook the blanket afterward to fold it, the horse twirled around and thundered off in fright. They were demons together to it. They could see only its dark silhouette in the night, galloping away. She hoped it wouldn't tear itself on the barbed wire fence.

A seagull floated, awkward, to the roof of Moby Dick and landed above the rain drain. Out of sight of her eyes. The people at the tables were squinting out the windows with their faces, watching a pleasure boat head out of the harbor thickly. And a fishing boat, larger, came back smoothly. She now saw him going into sleep and quivering as he did, with his thick arms stretched out and herself in between them. And after he was asleep she was brave enough to put her hand on his cheek tenderly to turn his face so she could see it. He awoke and said he'd like to stay there about a week. But it was like blackberries to her. Just enough and scanty to find.

There were no weeks of gorging. He would be married before Christmas and she would be back to work with him in her brain, steaming, alive, while he walked down the Mormon aisle into the life he wanted. She ate a lot and made herself a new pair of pants to wear after that. And looked forward to a whim when he might drop in. And treat her to himself. She had told him the last time that he was a golden bull and she worshipped him and she was not even Jewish. He did not respond to the last part. And to the first he said only, a golden bull, huh. He was blond but there was never enough light to see him in as she would have liked.

Scatterings of well-kept worn-out people ate fried potatoes and eggs, not getting up all of the yolk. And it was the vitamin A they needed for the shortsightedness that brought them here. The husband did not look at her. She was like a mirror to a parakeet, there across from him. He saw only himself and his side of their life if his eyes happened to fall on her. He thought about important things. The things that brought in money for her to spend, while smoke poured from his mouth and nose. It was that posture that had made her marry him. A strength was in a man who looked off into the distance and thought a lot.

She knew that what she had waited for was out of proportion to what she eventually got. And it was back then that the anticipation outweighed the actuality when he finally did come back. His tiny penis. His aloof touching. His heart being with his new wife. Coming to see her like driving by a nice spot on his way to somewhere else. The hair of his body bumped under her palm momentarily. And she asked him if he could feel the calluses on her hand as she rubbed him. He asked, calluses? And did not understand that she was a person. A live one.

She wiped sugar onto her neck accidentally off her cheek as she ate a jelly doughnut. He had guided her head once, to give him pleasure. It would give her pleasure to think of it for the rest of her life. To be wanted for something. By him.

The husband's eyes were full of how to save money on his taxes. He visualized a new car and a saw from Sears and a calculator for adding, subtracting, multiplying, *and* dividing. The dividing was important. And rare, he said. To find a machine that could do it. And a full height filing cabinet. She could have the small one. That would make up for his not wanting her to close the door of the car so hard. And he would mark it all off for the business. Even the gas. She joined him and suggested he invest in another piece of property for their future home now. And maybe plunk some down on the house to get the payment on its way and the interest down. It struck him right. They communicated for the first time that morning. She did not feel stupid to him anymore. She had made a contribution.

His blond hair was on not as big a head as the other guy. And there he was again.

Just a gesture or a color brought him back. To take her away from them. The ugly people.

And herself. The ones she belonged to and must accept criticism from and must love. So she nestled next to him in the back of the truck, because he had been young then and owned no bed somewhere. She remembered all the details again, while a little old lady sat eating a salad bravely alone and dropped some off her fork onto her lap.

*The house they lived in: He was going to make the house bigger. That was three years back. And now it is bigger. He had never built a house before but she figured it was in every man to do so. An instinct. And she watched without awe as he removed walls and built new ones, hoisted beams overhead or knocked out the other side of the fireplace. The construction went on and on and there would have been no end to her awe once she started it, so she yawned and bordered on boredom for self-protection. And when he was finished there was silence in place of cheering. No one noticed that he was a hero.*

# *Reform*

Alex is 44. He is annoyed by everything. One morning nothing is right. A smear on the oven causes him to curse. By this time he had planned to have all the smears out of his life. Cat kibble on the porch causes him to swear. She finally approaches him in his frustration and attempts to help. She has a notebook and pen. She takes notes. It seems official to write what he wants down. He recites a list of changes he wants in his life. He calls it Reform:

Organize yourself first by having breakfast at the table and discussing the day.

Get up at 6 AM (should have been no. 1)

Eat no food between meals.

The bedroom must be kept sacred, no kids in it. "Why, when I was a boy we wouldn't have gone into my parent's bedroom…"

The storage room straightened up…

All the broken stuff thrown away. If it's wood, burn it.

Put up more fences, stain them…

Have more togetherness …

"Everyone is going in a different direction, we never get together anymore…"

Then we'll have fun… "Once we get regulated like we should. We can't have fun being out of control…"

She reads the list over, tries to analyze it. It is the list of a man who has been cinched up tight all his life and now, wanting a change, he cinches up tighter. She reads the list back to him. He is smoking, nods in approval, turns to her and counts on her to carry out the nine points of Reform. First she goes to the storage room and opens the door to have a look. Things they believed in once are strewn about, jumbled. She feels sorry for all of them. *I cannot throw them away.* She closes the door and believes she will get to it when she feels angry. She can throw away everything when she is angry.

On the way back into the house from the storage room she trips over a piece of dead bamboo that has dried and fallen from the green forest of bamboo which grows along the leach line. She has heard Alex say at least twenty times over the years that he will have to dig the bamboo out before it chokes off the leach line altogether. She remembers how it started. She was walking on the beach once and found a little sprig of bamboo. She examined it and found it had a tiny root. It had been broken off from the whole hillside of bamboo lining the beach. She brought the sprig home and put it in a pot.

It doubled, tripled and was soon too big to stay in the pot. One day she dug a hole in the backyard and emptied the pot of bamboo into it. Then years later Alex is cursing the ever-growing forest, which threatens to choke out his leach line and cost him hours of digging and hacking to get it out. He has forgotten where the bamboo came from. She wonders why it isn't on the list of Reform. Get rid of the bamboo. But he has to be realistic.

Thinking of the list Alex has had her draw up causes her to want to eat. Makes her not want to get up in the morning. She thinks of his version of fun. One of the things most fun for her is to have all the kids in the bedroom and lie around and talk and laugh and eat and watch TV. She folds the list in half and tucks it away in a book and goes to the refrigerator. She wonders why it is that what she does as a whim turns out to be a curse to him.

# The Spill

Looking back she thought it couldn't hold. Certain phases would crack and spill her out.

But she sees that she was held by an unspillable thing. It would go on and on containing her.

The spill was suppose to come by now. And she would be viewing everything as *before the spill* and *after the spill*. It would be her personal calendar for her personal savior. But it hadn't come. It would never come. She would never be poured loose from this thing she was attached to. It would hold her tight and she would always have to view everything from *here*.

She had visions of causing the spill.

Every time she passed by the glass table she went through the mental act of raising a hammer above her head and bringing it down through the smooth transparent surface and sucking her head down into her neck to cringe away from flying glass. A bludgeon, down and through a surface with a force that twitched and welled, making her arm itch for action.

*I am afraid for him to come home. I don't want to hear him tell me things. As he talks I will realize my separateness. It will come to me. As I see his fullness, his new enthusiasm, the new information about movies and books he "picked up," away from home. Out there. With people out of their own towns, in somebody else's town. Carefree. Careless. Reckless. Greedy. Accident-prone by will. "Oops, I just slipped my dick into you, excuse me." "Oh, that's alright. I don't mind at all."*

*I've seen the eyes of travelling men. And women. They're eyes of animals on prowl. Even my own eyes are, away from home. Everyone becomes prey.*

*tAnd I can smell upholstery on him when he comes in the door. The smell of somewhere else where I haven't been and where he doesn't care to show me. The smell of things I fear.*

# The Male

Alex said, "Let's get in bed so I can hold you and be close to you. It's the only way we're going to get anywhere."

"No," she said. "I don't want to be near you."

"I know, I know, you can't stand me, I'm repulsive, but take off your clothes."

"No," she said, and watched him from the other side of the room on the other side of the bed. He had begun taking off his clothes.

"I'll rip them off then. They're old anyway. Hurry up." He took a step in her direction and she wanted to laugh, to giggle and to run away from him. To play.

She said, "Oh, damn, not this again. Okay. You're the bigger animal. You've got the big muscles. Big deal. So I have no choice." She took off her clothes and beat him under the covers, hugging the wad of sheet to her breasts, pressing on them so he couldn't touch them. Alex crawled in beside her. She felt his cold feet. She left her cold feet straight down between the cold sheets and did not put them on his warm ankles.

He put his arms around her body and pressed himself into her side. She lay on her back, stiffly pressing the sheet into her chest, keeping her body straight so it wouldn't conform to his.

"Now, come on." His soft lips nibbled at her cheek.

She sighed. "Ooh, that's sickening."

"I know. But, you'll have to put up with it. I want to be warm to you. We can't go on like this. It's destroying us. You're destroying yourself with all this sourness."

"I'm discovering that I've got a great capacity for sourness. A big empty place I want to fill up with sourness. I've learned that that's what I want to do. Hate. Uh, how I hate."

Alex was kissing her neck and it sent goosebumps of revulsion over her body. She wanted to continue to battle. She wanted to keep them on the unpleasantness until it solved itself. She was not able to define what it was that had to be solved.

She said, "The god-damned male ego is what has held us all back from the beginning of time because it can only reign by smashing down small dark men, poor whites and women and any other wretched creature it can define away. Anything threatening your power. Well, you wouldn't have any power without us."

The desire to cry had left her throat and the anger loosened her tongue. "Then it can feel big. It can only feel big by comparison. Only if there's something around it can make feel inferior." Her hands still clutched the sheet over her breasts, the only soft vulnerable thing about her, she felt. Those ninnies, that soft tissue. The most tender and sensitive place on her body. Like his testicles.

"Open your legs," he said. His voice was too soft. She would rather have been ordered to.

"No," she said and clamped her feet and locked them. He brought one arm down and threatened to press his thumb into her waist. She opened her legs and he nestled between them, closing his eyes and breathing his sweet male breath into her neck.

Her nose was in his hair and she inhaled because she had always liked the smell of it.

"Go ahead," she said, "Bigger Animal. I'm merely a thing here for you. Something for your ego. Your god-damned male part. Do what you want. But you can't make me like it."

Alex made love to her and she rubbed her eyes in order to cause a sensation there to distract herself and resist him. She lay limp and concentrated on making her eyes itch. She rubbed them until they watered, and then rubbed them some more making a snapping noise and created a new soothing sensation which made her see black and purple with microscopic red and white specks, small dots and bits of lightning and some green. She rubbed up until her eyelids smacked loose from her eyeball and smacked back down again. She went up into her eyebrows and forehead and into her scalp and back to her eyes.

She said, "Hurry up and get finished will you."

He said, "No, I'm waiting for you. Even if it takes all afternoon. I'm giving it the whole afternoon if that's what it takes. We're not going to go on hating eachother. It's worth an afternoon." She looked at the clock and saw they had already wasted twenty-five minutes. And she had a lot to do waiting for her. Beside the work, she wanted to go for a run before the sun went down.

"So, you think this is going to make everything all right again." She flattened out her knuckles over her chest because he was pressing down on her. She did not want to dig them into him. She did not know what accumulative discomfort would do. "After the big climax I'll think you're wonderful, huh?"

His head rested on the pillow beside hers. "Yes, it'll help because you like this. Now, tell me what you want. I want you to want it. You can't say you don't like this." He looked into her eyes and there was a tenderness she did not trust anymore because she had also seen the anger. A floating rage that could alight instantly in a hateful, criticizing temper. His level of frustration over life in general made her edgy.

"Yes I can."

"We've got to work at it." The pleading note was temporary. She knew she could not push him forever; but she could not break out of the resistance. They would make love again and like it then. But not now. There was something to be said for contrasts. Perhaps the resistance was an experiment. She had never held out before.

He said, "You know, if you really wanted to be master here, you'd ride the Hell out of me and take what you want. You could have me serving you so easy. And you've never learned that. I want to please you. That's all I want. My whole life is spent trying to please you." He had reared up, straightening his arms for props and talked as if giving a lecture on stage. She thought his whole philosophy about life would follow, but it didn't. He was given to theatrical rhetoric with the waving of the arms. How certain elements in a society did this and that and caused this and that to react and exactly where he stood in it all and where she stood and how, if there were injustices, nature and its laws of the survival of the fittest was to blame. He'd majored in philosophy and political science. His family held serious political discussions. And he had a penchant for pointing the finger so the world was at fault, never himself. He saw elements, not individuals. But, in the mean time, they would have their afternoon of sex and perhaps stay together because of it. He didn't usually try to solve matters so simply.

She wanted to get back to their original argument but could not remember what it was. "Well, what do you think I spend my whole life trying to do."

"I know, and you're a hard worker and that's why I love you."

"Oh, God," she said, "for my strong back, of course. What else?"

"What else do you want to be loved for? What do you love me for? What do we love anyone for. For what they can do. You can't separate it."

She thought of all the other wives she knew. Their husbands doted on them and they didn't do a thing to earn it. Spent all the money hiring things done while they went out to have their hair done. Where did she learn she had to earn love? And Alex a workaholic. They made a pair. There wasn't enough time in a day to get all the projects done that he had scrawled on a slip of paper. Lists of things that'd take years. Where was the fun. His constant urgings to get more done and her need for approval.

It came back to her. She remembered the argument. They had gotten up early and went right into their chores. Later in the morning he had stretched his arms out to beckon her to come. She had walked over to him and he hugged her saying, "Now, don't you feel better getting up early. You did so much in just a short time." She kissed him on the cheek and leaned against him and received the pats he gave her, and together they surveyed her work, the raked yard and stacked wood. He'd cut it on his band saw a few days ago and it sat waiting for her to load into the wheelbarrow and carry off to stack into a wood pile. And then they surveyed his work, the progress on the new deck. The sun was not even directly overhead yet.

She did feel better. That was the funny part. The pat on the back for her work did satisfy her. She felt that she had the right to be against him now, buried in his approval. She had said, "I do want to do my share. I don't know what's wrong lately. Maybe I'm just tired of working year in and year out and nothing ever changes. I don't know."

"It seems that way," he said, shaking out a cigarette from the pack in his shirt pocket and lighting it by squeezing her within the circle of his arms, blowing the smoke away from them. But, even in his approval, she suddenly became irritable. She broke away from him and, though she knew it was irrational, said, "I'll bet if you were married to Alice you wouldn't expect her to work like this." She let the feeling of being "put upon," out. It was an expression she'd heard from her mother.

"I didn't marry Alice, now did I?"

"Only because you know her little delicate piano fingers wouldn't be able to lift all this wood."

"That's right. I didn't want some weak spoiled little thing." She wondered if he meant that she had looked like a work horse back then when he met her. At that time she had thought of herself as a delicate, gentle thing, too. Like Alice. She had always wanted to be like Alice. She had always envied the girls like Alice who were being groomed to be ladies one day. Back then when she had first met him, she thought she had become a lady in spite of not having had the grooming Alice had. Now, she saw that he drew a line between them, the Alices and her.

She said, "You couldn't have handled someone like Alice; that's why you didn't choose her. She was too perfect. She was too good for you. You married me because you felt sorry for me." She remembered it now. The argument that morning.

She looked up at his face above her and said it again, "You married me because you felt sorry for me. You felt superior to me." She turned her head to hide her face as it broke. "You

**107**

were so bad off yourself that you had to marry someone you felt sorry for so you could rule her and intimidate her and not feel inferior yourself. Be a big man. Well, good, then you're getting what you deserve...." Her voice was gone and a continuous whine was in its place.

Alex was silent, watching her for awhile, not knowing what to do. At last he said, "There were other reasons, but, yes, that was one. I wanted to comfort you. You were so shy, you used to blush. But I liked this big body of yours, too."

"Of course, the body. For sure. What else?"

"You like to know you've got a good body. That's important to you, now, isn't it? It's important to all women. They like to know that men like their bodies. All these exercises you do. And, I do like yours."

He was down by her ear and talking low. She could feel his warm breath. She didn't know if she meant anything she had said all day, or all her life. It all seemed like a big act, even making love. And beside, she had to go for that run to keep her legs in shape. She put her arms around his neck.

Alex said, "That's better."

> *A tiny fire. As if on the plains.*
> *Perhaps smoke from the campfire of*
> *a singular traveling man. It is Alex's*
> *lone cigarette in the bedroom sending*
> *up Indian signals.*

# The Amnesiac

I vaguely remember buying this house. I have to use logic rather than memory. We must have been driving around in Alex's mother's old Ford or Studebaker which I had bought from her before we got married. Alex was driving. We used to drive around looking for houses to buy in those days, after we got married. We lived in Alex's little trailer for three months; and on weekends we would drive around looking, just looking out the windows of the car at the passing houses and scenery. One time, on the foothill roads we saw a deer. It was right after seeing this house down below. The foothills were just above it, and a deer was leaping across Foothill Road as we drove and I said, "I'd love to live here where deers are." I do remember that. That isn't logic.

Now I do begin to remember how I got here. Alex was wearing a blue shirt. That's logic, not memory. He always wore a very light blue cotton button-up short-sleeved shirt. The color matched his eyes. And khaki slacks. He had been in the Air Force. Blue and tan, and he, so blond. He looked pale to me. He never wore strong colors. And I must have been wearing, in those days, at twenty-one, my black elastic slacks and a pull-over sweater. It was in style for some class of women to dress in a Beatnik style. I owned a giant turtle shell, a bongo drum, and a canoe, and a paperback of Jack Kerouac. I liked simple things. This is not from memory now. I looked at an old photo. I had a good body. The sweater was bright orange.

We were driving around in his mother's car. It was a white car, all white and proper and clean, and Alex was in blue, and I was in black and orange, and for some reason we were looking at houses because we had just gotten married and were living in his old and very small trailer. We could lie in bed and reach for coffee then. I don't remember that we ever thought

**109**

about what we were doing in those days. I don't remember agreeing to buying a house, or Alex suggesting it. We just did it. Now I wonder why we didn't do so much else? We simply took that step after marriage, or Alex did. I would have done anything he wanted back then. Like the Manson women. I belonged to Alex.

So he was driving and I was a willing passenger. We were gelled in our roles like those bits of pigs' maws in lunch meat. We were those specks of gelatinous material in that man-made cold cuts loaf. And sliced.

I don't recall a conversation. I have to use logic to remember now that there was no logic behind our decision to buy that little house on Serena. The Smiths own it. They had just put in a new carpet. The place looked beautiful to me. I had lived in old tumbledown houses all my life. I never even thought in terms of buying a house. That was Alex's style. His family always bought. Mine always rented.

I do remember now, entering this house for the first time as the Smiths let us in. They were an old couple, grey and retired. This was their investment property. They had fixed it up. I remember feeling very young and beautiful as a new wife. The way the Smiths smiled at us and made something about our being married only a month, and how this would be our "first house." "Newlyweds," they said. It was nineteen thousand, five hundred dollars. I had the five hundred dollars, and another five hundred from teaching. I had saved my last two checks. We drove to the Smiths' house, a white old rambling well-established kind of house, and paid them my thousand dollars for a down payment. I didn't think of it as my money. It meant nothing. Alex had no money. He was going to school on the G.I. Bill and driving a school bus and city bus as a part-time job.

Alex and I felt so young next to the Smiths when we handed over the thousand dollar down payment and signed the papers. We got into his mother's old Ford and drove away. We parked at our new little house. I marvelled over the tile in the bathroom and the brand new rug. Alex looked out in the back and saw the fine horse stall he would turn into a

110

workshop. We held eachother. Or did we? I am using logic. None of this is memory. I vaguely remember standing in the big bathroom and feeling the coldness of the white tile and liking it. Mr. Smith had just laid it and the excess grout was still crumbling out. Alex used to have a habit of holding out his arms to me and I would go to him and be encased. It was a good feeling. I felt safe. It smelled clean like a swamp (the bathroom). I don't remember moving in. That's logic. I know we did because I am here. I do remember the trip in Alex's old panel truck over to our new house. All the stuff we owned was in the truck, and I remember that we had a whole shoebox full of pencils. He had a few hand tools. He wore his old military clothes; fatigues, big boots, tan shirt, baggy-legged uniform pants. I never liked his clothes. And he never liked my clothes. He thought I was gaudy. I thought he was too plain. We must have unloaded all our stuff. I must have hung all my high school clothes up, and my wedding dress, and the formals and chiffons from the Pageant. Over the years they all disappeared. My daughters played house and dress-up in all of them until they were in tatters. I never wore them again myself. I wore black slacks and pullover sweaters. But I don't remember wearing anything intentionally. I got so busy. There were babies all over the place and I would throw on anything. The house filled up. Soon Alex was crawling all over it with a hammer and a saw, building on. The little horse stall exploded into a gigantic workshop. The house expanded. Alex expanded. The babies expanded. We all got bigger and bigger. And then everyone left home, including Alex and me, in turn. And then I came back. I used to drive by Serena when I was out and Alex was in and I thought I would never be back again and marvel over it just being a place, and how, no matter how much I tried, I couldn't equate all that took place in there with the place. The events, all that had happened *there*. But where they happened meant nothing. I'd go in and see all the familiar things and be confused. They were so familiar yet it didn't matter. It was kind of like trying to be sentimental over the vase of flowers in a doctor's office when he was about to stick you with needles. Even now, the familiarity of the place doesn't register inside me. It's as if I am anesthetized in part of my memory, and I simply go on, making plans to fix the place up, as if all my life hasn't taken place here.

> *Later, over coffee, Alex's eyes are snapping. He is exhilarated. He says, "Life is, is, is...." and his hands come forward to express it, cupping up a precious portion of air... "GLORIOUS." The aerial has been repaired and. information about the world has come in.*

# As Bodies

She and Alex keep eachother warm at night. For hours they are embraced. Limbs, torsos, soft and hard parts, bony plates pressing together, entwined, interlocked.

Together. Their bodies are good friends that seek eachother in the dark. They like the other's company. The presence speaks in a wordless language like prehistoric life, mute, blind. Their minds are clicked off, eyes shut down, mouths not in use. All night for six to eight hours they are mindless creatures, combined as one large lump under covers.

Drawing warmth, incubating, latent consciousnesses. And then they stir, awake, draw apart. Their eyes focus turning on the minds and mouths. They see and speak and separate. They look at eachother and the timelessness of body warmth cools and hardens into a day. Today. Now. The blind probings are stashed for sixteen hours while their bodies travel in opposite directions getting twice as much done, until it is time to sleep again.

# A Big Joke

No man has ever come to her, as they do in historical movies to beautiful women, and said, "Choose one of us." Because of this she has felt left out of the big dramas one could have before they die. There was never that moment when her one decision cast her fate in one direction. But a man came to her house once and told her husband, "I love your wife," which caused the husband to cry out, "Who am I to stop anyone from loving; we only have one life…" Tears sprang to his eyes and both men sat down on the couch together to discuss it while she served them drinks. They got drunk with their arms around the back of the couch and sometimes coming to rest on eachother's shoulders.

Friends. Her two men. While she brought more whiskey and watched them: the German and the Irishman. They discussed her as if she were theory. With tears in their eyes and frogs in their throats, filling ash trays and spilling liquor, while she finally tried to curl up in an armchair and get some sleep, confused that they left her out of their reverie. She believed they should have consulted her, spoken to her directly, since she was the cause of their emotions. The reason they were sitting side by side. She had only waited on them like some servant girl. As she drifted into sleep she heard coarse laughter. They were calling her Miss American Pie and cursing her for being able to close her eyes and leave them in their drunkenness. They laughed as if she were a joke. As if all women were a big joke on all men. The horizon began to lighten in the east. It was a new day. No decisions had been made. Only understandings. The two men understood eachother better than they understood her.

# Out in the Middle of the Ocean

It was the deceit. No one can live with that kind of deceit. She lied about everything. Not only the men but the dog shitting on the rug. He would smell it and she would stand there, denying it with a rag in her hand. She brought in every stray creature she could find and let it shit on his new carpeting.

She never had anything as a child. She lived in old houses and he thought she would appreciate nice things. He liked making nice things for her. But she didn't care about them. She didn't take care of them. She didn't know how to. He realized people, some people, can't be made to change. If they don't have the training early, they can't learn. They don't want to learn. They want to continue in their own ways. It's a kind of pride. She was determined to hang onto her ways.

He worried about the children; he saw them taking up her traits. He could see it repeated in their lives. Another generation continuing her habits. At times it sickened him and his breath caught as if trapped, but those moments passed, and he did what had to be done each day.

The deceit and the way she argued her points. She believed only poor people could feel things and rich people could not. It was her reason not to change. She wore rags when they were first married. And went barefooted. He was embarrassed to walk down the street with her. Her hair was frizzled. Only after younger people began to go around that way did she put on shoes and use a cream rinse and buy clothes.

All on her habits annoyed him. Her fetish over food. She would not eat all day, refusing food at mealtimes and then wallow in a fried egg sandwich at midnight, sucking at the yolk, making noises. Slopping around in the kitchen, hunching over a bowl of cereal. Eating with her fingers, getting it on her face and shirt.

He turned on the stockmarket, picked up the newspaper,

read *Science News*, made tape recordings of classical pieces, anything to stay clear of the way she was. He wanted to get away from her. The extent of her bad habits alarmed him. Her quick, hurried forceful movements. The destruction she left in her path. Broken glasses. Burnt food. Clogged drains. Door knobs twisting loose. Electric cords fraying. Tires worn off on the sides from cutting corners. It frightened him. He did not know where it would lead. He wanted to get away from her but he could not desert the children and he could not take them away from their mother. She was their mother. They needed her; she was good with them. He taught them table manners and to lower their voices, and she took them on walks and turned over rocks to see what was under them. She read to them and sang to them and taught them to draw. She had her good points.

When he met her, she had a kind of enthusiasm that attracted him to her. She got excited and happy the way he never could. But that was in the beginning. Later, because he had had to train her to do things his way, and because she resisted training, she lost some of her spirit. He had had to break her down so she could take instructions. He had to get critical and mean. And that had taken away some of her enthusiasm. She had lost some of her fun. Sex even went bad, during the time of her training.

It was at this time he found out she was seeing someone else. There was a scene. She looked stricken at first, wanting to keep lying, and then defiant. She ran away from him on foot into the night. For ten miles. At four in the morning she called him and he wanted to come get her and bring her back. Her fear touched him. And his compassion gave her courage. She told him that she needed someone to tell her good things about herself, because he never did. That she couldn't live like that, feeling inferior to him all the time, because that was the way he made her feel. The accusation enraged him. He told her she was a product of her environment. That she was trash and that was all that she knew to do.

After that there was no more to say. What he said stuck. She accepted being trash and that he was a gentleman. And that he had mistaken her for a lady in the beginning. If he had known who she was, he wouldn't have married her. What more was there to say.

And she began to lie about everything. The washing machine broke and she swore she didn't wash the big bathroom rugs in it when he could see that they had been washed. They lay fluffy and smelling of freshness where before they had been flat and soiled. She lied about dents in the car. About speeding tickets. About dulling his razor blades, bleaching his dark shirts, spending money, scratching records, dropping the iron, squeezing the toothpaste from the front, mailing his letters. He grew tired. Tired of her. Tired of fixing the things she ruined. Tired of hearing her lie. And tired of making an effort to correct her and instruct her in how civilized people live. He was tired of hearing her say, "You are trying to change the very thing you require—a scapegoat."

It had been twelve years. Twelve years ago he walked around the harbor dreaming of getting a boat and sailing away. Instead he bought a panel truck and drove to Alaska. He came by to tell her goodbye. She crawled into his truck and turned a package of dried figs over in her hands saying, "So these are your supplies, huh?" They had never made love. She saw the hammock he had rigged up on one side, She sat down on it and rocked and smiled. She knew he wanted her. She liked not letting him have her.

They waved goodbye. A year passed. He did not find what he was looking for in Alaska. He lost his camera and ate up all the figs and everything else he could get. In the fall he knocked on her door and she answered. He asked if she was home because he had rehearsed the way he would say it.

She said, "I'm here!"

He married her the following summer, after she graduated.

He had had his adventure. They drove around looking for a little house to buy. And because they wanted one, they found one.

It was twelve years ago that he came laughing through the door with her. She was laughing and he liked the sound of it. Laughing as they began the journey to where they were now.

Into her lies and to his wanting away from her lies, wanting the boat again. But doubting if that would do it now, fearing that he would get out in the middle of the ocean and ask himself what in the hell he was doing out there. What possible adventure could there be in it now. He was tired.

*A big boat about to be launched. It has reduced us to ants, scurrying around a larger body. It dictates, becomes a monster. And men tremble with fear lest it fall and crush them. Women stand back out of the way. Pulley and jack cars are readied. It waits, fat, content over the attention. A smirking, yellow-eyed contentment that once again man has* done it to himself.

*Our hearts lurch when we see a Large Life of some sort show part of itself in the ocean. A black back, humped, a glistening head. For an instant, and our breaths catch. Our eyes scan. They dredge the area for awhile after that. For another glimpse. Of what we do not know.*

# To Escape

He wants to turn everything into money. He wants to turn himself into money.

She tells him, "You are handsome." He asks, "How much is it worth? Can you sell it for a hundred bucks today?" She tells him he is talented. He tells her that nobody is buying any of his ideas. She watches him, year in and year out, saving money by fixing things around the house. He does not bring in money with this skill. No one gives him money for it. But he does not let go of money to repair men by doing his own repairs. It is almost like getting paid. He pays himself. But it is not good enough. His skill has to mean more than that.

He wants evidence that *they* notice his worth by paying him for it. For what he is: his health, his talent, appearance, love of warm furry things. It is of no worth to him if *they* are not buying it. How to turn himself into money is his main concern.

Maintenance has become his style. His slogan is, "If I can't move forward, at least I will not slip backward."

She draws a verbal graph for them. Across the bottom is for time. Up and down is for enthusiasm. There are fourteen squares. One for each year he has been working as a married man toward his goal: to get rich. She says, "You start out going upward at an incline of one square-per year until Year Thirteen and then what happened?" He is smoking and gazing out into the air. He sighs and says, "I lost belief in my efforts. My back is not willing any-more because my brain knows better. Why do anything? I have ideas, but I've had ideas before and what happened?"

There is a half-built submarine in the backyard. A new portion built onto the house. Everything is functioning. He has kept all the machines and structures in good repair. Everything works. Can be used for the purpose it was meant. He has thrown out nothing. Wasted nothing. Except for time.

Now he spends long stretches in bed with headaches. Waiting for the next cable to snap, generator to give, fan belt to wear through, gear box to crumble, pipes to erode, termites to chew up an overhead beam, baseball to sail through a window, guest to flush an unflushable down the plumbing, hand to wrench too hard and pinch a washer on a faucet to pieces, dog to vomit, cat to shed, vacuum to beat itself to death. The machines and structures move in, a formidable wall, closing him into a smaller and smaller area.

Restricting his movements, confining him. Enslaving him. He hides under the covers away from his version of the boogey man. In a manner in which a grown man can hide: ailments of the body.

She asks, "What if you woke up and found out it was all just a bad dream?" She has brought him his first feeding for the day, as he props himself up on pillows. It is a bowl of shredded wheat. He can no longer eat eggs, peanut butter, bacon. He has to watch his cholesterol intake. His own machine, his body, is breaking down. He must maintain it, too. He is not humored by her question. Annoyance lines form between his eyes. "Oh, God," he groans. "I think I would not have the courage to go on if I woke up right now and saw that it has been a dream It has taken too much out of me. I'd be afraid of it happening again and I know I wouldn't be able to do this all over again…"

She knows he needs to have fun. On a weekend she dragged him to a hot tub party and they stood nude in steaming water and then traipsed across an ice cold yard to get dressed. In a week he was in the hospital with pneumonia. They found he was dehydrated. He lay abed taking intravenous feedings of fluid and one million units of penicillin. She looks at him now as he pinches the bridge of his nose to get at the headache. And remembers that all he ever wanted to do when they first met was to "get a boat and sail away to an island."

# Fourteen Years Ago Today

She was having her hair done for her wedding. She never had her hair done but for her wedding she thought she should. It was a thing to do. How could she be a bride without something being done differently than what she was used to. Something that would set her apart from other days. They didn't have time for her at the beauty shop. It was a shop where she worked after school. They gave her the shampoo girl. This girl gave her a shampoo, set her hair, dried it and combed it out painstakingly. It was a bad job. One side turned one way, the other side turned the other. After the hair style she went to the florist next door, during her coffee break, and ordered a flower. The florist was a woman who came to the beauty shop to have her hair done. She looked at her, closed her eyes, opened them, and said, "I see an orchid." She hated orchids. They reminded her of old ladies' breaths and middle-aged ladies' excitement. They were fibrous, hard-petaled, formal; but she did not protest because she thought she should do what the florist said.

She brought the orchid and carnation for Alex back to the salon and put them in the refrigerator with the bleaching formulas, snacks, cream for coffee, and the oil shampoo.

After her last lady, as the lady went out the door with a shiny crown and a halo of tight pin-curl curls, she cleaned up her station and said goodbye to that whole lifestyle and walked away. At seven o'clock she was waiting at one of the oldest church buildings in town. It looked like a chapel. It was her family's traditional church.* *Church of Christ* was posted above the doorway and also on a sign on the front lawn, along with the times of the service, attendance, and levels of Sunday

*Forty-seven years later, she and Alex would be at that building again for their son's death. It had been turned into a mortuary.

school. Her father and brother milled around making clever comments. A wedding was a thing to joke about.

They were the last of the family at "home." Home was a rented house on the beach side of town near the park. Everyone else was either married, in the service, working, drifting, or living with her mother and her mother's husband. She, herself, had just graduated, gotten her first teaching job and was finally on her own.

She stood on the church steps now, trying to be a bride. She believed all kinds of things about the way a bride should be. She had heard tales all her life. And now when it was her turn it was empty. Her face was hot. She was numb. She could feel nothing.

People began to show up even though she hadn't invited anyone to the wedding except Alex's best friend and hers from school. She kept posing and pacing and feeling nothing and waiting for Alex and the preacher. And knowing that marriage was going to be like everything else. It was going to happen to her like an accident. It wasn't going to be any different than doing anything else.

Alex drove up in his blue Chrysler convertible. He had a rubber band around one shoe to hold the sole on. There was a slight flap flap as he walked toward her. He felt his back pocket to make sure he had brought his wallet so he would be able to slip the minister a bill for his trouble, at the appropriate time. The minister was late. Her brother took some pictures of everyone milling around. The church was open. They were inside standing in front of the colored glass windows having their pictures taken with his 35 mm when the minister finally showed up with his wife and four daughters. All the little girls wore patent leather shoes and their party dresses. The minister was a man she had always liked. She had liked the steady tone of his voice and the sense he made from the pulpit.

He wasn't doubtless like the other preachers she had heard in that church. And he looked like Abraham Lincoln.

He hurried around, opening back offices, arranging things, opening a Bible, while his wife talked to her about the wedding she had had twelve years before. An extravagant, thousandinvitationed thing. She listened, polite, sweet, innocent. It was an image she tried for. She felt sick to her stomach. She could not remember ever having decided to get married. The choice had happened to her. The decision was some automatic silent clicking that had taken place without her knowing it. As the minister's wife chatted and described in detail the bridesmaids' gowns, she smiled and nodded and knew that she would not be able to stop this thing that was about to happen to her. She was Here. In the church, with Alex, in a white dress, The minister was fussing around. It was all set to go. But it was not where she had planned to be one day. There was a resistance going on inside her, like a prisoner beating on the sides of a cell, begging not to be given another sentence. And she stood ignoring it, a part of her that believed in winning prizes at the carnival and stood solid, waiting to win a husband.

The ceremony took a matter of minutes. They had but to repeat after Mr. Truex, the proper vows. They tried to take hands, bumping knuckles three times before they got their palms together. They were processed from one kind of thing into another. And they came out on the other side appearing as if nothing had happened. It was the end of the first step in a direction she knew nothing about. A step made with the force of compulsion. In a white dress she had bought with her first "teaching" money. Alex was kissing her on cue, to end the ceremony and she was feeling embarrassment because her father was in the same room. He had spent 23 years insulting men who pursued her, chasing them away, and preserving her virginity. She winced. Then she and Alex were running down the steps of the church and getting hit by rice. She was holding the front of her dress shut and Alex was sucking his neck down inside his collar like a turtle. Then they were jumping into his old Chrysler and swinging away from the curb and wondering where they should go now. The dozen people were following them in their cars. Alex drove. She watched him or looked ahead from the passenger seat. They followed the main street of town all the way up, and on an impulse, while passing Uncle John's Pancake House, pulled into the parking lot. Everyone pulled in behind them. As if in a mad frenzy they all pushed into the entrance of the restaurant. Two waitresses glanced up in surprise and then curiosity. A busboy was called and four little tables were pulled together to make a long banquet size place to receive the group. Alex was at one end, she at the other. Forced into positions. Carried by an energy she didn't understand. They ordered coffee. Alex conducted the wedding party in a way that surprised her. She had never seen him around so many people before. He took over, tied everyone together in one big jovial conversation that took the form of one humorous comment after another about marriage.

They chatted and laughed for an hour and then everyone began to fade away. She and Alex went to a place to dance. Everyone kept glancing at them in their white chiffon dress and navy blue suit. She blushed, Alex led her in waltzes. She stepped on his shoes. He adjusted his rubber band several times. And then they drove to Punta Gorda street where his tiny trailer awaited. He had stretched red corduroy material over everything that needed prettying up - the couch, the bed. A chair. He even hung some up for a curtain.

She looked around, still confused. They undressed, made love, fell asleep and she tossed and turned because she was not used to having someone in her bed. She woke up saying polite things like excuse me, I'm sorry, are you comfortable or am I in the way... And was careful not to fall into a deep, greedy sleep, to escape from her body.

She worried about waking up with crusts around her eyes and mouth or mascara under her eyes from sleeping too hard. She slept prepared to never lose consciousness.

Fourteen years later they wake up together. The trailer and the red corduroy are gone. She has a sore throat on the left side. It's either one tonsil or the other. Alex squeezes her. She says, "Are we still together?" He contorts his face in laughter and says, "Unbelievable, isn't it?" They try to remember exactly the way they felt that first morning fourteen years today. He was in a hurry to get to work. It was a new job. His first real job. She cannot remember except for being afraid she would look like a Chinese to him. After sleep. And that she wanted to fix him a good breakfast now that she was his wife.

They lie side by side. Nothing more comes. Fourteen years before is blocked off by time the way fourteen years ahead was back then. There is nothing about it, except a kind of surprise that they are still here. That she is still where she never planned to be. That it has been like watching a movie about some other woman's life and she has not been present yet.

# What Do You Want?

"I've got to quit smoking," he says. His turquoise shirt parts just under the last button and does not reach his belt. "And quit eating so much... God, what's left?"

"What's left?"

"What do you want?" his wife asks. She is mature, ready to listen to any request, any dream, because she thinks of herself as an understanding person. He is silent.

"Adventure?" she coaxes.

"I don't know," he says.

"I do," she says. "Success. That's what you need."

He is nodding slowly. She knows what he needs. They have been over it before a hundred times. She is getting pretty smart. He can admire her for it. There was that time in the beginning, about the first five years when he wasn't sure they'd make it, but now she is shaped up. Her voice comes out thin because of a tenseness in her throat muscles place on the air across her trachea. It is a trick to sound intellectual. She is saying, "The timing is off in your life. You programmed it subconsciously, I think, to be successful about this time, or even a few years back. You were supposed to be enjoying your success by now, the results of your efforts, rather than still being in the process of getting there." She inhales and looks down at him. "You're impatient. Impatience breeds boredom. Look, you can't even get off the couch. You want to skip the present."

Alex has heard it about a dozen times before over the past month. It is her current thought. She says it differently each time, but in the same thin strained voice and eagerly, as if it were a sudden revelation each time.

His wife leaves the room and he can hear her rattling drawers in the bedroom. He says, "Maybe you're right," but she cannot hear him. He sighs. "Well, back to work." He raises his feet into the air, drops them down, and then moves his body into a sitting position. He stands up and walks toward the front door, but does not go out. He goes to the bedroom door and stands there looking at his wife. She is moving around, rearranging things. He wants to hit her so that she will have to lie down on the couch again. He says, "Maybe you're right."

She glances around, surprised that he is there, but does not comment.

He says, "You know, you're getting saddlebags."

"Saddlebags?" She turns around. "What do you mean?" Concern fills her face as she studies his eyes.

"Your hips. You're packing it on."

She rubs her hands down along the sides of her body and attempts to look down to see herself in perspective. She goes to the mirror on the back of the door where he is standing. He watches her as she looks at the back of herself. He sees anxiety appear in her face. The pepper sensation begins to lessen inside his sinus.

*You put everything out on your front lawn. You take it out of your house and spread it on the lawn and people come by because you call it a backyard sale. And they do not buy most of the things. So you take it all back into your house and live with it, but now you know no one else wanted it. You have a new relationship with it. With all of your stuff.*

# The Cabana

Gertrude called it a cabana because it was as close as she would be to living that kind of life. Marty called it a bathhouse and got undressed in it to go swimming. There was a whole row of them along one side of the pool. With keys. And inside was a basin, a mirror, a hook with wire hangers, a chair, a waste basket and a wooden bench. And a throw rug. Gertrude's swim wear and tissues and emollients for the sun were all around in neat order. Her key was number twelve. Marty was happy for Gertrude, Alex's mother. She should have nice things. She lived a good life. At almost seventy-five, she should be getting some of the pay-off. Gertrude's life was just the way they taught you life would be. If you were good and did everything right. It would all work out. And:

Gertrude had been good. She was the most virtuous woman Alex knew. Which was good for him. It can't hurt a son to believe that about his own mother. It can only hurt his wife. If Gertrude had only sinned a little, Marty wouldn't look so bad. Sometimes Marty would try to take that idea of Gertrude away from Alex.

She would say, "Gertrude never wanted to be bad. She couldn't have done anything wrong. She didn't have it in her. She did exactly what she wanted to do. So she wasn't really good. Being good is making yourself not be bad when you really want to be bad. If you never have any desire to do anything wrong, and never have to sacrifice what you really want to do and do what you don't want to do, then you're not really being good."

To this Alex would usually say, "She stood by us after the divorce and worked hard. She never wavered from her duties to her children. She gave up everything else that might distract her."

He meant she never went to bed with another man. After

the divorce she kept her legs together. To a man that means so much. A woman who is celibate forever after. The idea could almost bring tears to his eyes at times, when, by comparison, he heard of other divorced women going from man to man, their children getting dizzy from the parade of males coming and going to and from the door.

"But she was never even tempted," Marty would say, during their sessions when Gertrude's virtue was in question. "If you're not tempted… it doesn't count.… If she had had to go out and earn a living by sleeping with men, then that would be different. Then she'd be good… because it would be against her grain. You can't get credit for nothing. She was really selfish when you think about it. Everything went her way. Good was what she was. Not what she chose."

Then she would give her old example of how foolish a man can be in judging a woman. "Remember Eddie Banner who divorced Audrey because she had sex with her boss? Audrey had so much energy. She earned half the living, kept a beautiful house, played the piano, was a good cook, efficient, talented, and had a pretty face. Remember? And he threw her away just because he couldn't take that one tiny flaw. Then he married Vicky who has been faithful to him all these years. But what else does she do? Moves like a slug, looks like one. Everything is more than she can handle. Laundry, meals, even a cup of coffee is outside her capacity of performance. The house looks like a bomb hit it. The kids all turned out bad. But Eddie clings to her for that one simple thing: faithfulness. And she wouldn't even be faithful if anyone else would look at her. Can you believe a man can be that stupid? That one quality should outweigh all the others? It tells on him, doesn't it?"

Alex blinks about now and has to agree about Eddie's stupidity, remembering.

Marty can talk this way endlessly because it is in self-defense. She, herself, looks shady next to Gertrude. Even in body. Gertrude dresses in whites, lives in an apartment decorated in white on white. She gets white stuff in the corners of her eyes, as well, as if her very soul is oozing pureness. And she wipes it out with white handkerchiefs. White, to Marty, is nothing. A non-commitment. You cannot tell anything about a person except for what white means. Next to Gertrude, Marty is totally exposed in a multi-colored bathing suit, sun-burned skin, and polished red nails. She has worn every color there is over the years, gradually moving back into the shades of greens and blues, out of yellows and oranges.

When Gertrude decides it is time for her to change back into her clothes from her swimsuit, she goes to the door of the cabana, turns the key just so and disappears without a sound. She comes out minutes later in white nylon slacks, white pull-over jersey, white belt, white shoes. Her white hair and white skin dazzle in the late afternoon sunshine, as she walks to her white car and drives away, leaving Alex and Marty to enjoy the pool and the use of her cabana.

Marty is left with the twitching in her right eyelid. She has had enough sun. She gets up and enters the cabana, takes off her suit and wraps it in a towel. Gertrude's perfect life is all around her naked body. A sinful body inside a sin-less place. Her nipples rise. The power of opposites meeting tingles in every part of Marty. She stands boldly naked and her nakedness becomes blatant in the exact place Gertrude held her towel around her lest anyone break down the door. Through the slits of the louvered door she speaks in a low voice to Alex, who still leans back in his poolside chair with half-closed eyes.

From out of the center of Gertrude's virtue, from the depths of the pure white cabana, she says, "It's really nice in here. Why don't you come in?"

At first there is only the sound of swimmers splashing in the pool, and then she hears the scrape of aluminum chair legs on pavement. Alex has gotten up and opens the door a crack. Marty is smiling, waiting, about to laugh with glee over the possibilities of it. The sacrilege. She suddenly remembers the story of those Catholic boys who snuck into the church and peed on the altar. Making love in Gertrude's cabana with Gertrude not knowing, with Gertrude believing nothing is happening in her cabana except what should be happening is an act of indecency that Marty is compelled to commit. She hopes the flimsy cabana will rock wildly back and forth.

Alex's wet suit drops to the floor with a soft smack. They are both damp, sticky. Unclean. They are eager. Greedy. They kneel. On hands and knees on Gertrude's stark white throw rug. There is no room to move. The cabana is as small as a confession booth. They lean against the wooden bench. Marty's nose is pressed down into Gertrude's wicker waste basket full of wrinkled white tissue. Marty wonders what Gertrude would have to wipe off. They do what Gertrude has not done for thirty years. All over the inside of her private cabana. And at the very last, in short breaths, Marty sighs.

"Let's leave a big splat of it on the floor so Gertrude will step in it when she comes in…. All her little white half-grandchildren squeezing up between her toes… all that white froth… ha, ha, ha…." She is half whispering, as if she recites a prayer, and then she collapses in weak laughter which turns into tears, and her shoulders shake because she does not understand what she has just done.

Alex has not fully heard what she said, caught up in his own thoughts, wondering if they made any noise, perhaps everyone knew. He hurries to dress, buckling his belt, and reaching for the tiny brass door knob of the thin white door. The pool lurks beyond, a giant audience about to applaud when he steps out. But there is not an unusual sound as he opens the door and leaves Marty by herself.

Marty makes sure Gertrude's cabana is left spotless. She puts all the tissues she has used inside her own beach bag to deposit them in her own waste basket. Then she leaves the cabana, turning the key just so and locks the door against what they have done.

# The First Evidence

The first evidence of being a social creature this morning. I arrange my lower face so it won't hang funny on the pillow-less place I've slept all night. I hear Alex in the bathroom, splashing and splashing, and if he passes by my door he'll look at me and I want him to see me in a certain way. I don't want it to flash across his mind, the part he isn't aware of, of "Ah, is that her? Funny, her jaw is looking like any woman now." I have had those flashes of him, catching his aging over the twenty years we've loved eachother. But he doesn't know he thinks that way. He feels things apologetically and lets them pass. Never saying them except under pressure. (If I'm crying maybe or begging to know if he thinks I'm ugly now.) He doesn't catch a vision and hold it about people. He does that with machines: sees for an instant a perfect or imperfect product pouring from his lathe, or sees a part breaking instantaneously.

So I move my cheek; he doesn't look in. I am on the couch where I read last night.

Then fell asleep and lay pressed hard by the atmosphere, like a bug under a rock all night.

I slept flat, mashed, heavy, deep. Alone. My hair, damp at the neck from the bath. And all night my throat swelled. In the morning I awoke in a fever, wet now from sweat. What a place sleep was. Where no human beings were. Wilderness. A savage, uncivilized place, and I, making my way along a beach (again). Like R. Crusoe. Alone, scared. The ocean waves playing with my fright. Lifting large and threatening to roll up with the incoming tide and smother me in turmoil. The tide is always incoming in this dream. The waves always high as the sky and their tips being whipped by wind. I am always planning my strategy, eyeing the place in the rocks above the beach where I can leap to safety. Or a trail leading inland. A trail always is up ahead if I can reach it before the tide comes in.

The trail is through the ugliest terrain. Swamps, ugly hills, filthified and chopped up by trailer-living kind of people. Poor. Unsightly. Undesirable. People who have poor houses, poor yards, poor animals, poor faces, poor hearts, and poor souls. I am afraid of these people, yet more afraid of those gleefully whip-tipped waves which are like crazy hell-raisers. "Ya-ha," the waves say, with reckless depthful lashings. It's the way their tips rise up and ride high on such a body of water. The solidarity of that moveable water. It's wall-sized crushability. On land there are evil-hearted people but I have a chance. I can dodge them, hid, peek out. I can run fast along that gloomy trail, past all that hacked up landscape. I am always on my way to safety, which is a big house on top. With rooms I've never decorated. Big elegant rooms to fix up. Safe rooms. And I have redone only a few. The rooms I have done, which are up on that hill in an old house are on the edge of being luxurious, but handmade. And always attached to those junky room which I have not gotten to yet. That house is up above all that lower poverty. It is in another kind of neighborhood. Estates, not shanties.

I veer off the beach and see my escape up the trail, but I never take it. I awake cold, sweating, swollen-throated, swollen-eyed. I've been there again. That place. I hear Alex splashing in the bathroom. And I arrange my face. I'm back. In civilization. I need to look right. I want him to see my newly-slept face and for it to flash through his mind, "It's pleasant." And for him to go on knowing I am not losing my hold. Not slipping into the clutches of time. That life is being kind to me...

# His Face Was Red

His face was red and moist like the ball of a finger after a fire cracker goes off on it, and he bent over in order to squeeze the last bit of air out of his lungs to say the angry words he had to say, rolling his eyes up and shaking his face at her as if it were an extension of his hand. She watched him like a child watches its mother, seeing the anger physically, the color of it and the moisture and the way it shook him and she wanted to laugh because he looked funny. But she was afraid. She did not trust the anger to stay in him. She sat on the couch and said, carefully, "You're a tyrant, you know."

He said, "Why can't you just admit you were wrong? You sit there smug wanting me to feel guilty being angry with you."

"Because anyone can make a mistake. I didn't do it on purpose. And I don't want to encourage your tyranny and I can't believe you're so self-righteous. As if you never leave windows open."

"God, why didn't I pay attention to your IQ? It was a good fifty points below mine." He flung his tie around his neck and tried feeling with his hands the lengths of each end. One was too short, Marty knew, even though she had never learned to tie a tie.

He stomped away to stand before the bathroom mirror, leaving the door open so the anger would have some place to go. Marty turned the pages of her check stubs and sub-tracted from the balances and sat as still as possible, warm from his anger flying loose and stinging her with the differences between their IQs.

She said, "Yes, we both know how much you believe in IQ tests. At least until you compare yours with Edlin's and then suddenly they're not valid."

"If you could only say that's all right, I understand why

you're angry. I was in the wrong. But you sit there wanting to be hurt. Making me hurt you. I've got to suffer just to keep you in line. You think I like to get mad."

"Some men can conduct their role of husband without terrorizing their wives."

She sat steady and spoke watching him and gauging it. "You don't have to ever get mad. It's all you know. It's your way. Don't say I make you do it." Her voice was getting as loud as his so she lowered it at the end and he glanced over waiting for the tears after it dropped.

He always sought her face at the moment before it broke. It was like an artist standing back and looking at the effect of the last stroke on the canvas. Marty took a deep breath and looked out the front window at the cat sitting on the seat of the bicycle where it perched in order to look in. Eleven thirty and she had to take it to the vet for its appointment to be spayed. In another hour. The cat was watching Marty in expectation of being fed. Marty pressed her fingers against her old appendicitis scar and thought of the tender pink uterus and ovaries and tubes sitting small and utilitarian inside her cat. She saw the high intensity light on and the veterinarian with stainless steel snippers and she pressed into her own side harder and harder. He would be snipping her life bearing organs loose, to be thrown into a dry waste basket while allthe cars in the street drove by and people milled around and no one would stop and say poor kitty. Marty was crying and the cat looked at her expecting food and not knowing anything but the flow of saliva as long as she looked at Marty.

Alex came out of the bathroom wearing his dress coat and tossing it into place with his shoulders several times. He sat down by Marty and said, "You know I don't like to hurt you. It's just that I'm sick of that cat getting in the car and spraying it down because you forget to close the damn window." She swallowed hard. Alex wanted to get his anger out again but held it back. He said, "Don't you see that?"

"All I see is that you have left the window open yourself before." Marty folded the checkbook, pushed it into her purse and went out the door with the shoulder she thought he would grab ready for him. He let her go, standing there ready to leave himself.

"Now I have to go to work smelling like that cat." He was yelling again, as Marty picked up the cat and got into the car and drove away.

She dropped the cat off and then went to the Stretch and Sew store. She browsed around looking at material. She looked at the prices and rubbed the cloth with her fingers and her hangnails caught at it. There were other women browsing too and Marty looked at them and thought that they probably believed in Stretch and Sew. She knew that they would make the clothes and wear them and everything would be fine. She examined the samples of the polyester fabrics which had been made into bathing suits and T-shirts and children's outfits. And she knew that even if she made every item in the patterns out of the most expensive material in the shop, she would still not care if the window of the car was left open or not.

Marty left the shop with the vision of the sales ladies and the customers wearing all their polyester clothing, the pastel wrinkle-proofness of it puffing full and smooth on their full bodies and she wished to see the poor people of Mexico in rags again, the ones she had seen once. She felt sad then for them, but not as sad as she felt now for the women wearing their brand new wrinkle-free Stretch and Sew fabrics.

Marty drove to the beach listening to the rock music and letting it beat off her feelings about the window. She parked and walked to the sand and broke into a run. It was two miles to the point and back and to the other point. The day was overcast. It would be comfortable for getting hot she thought. She paced herself although she could have gone faster. In the beginning it always seemed as if she could run fast and forever.

Her ankle bent instantly into a hole and straightened and she did not stop. They sky was big above her, bigger than before with her own blood pounding in her head behind her eyes and ears, rhythmically cutting off the sound of the ocean. She rounded the point losing several dozen feet that way because of the rocks. She did not like to cheat on her own legs and decided to run an extra stretch to make up for it and thought of Alex in the cockpit smelling like cat musk and the other pilot flaring his nostrils as he picked up the scent. She knew Alex would remain silent and humiliated stinking up that small space as they took to the air for a four or five hour flight. Alex liked to "keep a low profile" with his company. Cat musk was like yelling in a coworker's face. Alex had only the one uniform, as an economical young pilot. She remembered her pride meeting his plane for the first time and seeing him step off the with the rest of the crew and walk toward her. The old captain was rounded down with a dog-eared brief case and a cap conforming to his gray head, while Alex's shoulders, hat and briefcase stood out, squared off, brand new and shiny.

He was her man then. But he lacked humor over most things she thought funny.

*Transitions take place silently*
*between us. I feel a switch of* burden.
*I carried it all morning, the weight of*
*being in the wrong, and then he made*
*a mistake and even though we go our*
*separate ways, I detect a transferal*
*and he carries it all afternoon.*

# *I Sit Around Now*


I sit around now, wanting all that. I get Alex in close and try to get him to give it all to me in a few sentences. To convince me that I am everything I ever envied. In words that do not really say it, I tell him I am *easy* to be with. I do not want anything that is hard to give. That my tastes are simple, rustic. I prefer corduroy over silk. Suede over fur. Wood over suede. Monks cloth over wool. Wooden beads over jewels. Plants over sculpture. Burlap curtains over knit. Sandals over heels. Don't buy me anything. But don't look away. Don't look at women in White Stag Bermuda shorts in Las Vegas, or blondes, or sorority girls, or only daughters, or women who leave most of their steak, or girls squealing in the arms of their boyfriends on the Ferris wheel, or anyone being kissed at the stroke of midnight or under the mistletoe or someone being cheered into the dining commons somewhere.

# Where to Find Women

…who are desperate for men. She hears men discussing it now and then, here and there. A young man who has a body to offer says, "Down along the highway, hitchhiking. Women will pick you up. Rich women, beautiful women, who have old husbands who aren't any good anymore."

Another man who believes he has discovered another source is spreading a story. He is a husband with a talent for fixing things. He has heard it from another man, an old man, who also knows how to fix things.

"Go to that class in How To Fix Home Appliances. It's packed with divorcees who are begging for help. They're being eaten up by repair bills and will do anything to get a man who knows how to fix things."

# Seven Things that Happened One Day

## 1

I put on the wrong pants; They are the ones I wear when I have eaten too much and want to conceal my fat. They fit loose and I feel skinny in them and eat more trying to fill them up. The only thing that matches them is a white blouse which I bought once as a mistake. I thought it was a fashionable blouse and found it to be old-maidish on me. I felt homely going to work as a substitute teacher.

## 2

I am too early to go to work so I drive to the beach and take a walk out on the sand in my street shoes. It is only 7 AM. I had to drive my son to school early and it is too late to drive home again so I try to kill time looking at the ocean in October when no one is getting tans. It is cold and the wind blows. A large-legged girl is making her way off the sand and is being eyed by a lean older man, who has a German shepherd on a leash. He watches her until she is out of sight and then he ties his dog to a faucet and makes his way down the beach. I stand and try to get a feeling out of the windy cold beach, where just two months before I had lain on a beach towel beside him (a man I loved), both of us thin and brown, laughing and almost naked. Now I stand fat and white, covered up, alone. It is not the same beach. As I turn to go back to my car, I see another older woman sitting in her car, staring out blankly. And I remember all the times I drove down to the same spot to feel sad and dwell on how my life was tragedy. I drive to work thinking at least I am out of that phase.

## 3

Twenty-five five-year-olds are looking at me. They have lined up neatly on a piece of tape stuck to the rug. A few of them squirm because my face is new to them and they want me to look at them. I know I am suppose to speak only in positive words. No one is allowed to say mean things to kids anymore in the classroom. We have decided that even though negative reinforcement is effective and quicker, positive reinforcement is healthier. One child is an albino. He wears dark glasses inside the room. A volunteer mother hovers over him. It is the first year he has been exposed to a social situation. He does not know how to behave socially. I face my group of five-year-olds as their substitute teacher for that day and begin in a voice I like in myself which seems to come out when I am talking to a group of very young kids. It is warm and sweet and uses down-to-earth language. It is reasonable and wise and eager to expose new minds to new thoughts. I hold a schedule of things their teacher wants me to teach them. First off there's a marching song in place of a flag salute, then a good-morning song. Several mothers appear in the background during these routines. I look up and see their normal faces and something wells up inside me and does not want to go on. A kind of shame comes on and I grow awkward, as if they can see that I am not fit to be in front of such pure and young children. I falter in my speech but go on, emphasizing my teacherly tone so not to lose authority and control of the class. I feel their eyes penetrate into my core and witness this self-consciousness and my face grows red. I get through the whole day, fighting humiliation. Mothers come and go, filtering through the classroom in various capacities. Getting out of their kitchens. Helping with cutting, pasting, and coloring. Following albino children. Using the positive reinforcement language teachers have taught them. A speech therapist, a child psychologist, a math readiness, and the principal all make their way in and out of the room in the course of the day and I never give in to wanting to hide my face from them, as if there were something about me that is a terrible thing to know. At the end of the day I make a mistake. I crack and send home the papers that were marked on the day's lesson plans to save. I feel stupid. I confess this error to the aide. She laughs. The team teacher smiles big and raises her eyebrows. Everyone thinks how funny it is going to be when the regular teacher gets back. I can almost hear their laughter and her griping in the teachers' lounge on Monday about the stupidity of substitute teachers. I get an urge to call all the parents of the kids and go around and collect the papers up, but shrug it off with a kind of hidden gladness that I did not do a good job. Glad I did not give in.

On the way through the office to sign my card, I run into the principal. I ask him if he will write a letter of recommendation for me so I can be accepted for Graduate school. He steps back and cocks his head in curiosity. I falter, trying to explain myself, that I want to get into child psychology. He asks, "What?" as if I have said an absurd thing. He wonderes what I want him to say. I tell him I don't know what the University wants to hear, that I really don't know what he should say about me. He makes a deal. He says he will write it if I will give him a stamped addressed envelope for him to mail it. I do not have an envelope on me. I have to ask to buy one from the office. He laughs and says he guesses the district can afford one and has the secretary find one. My recommendation has become a big joke. Everyone is happy, rummaging around for envelopes, thinking of what to say. Shame burns hot. I think of my family, all the relatives. They are all so proud that I became a "teacher." They picture me strong. I would make them all embarrassed. I leave the office and hide inside my car. I have brought disgrace onto everyone who was ever proud of me. If they knew the way I really was, that I could barely hold my class together.

I drive by my daughter's school to pick her up. She is the fresh-man track star in girls' track. She runs cross-country faster than any other girl. But she is temperamental. Sometimes she wants to be begged to run for her school. She wants everyone to want her and to show evidence that they want her. She has missed one race because she was testing the coach. She told him she didn't want to run and he said OK. So she didn't run. She thought he would make a big deal out of her not running, and then she would give in and consent to run. He is talking to her as I drive up to pick her up. Her face is red and she looks as if she is trying to keep from crying. When she gets into the car, I find out the story and grow angry with her. She pierces my eardrums with a shriek that makes me lose track of what I am doing. I forget where I am. I look back and see that she has surprised herself too. She tests me further. It is only this year that she has begun to see who she is outside of me. She screams that she hates me, that she is ashamed of me, that she is embarrassed around her friends for them to know that I am her mother, that I am weird, that something is wrong with me. I can do nothing as I drive. Even if I wasn't in the car I could do nothing. Maybe chase her out the door, but she can outrun me. I taught her to run. I taught her to talk of hate, and being embarrassed and ashamed. Of testing her coach. I taught her to scream. She is everything I am. We are told we look like twins. I don't know what to do about her anger. I know she is angry because she made a mistake and her coach is mad at her. I feel like saying, "Oh, God." She rides in the back seat and needs me to understand. I drive in silence. Now I know why I should have tried to change myself.

We arrive home and go in different directions. I eat. I have not eaten, trying not to stretch the pants that I wear when I'm fat. I (suppress the feeling ) that I am ugly. Being ugly bothers me even when I am worried about what to say to my daughter. I decide not to try to talk to her. I remember hating my own mother now and then when I was fourteen. I am thinking that I will trust that she will figure things out for herself the way I did. That maybe it's good to feel like you could run away and never come back. A kind of cleansing of all the angers. Then I remember that I am supposed to have her on a plane to Reno at 6:30 PM. We have both forgotten, in our emotions. I go find her. She is riding away on her horse. Her eyes are red. I try to be tough. "Hurry up or you'll miss your plane," I command, now in position of authority again. She remembers, gallops full force down the field to put the horse away. She comes into the house with a new attitude. She will be getting away. She won't have to be here. Something could happen. Maybe this is the last time she will see her mother. I can tell what she is thinking as she glances at me helping her pack. Then we remember that she is suppose to take the bicycle. I get a wrench. She opens the bike crate. It is cardboard and does not stand up on its own. I cannot turn the bolts to get the handle bars off. I take off the front wheel instead. Still the pedals are in the way. I curse. My daughter watches my anger. She laughs, says I look funny, red in the face, straining at the bolt that holds the pedals on. We throw the whole bike, wheel, and box into the back of the car. I will find someone at the airport to take it apart and crate it. She barely makes her plane. She was invited to spend a weekend with her cousin. The girls are the same age and have a sisterly closeness. They talk about their mothers' angers together. Their mothers are sisters. I pay a young man a dollar to turn the bolt for me. The bicycle is crated and loaded on with the other bags. I tell him how to pass the crate through Security. My eyes brim with tears. I know she is playing voodoo about foreverness. Last times, etc.

I hug her. She hugs me back. She does not take her eyes off me as she stands on the other side of Security. We are both sorry about all the hate. We know it without words. I smile with a lump in my throat, wondering why everything is like this when there was such a promise for it to all be better. The passengers board. She files on, a passenger now, turning to wave three times. The engines reach such a pitch that I cover my ears. The sound sucks something out of the air and leaves me empty. I look at the row of windows and do not see her face. It doesn't matter, I am thinking. Goodbyes don't matter. It's all the rest that matters. What you did before the goodbye. We all stand as if saluting as the plane takes off. We stand in awe facing what we understand in fact, but not in the mystery of it. The plane disappears into a solid cloud bank, into the sunset. It is a dramatic view. A man who looks gay, stands with a friend, wearing a strange fur coat. Even though my daughter is being whisked into the sky, I look at this man and miss all the men I've ever missed in my life. I turn away before I let myself cry.

6

At Fed-Mart, because it is near the airport, I kill two birds with one stone. I go in and look to see if my film is ready and I try to shop for anything we need. The film is in. I open the envelope before paying for it and look at all the reproductions of our life on film. There is my daughter in her school track shorts the day she took first place in cross-country. There are all of us doing what we do. I put the permanent record of our activities in the basket and wheel past the clothes racks toward the food. All the clothes are the same old things. Even though I am wearing the wrong clothes, I cannot stand the thought of ever buying another garment. I have had too much bad luck. Everything turns out bad. I have been through all the stages of dressing, from those little tailored blouses to those loose baggy monk's blouses, or is it Indian cloth. All the pants. All the dresses and skirts, suits, etc. There is nothing to wear anymore that doesn't remind me of all the wrong ideas I had at one time or another. Nothing ever being what I thought it was. I pass the wigs and remember that once, in my efforts to be something right, I bought a hairpiece that had a comb in it to attach to the top of the head to give height to the face. Also false eyelashes. I thought, at that time that if I had height to my face and longer eyelashes everything would be better. Everything would work out. I turn away from the wigs and clothes and pass by the cheese. I know the price of everything. It is one thing I do know, even though it keeps fluctuating, I do know what is a good price and what is robbery. There are no good prices on cheese. I am relieved. The thought of buying cheese clogs my throat. I could gag if I gave in to the thought of it. I suddenly do not want to see any food. It is like the clothes. I have gone through everything already. The big dinners, the small ones, the snacks, picnics. All the thought put into feeding people and entertaining at one time, thinking that was going to make a difference. Have people in. It is what you do when you have become something. You invite people over, feed them, and sit and talk about things. All the nice pieces of meat we forked down while making nice conversation. All the butter. All the creams, sauces, rolls, desserts. And on the other end of it, I coming out lonely, a joke, nothing ever being right. I drive my cart, with the pictures in it, to the check stand and get out of the store as fast as possible. Its commonness heckling me. My commonness heckling me, pecking at my back, over the mistakes that were my life.

7

Back in the car, I want to faint. There is a weak trickle of nothingness flowing somewhere inside, up and down my spine. Instead of leaning over in the seat, I drive next door to the Post Office Annex and mail my application for Graduate school. Working with kids one-to-one. Maybe that will do it. No more facing 25 kids and trying to teach them something while their parents watch. Finding out instead how the parents have messed up one kid at a time. Talking to the parents.

Going to why the albino kid has to take half the day of another mother's time to be able to sit on a rug with 24 other five-year-olds. Just because he is a different color. I think of how white his tennis shoes were. Was his mother hung up on white. Couldn't she even get pigment into this clothes. Or was she dressing him whiter than he was so his skin would look a shade darker by comparison. Dropping the application into the right box was an accomplishment. Finding the right box, not applying.

> One lingering syllable that gets caught
> in your throat and you can't get it
> out. You see eyes trying to look away.
> And you know you have shown
> the world once again your fear of
> speaking to it. The rest of the day you
> cannot forget.

# Ten Years

*I want to see things and feel things and hear things and say, "Oh." And not care how they affect me. I like men with hard chests who are not afraid to get socked there.*

# *Does He Love Me, Does He Not*

She did not put sugar in her coffee. The bitter taste was what she wanted because it was cold outside and she could not get to a point of feeling settled. She could not make a statement about anything and believe it for sure. Later on, at home, she would nibble from the jar of plum jam preserves to make up for abstaining now. There were chunks of peel she could hook out with a fork.

Besides, they had told eachother during dinner about imagining the other's death as a way of being free again. She had brought up the subject because she thought if they had those thoughts they should admit it. But he had gone a point farther than her and even imagined the location. She looked at her napkin, wrinkled and stained in her plate and did not want to touch him. She looked down at her strong brown legs, the ones she had worked on for fifteen years so they would be strong and brown and she thought of them decaying and him-not caring if they decayed, not liking them enough to want them preserved and next to him in bed forever, and she did not want to look at him.

She told him, "When you think about my death, it's as good as if I'm dead because your thoughts are valid. You're you. I'm just me, no one. It doesn't matter what I think. It's like bbs to cannons."

We're all equal in the eyes of God," he said, winking. And then he leaned forward on his elbows and said under his breath, "How much change do you have?" He had his wallet open and shuffled through only large bills. He needed money for a tip. Marty opened her purse and unsnapped her coin purse and glanced in, estimating after awhile.

"About one sixty-five."

"Are you sure. Now make sure. Count it again."

"OK, I'll count it on the table," she said, dumping her

**151**

coin purse up-side-down. His face tensed and she counted defiantly, "A dollar twenty-five, forty-five, fifty-five, sixty, one, two, three, four, five."

"You brat," he said. "You're just a brat. A thirteen-year-old brat and you'll never grow up. God..." And his lip began to curve down.

He drank his coffee with a stiff arm and smoked at a side angle instead of facing her, turning as if away from a dog turd on the other side of the table. His mouth was held in repugnance.

Marty had always cringed. She had always flushed herself with shame to cleanse herself. And she had tried to make it up to him by apologizing or something. But now she stiffened her face across the table from him and said loud enough for him to hear and for the young unmarried couple at a table beyond him to hear: "Dr. Anthem said it took him half his life to learn to say screw you. And now I know what he meant. Screw You!"

Her breathing was short and her face was hot. She said, stumbling over the words, "You sit there thinking you have the right to be mad at me because I humiliated you in public. Well, *screw you*. I'm not going to be ashamed. I'm not going to be thirteen anymore. You want me to be thirteen."

Marty swallowed and pictured herself on the outside of the warm walls of their house. "Why do you suppose you asked me again if I was *sure* I had enough for a tip. You can't take my word. I've got a long history of doing the wrong thing, right? Of making mistakes, of not being accurate?"

She put her cup of coffee to her mouth to stop the words. She swallowed the warm fluid with a thick throat, and looked at the far wall where illuminated figures of Little Black Sambo hung in succession. She wondered if it was a joke. Those figures, while she was saying things she had always wanted to say. This is where it takes place, she thought, anywhere, even where pictures of Black Sambo hang. This is where we change so later when we look in the mirror we see someone else. She wanted to give birth to the lump of food in her stomach to get rid of it too. It lay dead now. All the juices were in the redness of her face.

Marty finished her cup and the waitress did not come with the coffee pot. She was glad. It was time to get up. She walked away from Alex and stood near the glass doors near the cash register. Two girls walked in and took stools at the counter. With her heated eyes, Marty noticed that one had a special beauty from the front view but her profile became a small homely child. The other girl had an elegant profile which gave her an air of wealth, but straight on she was coarse-featured. Marty swelled with composure, the composure of being on a perch and not of those of a low down flat land, as she watched Alex walk toward her with his shoulders like those of an air force officer in uniform. He stopped at the cash register and took a toothpick and two mints and rummaged in his billfold, holding the check between two fingers that weren't in use. The young pert cashier cheered him up.

Marty folded her arms like an Indian, Alex held the door and they went out looking at the tall metal flowers in the foot light along the entrance wall. She said, "I wonder who made those?"

They got into the car and she did not know if his stiffness would enter his hand and fly to her mouth.

She said, "It's a cycle. And it'll continue forever until I stop trying to second-guess you. Of course it was stupid to dump the money out, and if I were alone, directing myself I wouldn't have done it, but I do dumb things trying to read your mind."

He put his hand on her shoulder and the lightness of it surprised her and did not please her, but there was a certain relief in it. She went on.

"You wouldn't have asked Gertrude to count her money to make sure. She would have snapped your head off with her pursed lips. 'I know how much I have, so just don't mind, never mind now, dear,'" and Marty spoke in the mincing tone of her mother-in-law's voice.

Alex smoked slowly as he drove. Marty saw it so clearly, the way they were together and why she had dumped her money out that she could not let it go. She said, "You can't trust me. You can't take my word. And it's not your fault.

Because I have done silly things before, so you'll always expect me to, and so I always will do them. There's no point where we can break the cycle." He just moved them along the freeway in silence and after she stopped talking, he said, "There's a knock. Damn, the piston's going out. That's another half day out of my life."

Marty wished she could fix the piston so he would have no reason to be irritated. When he was irritated she could not relax. After a pause of listening to the piston, she went on, "Of course, you'll say that I was embarrassing you from the very beginning. That you didn't make me into this kind of person by treating me that way. But all I'm saying is that it's the way we are together, you treating me like a dunce and me always living up to it."

He reached over and patted her shoulder and they pulled into the Falcon's parking lot, and he said, "Looks like a crowd here tonight." They locked the car even though the only thing inside was the manual in the glove compartment. And they entered the dark loud room, passing a mammoth aquarium where a long pink catfish floated beside them, waving and turning like a severed penis. Marty looked at the group on stage and saw three thin stringy boys at their electric guitars, a piano and singing with their mouths against the microphones.

Alex led, filing through the tables. The heads of people, waist level, turned as they passed, looking to see the competition or the prospect. A girl looked at Alex and followed him with her eyes and it occurred to Marty that she saw him as a male, a lover. A guy alone against the wall watched Marty and his eye was a male eye seeing a female. He did not see a mother or a wife, PTA co-chairman, science coordinator, math tutor or Girl Scout leader, or a thirteen-year-old brat. He saw her as raw flesh, raw fuckable flesh, and Marty's hips felt vulnerable and a little worn from all the walking and standing and routine usage.

They ordered what they usually ordered and Marty. wanted to laugh as she always wanted to when Alex hollered out of the corner of his mouth so the young blonde girl with the tray could hear over the noise from the speakers next to their heads. "A side car and a gimlet." He was pushing back in his shirt so his shoulders were erect and chest out, one ankle crossed on his other knee and his head tilted up. He did not look at her until after she nodded and then he looked at her face and glanced at her body as she made her way through the tables.

Marty knew she could not do it tonight. She could not get up there and bounce around. She could not place herself on the floor and let go of all she knew and believed in, and dance. She could not become one of the throbbing mob because she was alone and afraid tonight. But before the drinks came, Alex got up and held his hand out behind him to her and without touching, because she extended hers to him the right amount of paces behind, they squeezed their way to the dance floor separately. Alex went right into it, moving his arms and legs rhythmically. Marty started by bobbing her head with the motions of the other people and hoped it would work down. She found a place behind a large man in dark clothes and tried to hide her efforts of blending. She began bending her knees in beat but her shoulders were too stiff to move and her fists hung at the end of her dead arms like gong hitters.

Marty looked at the girl beside her who was snapping her fingers and bending her elbows front and back, so she tried that. Another girl was pumping her pelvis, so Marty added that. She tried not to look conspicuous. She looked with sober eyes at Alex and saw that he was giving it everything. Marty bobbed violently, determined to look like everyone else, but she let her eyes travel across the room to the cool dark wall and picked out the people individually and studied them. Her head rode evenly on the solid block of writhing bodies, and she was able to preserve herself. She began to laugh after awhile because her body had become a beating pelvis and her head was not able to tell the pelvis it would be free... really free to follow through with its movements. The separation struck her as funny.

Marty drove home in the early morning with Alex smoking on the seat beside her saying, "It's good to let go once in awhile. We need to get out like this more, break the routine. It's good for the spirit. We've been working too hard. Let's face it, I'll blow my heart out before I'm forty, so why not live a little." He stuck the cigarette butt in the full ash tray, sat awhile then and lit another and smoked it gently, meditating.

Marty looked over at him during the intersection where the street lights were bright. He responded.

"I like you," he said, "You're a good sport." He slapped her thigh like a pal.

"Do you love me?" Marty asked.

"Do you love me?" he asked back.

"I don't know," she said.

"Well, I like you," he said. "You're hard to love sometimes but I always like you."

"What do you mean!" she asked, knowing already.

"Love. What is love!" He looked up into the grey upholstery of the car ceiling as a philosopher would look at the stars. "You love someone in the beginning. I loved you in the beginning. Love is when your heart is full. It's so full it aches."

"And it doesn't ache anymore?" She knew it was not really a question but a way to keep the talk going, because hers didn't ache anymore either.

"We know eachother too well," he said. "You can't love someone after you know them as well as we know eachother. Love is believing in illusions." He flicked his ash out the wind wing. "We've had too many nasty moments. Too much trampling it down. Love is a tender thing. I kept telling you in the beginning to stop the moods. You can't keep trampling it down."

His words twisted her even though she knew everything he was saying before he said it, because he was speaking for both of them. It was ten and a half years. They were just used to eachother.

"But I like you, sport. Come on, what is this talk. Love? Yes, of course I love you." He was always able, at the moment of lagging, to grab ahold and give it punch. She always let it slide, limp at that moment. He was responding to her silence. It was heavy and he recognized it as a brood, one of those hurt moods. More trampling.

"But I want you to love me like in the beginning. Why should it ever end if it was ever real at all?" She played naive and tried to pretend she wasn't playing. She wanted to believe it could be done. That love could last forever.

"It's one of those things, dear," he said, sighing like a teacher who had to put a check mark somewhere and disappoint a student. "Nature screws us. Blame the universe." He crushed out his cigarette and leaned toward her like an imp and said, "Love me, Marty, like you did in the beginning. Come on. Please, Marty, feel that warm glow flood your heart again."

It was mock. She laughed instead of cried. Of course it was ridiculous, but she still wanted the safety of knowing there was a feeling that was constant, not relative to time and event.

She gave him the repeat reasoning, "But when you say you don't love me, it's real because you're real, the leader, the Big Man. I'm just me. So when I say I don't love you, it's not valid. It doesn't matter, and besides, you don't need my love like I need yours. And besides that, it's your prerogative to feel my way about it if you want to."

His eyes blurred, seeing distance without looking past the dashboard. "Yes, I need love, we all do, and I need it too. It does something for you.. But I'm not going to...Well, what can I say. Sure, it'd be nice to hold someone and be in love again, but it's not practical. That phase has passed for me. And I don't think I'm capable of feeling it anymore. I know too much now."

They were pulling into their own driveway and Marty still wanted everything that she could not have anymore.

# The Sky Over Alaska
# and Being Up in It

At Sambo's. It is ten o'clock. I am with Alex. It is nighttime. Thirteen years before, at night, we sat here. It was called Kerry's then. I was afraid to eat in front of him because food was emotional. I could not choose between etiquette and what I needed back then either. I drank something from a straw in front of him, as he gulped down a hamburger. I did not want to take a chance exposing what food meant to me. I did not want to bulge my cheeks or wallow or lose some of the precious stuff out of the corner of my mouth and recapture it with my finger. I did not want to chance spilling some of it on my chest. So I drank from a straw because it was safe.

I drink coffee now as he eats pie. I do not like to waste money on *just* food. He does not mind. There was some of that back then, too. I wanted to save his money. I didn't want him to spend money on me. It made me uneasy. I feel that way still. Plus, *food should be accidental.* It should be something you run across. Buying it always bothered me.

He and I sit on the same side of the booth. We sat across from eachother then. We wanted to look at eachother. To gaze. To read the eyes. Now we want to be side by side looking out at the same thing together. A common eye. I see what he sees. He sees what I see. We are in a fort together. A tank. Moving along. Over bumps together.

I say to him, putting my arm around his back because I know he is *with me,* "I was just thinking that we were here thirteen years ago. And I was remembering the way you were then. You are not much different. You haven't changed from the way you were then."

He is silent, chewing briefly and swallowing because there isn't much chewing with pie. Pressing the tongue and crushing the crust and berries. A boa constrictor act. Pressing it

158

down the throat. No grinding. His neck works. I am looking into the side of his head. Ear level to him. I go on, attempting to be explicit. "You still have the same eyes as then." I want to say more. About his compassion. His acceptance of the "way we are." I want to tell exactly how I feel about him back then and him now. And *us* then and now. I want to know the differences and the sameness about him and about me. I want to know *what happened.* And what will happen. I want him to tell me if he thinks I am the same as then. I want to be the same. I want to know if I have an indestructible core. If I cannot perish. If I am sill present in my life. If he and I are still left. If we are anything but the thing we have been doing for thirteen years. If we are still the promises we made to our individual selves. If there is a remnant of us from *then* to *now.* I think of the phrase "identity crisis" as I crave to know where we are and where we are going. Over coffee. And pie

He says, "I think we've changed. I think the years have taken their toll." I know he says that because he thinks he has had to do most of the work. It was his vision we were following. The future. I was a passenger. I sat and looked out the windows and counted the telephone poles going by.

"But," I say, digging my mental heels in. Skidding so I won't have to get there to where I know he will take us—into the tainted place. The mildew place. Where rot has begun to form.

I say, "I see you then and I superimpose what you *have* now over it. I see how your face then would have looked if the knowledge of having what you have now had passed over it. You were twenty-seven then. You owned nothing. Only a trailer. You drove a bus for money. And you were so idealistic. You believed in a fairy tale. That you'd meet *the woman* and live happily ever after because she could not help being satisfied with you, knowing what you know about yourself. Well, that's okay...."

Pause. "...If you could have seen our little place, the house, all the stuff you own. The workshop you had wanted then that you have now. The submarine...."

I watch his face. "And *me*," I venture, testing. "And the

kids…Wouldn't you have warmed if you had known then that in thirteen years all this would be.…" I drifted off, not sure now of it myself. Not sure if what he traded for it was a fair price. If he had paid more than it should have cost. If what he got was paltry little compared to his red-blooded idealism then that rocked him to sleep with sweet dreams in his trailer when he was single. If supposing he didn't know us and walked by and saw us. Would he be warmed by the sight of us. And knowing he saw the equivalent of us all the time. Little homes and little people in them. And he was not warmed. That he was warmed by the sight of a yacht from Alaska docked at the harbor. Or spacious, clean and fully equipped wood and metal workshops on back streets. Evidence of men putting their dreams into reality. *Means.* Evidence of money and ability doing exactly as it pleased. Every ambition.

He was not warmed by a mother and three little kids standing in the doorway waving goodbye as he went off to work to make more money, just enough money, for food and clothes and transportation and shelter.

I did not want to see it. I said, "Is it so different from then? Food and clothes, transportation, shelter? It was what you were doing when I met you." I felt defensiveness welling up even though he had not said a word. "You were just going to school and driving a bus and coming home and eating and sleeping. Then. Except for Alaska."

*That Alaska trip.* I said, "Right. You dropped your camera in the river. You ate dried figs. You pissed in a stream. You wiped on a lot of *Off.* And you dredged for gold. And you look the same now as then. Alaska is still in your eyes. *Everything is Alaska,* isn't it?"

He turned and put his hand on my leg and patted me. We sat in silence. I gulped goodwill in my throat. I wished to capture and imprison no one. I wished to leave the cage door open. *Go. Be free. Damn it. Don't do me any favors.*

In our silence I remembered asking him where he would *really* like to be once. Exactly what he would like to be doing if he had a choice. And he said, "Up in a little airplane over Alaska." His voice was tired and reasonable. And I had used what he told me to scoff, "Really? Why? Up in the air? Over a certain territory? What a bore. I don't understand what you could possibly get out of it. What does it mean being *on top of everything?* Or something?" He had smirked and shrugged and said, he guessed it did sound kind of stupid. A position in the air over a certain place.

As we sipped our coffee I wished his dreams could come true so he would see that they weren't anything anyway and could value what he had. And I knew that that was the difference that had taken place. The knowledge that *no difference* takes place. *Ever.* I was still hiding my eating habits and he was still wishing for what he didn't have even though he had more than he had ever had.

# Home Movies

There is Alex on the screen. First born and then a chubby toddler in a wool suit at the swings. Then comes the dimples and piles of white curls and a wide smile and bright blue eyes. Later, as the night grows longer and the reels turn, he gets large shoulders, long legs and the scowl and the knitted brows that stay with him forever. It passes before my eyes on film. Alex runs the projector knitting his brows. I sit beside his mother and we concentrate on the screen, attempting to see more than is there.

The home movies have left out all the fights I have heard about. I do not see his mother switching his bare legs with a hickory stick. Or his father taking off his belt for the beatings. Or the track coach telling Alex he can't play in the finals because he missed a meet. Alex, the top runner. And so the team lost to a neighboring town. Or the only girl he loved breaking his heart in high school. Having his baby and giving it away and coming back and dating older boys as if nothing happened.

We see well-prepared meals of chipped beef on toast served by a black maid and laid on a highly polished formal dining room table, set with plaid mats, silver, crystal, China, and linen and proper center piece. There is Alex minding his manners, ever watchful and fearful of his stern parents who are dressed for dinner and seated at the head and tail of the table. There are reels of Christmas tree rituals with Alex and his four sisters descending the stairs and entering the sitting room to admire the tree. There are rows and rows of old aunts and uncles and grandparents with young children running about. The adults stiff and reserved, breaking into modest smiles.

While I watch Alex unfolding, his metamorphosis into a young gentleman in white shirts and dark slacks, I see myself all along the way in comparison to certain points in his life. He is six years older but nevertheless there are parallels.

His family is in Chevy Chase building a new house, a two-story cold-weather house and filling it with expensive cherry wood, cedar, and oak furniture. Mine is in Porterville, living in the unpainted pioneer style, three-room, linoleum-floored pine house of my grandparents. I am falling into the river on the way to kindergarten at three and a half. Alex is being driven to a private school for boys. His father wears a suit. I am afraid of men in suits. They are foreign to me. Men in blue shirts and Levi's are familiar. I am sleeping in the living room on the daybed sofa. Alex is sent to his room, full of solid oak furnishings, for punishment. He is shooting small pebbles out the window with a sling slot and breaking the small windows of a green house which sit on the neighbor's property. I am afraid to break anything. There are too many broken things around already. Alex is learning to say the right words and act the right way and be a proper young man. I am leaping rocks at the beach like a young goat.

Alex is going off to camp. His family is renting a cabin at Cheley Camp in Estes Park in the Rockies to be near him for the first week. I am traveling across the desert to Needles, California with my father, and sleeping on the ground in my sleeping bag. Or on top of the car where there is a rack with a mattress.

The comparisons go on and on as long as the reels roll. And when they end and Alex tries to catch the tail of film as it flies loose and flaps several rotations, I wonder why he wanted to marry me when I did not do or have any of the things he did or had.

And why he could not tell I did not have them when we met. He thought I was a solitary rich girl back then, he'd said, the way I was holding myself aloof, never joining the crowd. Why he didn't choose a girl who had his background. It would have been a natural choice. Similar matching similar.

Later in the dark, in bed, after we are alone, after his prim mother dismisses herself with a brisk "good night fellas," brushing her cheek to Alex's, I ask Alex why he didn't marry someone else. Why he pursued me all semester so feverishly. He says, "Because I never agreed with what middleclassness said." I am very still and slightly numbed as I listen. It is the first time I have seen the films and had no idea that he'd come from such structure. "It didn't put anything of substance into girls. You knew and felt the way I had always known and felt and I liked that in you." I am warming. He goes on.

"I just didn't know how much you hadn't been trained in doing things right, though. If I had known how much you hadn't been trained...." He trails off. I am hurt. It was his severe training that soured him on life, making him envy my freedom that attracted him to me. He used to say, "You have a lust for life." It intrigued him. How'd I have the right to go around not caring what people thought. Walking barefooted, letting my hair blow in the wind.

I waited for him to say that in spite of my being of the poorer class I had a wealth of natural gifts. More than any of the girls of his uppity class. I disengage my tender, vulnerable, valuable self from his middle class judgments. He was middle class after all, no matter how he had tried to rebel. He just didn't like the restrictions on him, but agreed with all the rules and regulations on everyone else. He liked all the effort it took to stick to a career and be able to afford nice things. He just didn't want to be the one who stuck to it and bought them. His father's social position and prestige was a point of pride for Alex. He'd rebelled against all the punishments that came with status and confused it with the rest of the package.

I stay alone and defiant, filled with savage pride against values, illusions and fairy tales I attribute to his mother and all the girls Alex has ever known. He sighs over my silence. We have been over it a hundred times and he never catches on about what I want to be loved for. *For being poor.* For the lack of training in standard ways of doing things. Of developing myself by myself with no help from anyone. With making it. With surviving my childhood. He can't have it both ways. Attracted to my rawness and ungroomed-ness and expect me to mince and purse like his mother.

Alex cannot love me for that. He has twirled his short-fingered thick hand in the air and said, "You're a diamond in the rough.… " And laughed. "I just didn't know you couldn't be polished. I thought I could take your raw material and make you into a real gem. But, you are unteachable. Like an aborigine. There've been studies. That's why they're still sitting on the bare ground with their bare behinds. They can't be taught anything." I'd already cried over that view of me.

Alex tells me that he loves me in spite of those things. I tell him that because of those things I  allow him to *be*, the way he wanted to as a child. That I let him simply be without restrictions. The only restriction being that of loving me for all those things he can't love me for. We turn on the light. Alex reads a science magazine to escape. I drift into dwelling on the old scar of shame. Of being poor laid open again. Of Alex thinking that what it did to me was a bad thing when I think it was a good thing. Of Alex thinking that I want the impossible: to be loved for knowing none of his rules. I have already threatened him that there is someone somewhere someday who will value all of me. But that I just haven't met him yet. Alex does not act threatened. "It'd be your loss," he has said more than once. He is the product of the very thing he had turned against. Like an animal chewing off its own hind leg to get out of the trap.

# Away from Him

For awhile she does not think of what to do because it just happens. One thing leads into another. She has no choice out of principle. There are certain things you cannot take from people, and that is how it begins. You walk away.

Away from him and planned to go nowhere at all. Because that was what was important, to go nowhere in particular, as if one weren't going to take certain steps to find the way first. So she left before he had the chance to. It felt good walking away. It went on and on, this act, rather than a word that told him, *see, I'm as capable of leaving as you are.* But she turns back, though, because going doesn't penetrate. She was tired of making action statements to him. It got down to her having to ruin her own day, use up her own time, just to show him that she was separate from him, and that he could not treat her any other way.

She walked in one direction opposite from where he was, or where she thought he was and she eventually came to a doughnut shop. It was not her decision to enter. She entered because now that she was away from him, she had to do something. She had to enter and exit somewhere in order to appear under control. She never eats doughnuts but he does. She has watched him eat dozens of doughnuts over the years, and has swallowed when he swallowed, getting the same pleasure watching him as he did eating them because he was lean. She would not have enjoyed seeing a fat husband eat doughnuts.

There is some privacy inside the doughnut shop because of the way the counter and tables are situated, and because it is run by a family from Mexico who leave you alone and do not know how to interpret what you are doing after you make a purchase.

She orders a cup of coffee and takes a small table along the wall where she can watch everyone but will not be watched. She watches the people in her small town attending a rummage sale across the street in a parking lot. They hold somebody else's pants up to themselves. Women with faces as wrinkled as the clothes they buy go off to their cars holding their items under clamped arms with their mouths also clamped, as if they have caught their dinner inside.

She would have sat with her cup all day if it would not have looked odd. She did not want to look as if she were away from anybody. But twenty minutes is the time people give you to be finished and moving on to other things. She gives it a half hour and then gets up, still away from him in her heart and walks along the street. Where he is is of no importance, she tells herself. Not now. She passes the rummage sale and inhales through her nose to catch the smell of sweat in old sweaters. It is there. Or is it there in her memory.

A Greyhound bus comes to the crosswalk and waits for her to pass and then it passes her, going slow on the main street through town. She sees it stop two blocks ahead and wait. She begins to run. Her purse knocks against her hip. She runs casually in case the bus pulls out before she reaches it. She runs as if she is just running because she wants to, not to catch a bus. Only toward the last of the second block does she get serious and strain toward the bus and want it to wait for her. It is then she knows that she will take the bus away from him.

There is a good feeling, an empty bond-breaking feeling as she steps up on the bus and buys a ticket. The defiance of being in *transportation* when he did not want her to have transportation because it was a way to keep her from going away from him. The bus sits high up off the street, and gives a cushiony sense of moving along. It takes her all the way through her little town, past people she knows when she is in other roles, roles that have nothing to do with going away. It takes her past her own house outside of town, and *away* from him farther than she had planned to get. She does not look at her house. It is tucked back anyway, but she pretends it is not there. That no place is anywhere. No place at all. She does not want to be going away from a place. Leaving places hurts her more than leaving people. A place does not know.

It is a nice ride into another small town. The bus driver has an Irish brogue. He has chatted with her all the way. She has made inane comments back so not to appear to be ignoring him, but not because she wanted to talk. He has robbed her of a valuable silence. She could have felt alone. He made her appear to be just anyone on a bus for the usual reasons.

At the depot she alights and pivots away toward the main street of town, knowing that it is more *being away* from him than *being here*. She is *not here*. She is simply *not there* with him anymore.

It is early in the day. Just noon. The day stretches out and she walks on its long flat colorless belly. The sun comes and goes and comes again. She enters the mainstream of people walking up and down in front of the stores. No one's eyes are focused on anything. Each item displayed in the windows call to her. They speak of being the real thing. That if she had *it*, she would not need anything else. This blouse. This pen. She wants everything. She wants to have the *not having them* out of the way. The invisible scoffing that would be done somewhere if they knew she didn't have these things. They irritate her. She used to hold his arm and laugh with him over all the vulgar things they could buy if they really wanted to appear to be in vulgar showy taste. They only laughed. They never bought the things. They got past caring to buy them by laughing together.

But now he is *not here*. He is *somewhere else*. And she does not let herself look at the windows. They become background for her aloneness. She can pass them as she passed her house. As if they are not there.

Except for a pair of shoes.

The salesgirl is no one. She brings shoes to her and buckles them onto her feet. And then she watches her walk around the store looking at herself in different mirrors. There is one pair of shoes. A pair that are hers as soon as she sees them.

She goes out into the street again, wearing them, feeling the new places they touch her where her old ones didn't. They are her first shoes away from him, touching her in new places.

And his not knowing that she wears them sets her more apart from him than she had thought she would be. It is like the time he paid for the car license without her knowing it one year. It was the first time he went about their business without telling her about it. She felt abandoned. Now she was abandoning him, touching *their* money, a part of him, without telling him about it.

She stands before a rack of long pants for a long time. They confront eachother until she has taken what she wants from it. They are a pair of pants that touch her in new ways. New cloth bringing new sensations in places where her old ones had gone soft. She goes out wearing them, wearing the new feelings, knowing he cannot know what she is feeling, and they are not old feelings.

She does not like carrying her old shoes and old pants around. There is a church playground she knows about. So she hides them. It is in the playhouse and it is the wrong day for children to be playing there. She places the two bags just inside the little play door and sneaks back over the hedge and makes it away without being seen. There is a feeling of power in it, that she has been able to arrange to have her bags kept away from her even though there is no place to put them. She put them nowhere. In a place that does not exist to anyone when they think of packages. While he is with the car, which is *the* place.

Her arms know about their freedom. They hang and swing in contrast to six blocks of clutching. The new shoes and pants allow her new looseness. And for a moment she sees the town the way a primitive man views things when he goes up in an airplane. She believes her eyes. Everything away from her looks small and she knows that it is small. The street and sidewalk go short before her. They are too narrow for her to pass through. Her vision functions in one dimension. The sidewalk and street stick up, short, flat, impossible to be on. So she sits on a bench away from them, fearing she will bump into the end of the town. It is not a real town. Or she is not real away from him. And everyone is pretending to be only walking along. Or she is. That it is so simple to just *be* where they are. Or where she is. That is hasn't taken their whole life's efforts up to the last second to be *here, now*. Or hasn't taken hers.

She is being tricked. It is a toy town. A poster painted place. She pulls at a weed coming up to her from a crack in the sidewalk and holds the moist root to her nose. The smell of soil revives her. It tells her that the town is real. *Underneath everything.* It is still real. Or she is. She puts the root back into the hole and walks toward the art museum because it is a place to go before five. After that there will be the library until nine, and then the Christian Science reading room. It stays open all the time. There will be places to go even when he believes there is no place for her to be when she is not with him.

Portraits loom at her. She goes away with them. They take her away and look at her from different angles. She is held captive until they become familiar and then she is able to break away, entering another room where large canvases dominate her. Canvases as large as the walls lead her along diagonal lines, making her teeter and trip and fall into thick red places so that she tries to hold onto safe open green and yellow and brown spatterings of color.

A guard with a radio transmitter watches her as she turns a complete circle in the middle of the floor. He puts the speaker up to his mouth but she cannot hear him speak. She sees his lips move. She looks at him with sorrow from *where she is*. He is sad. It is sad. He is the weed growing in a crack of brown.

She goes away from him, past the statues of male torsos. She looks at the broken places on them for the hundredth time, because the museum of art is where she came with him for all those years to watch his face when he looked at paintings, to detect what would be there. It was animated twice, once with a metal optical illusion exhibit, and once with a roving slide show. She absorbed his appreciation then, of these things and drew strength from his *knowing* what was worthwhile. And once she was jealous when he went up close to examine a pop art porno drawing of very intricate Asian sexual acts. She was afraid he would long for an Oriental woman to do those things to him instead of her.

There was no certain time outside of him. No time to prepare for his return or his departure, or his food. No certain time to sit down or stand up or roll over or get in or get out. The same as there being *no place* away from him, there is *no time*.

She drifts outside the museum, not in step but in thought. About how she has not functioned around her *being* but around his, so that now she is left mindless without him. There are no decisions that affect her. She goes into the gift shop and buys three prints. One of a water buffalo, another of two elephants, and the third of a lion. There is something about these. And she buys a bottle of China Muskoil. And then, as if by a remote childhood control, she goes to the library.

The small print of books is before her eyes. She gathers facts and figures for awhile and then reads a story about a man who misses his dead wife but learns about his sexual perversions through a red-headed girlfriend. she holds the story as if it is a living creature and when it is over, she places it gently on a shelf. The lights begin to flicker over head, throughout the library. She watches them. This set and then that set. In waves of blinking lights the librarian tells her to leave the warmth of her chair.

She thinks of the story outside in the night air. She does not like the man or his girlfriend or what they did, but she liked the way he could tell about it. She wants to meet him. And for him to keep her warm. For a man like that to see her and know she needs help and to help her. If you are a woman you imagine a man saving you. The man in the book stays with her for awhile.

In the cold she reaches for the small bottle of China Muskoil inside her purse and opens the bottle and presses it against her neck. The warm scent of it encircles her. She hugs herself and inhales until she is filled with the promises of good things. She knows that while she is away from him he is *there* with himself, comfortable, safe, being the main person wherever he is so that it is impossible for him to *go away*. Where he is is where everything is.

It is the first time she has to think of where to go next.

Men pass her but they have become *the enemy*. Now that she is alone. After all the fantasies of being rescued by a strange male, she cannot look upon one now on the street after dark. The thought of his disease-carrying parts scare her. Where to put her body so that it will be out of sight is suddenly her main concern. To get herself out of the night.

There is a block of cars parking along the curbs and people walking toward a Catholic church. There is a determination in the throng of people making their way up the steps. The doors open and close as they enter and she sees a golden glow inside. She goes toward it. All the people are seated by the time she enters. The floor creaks under her step. There is a red carpet. A soft warm deep red. And a row of candles burning beneath a statue of Jesus in Mary's arms. His stab wound bleeds and the nail holes in his feet and palms bleed. Their faces are distraught. The message beneath says something to the nature of *Are your troubles any worse than these? Well, then if he managed so can you.* She stands in the back afraid to interfere in a religion that is not hers. No one seems to notice her, though, so she creaks to the nearest empty bench, and studies the figures of two Japanese sisters in front of her. They are immaculate. She wonders how they can stay so clean and still live. They frisk a "saying" book back and forth between them and read aloud with the congregation when the time comes.

She hears a man speaking about abortion and voting against it, through a microphone, and searches the altar for someone who looks like a priest. She cannot distinguish one man from another. There are several people in robes and others standing about. A young guitarist plays at intervals. Her sweet young folk voice is incongruous with the glitter of ancient murals and symbols. She uses new phrases for old sentiments. After awhile baskets are passed down the aisles and finally down her aisle where an old man beside her puts in a dollar bill. Not everyone gives. She is embarrassed. She wishes the old man's hands had not shaken. That that kind of thing never happened. Ever.

A mother takes her baby out because it is making noises. The congregation rises and sits as a unit and then they kneel on the kneeling place. It is a red vinyl padded unit attached to the bench in front of them. A couple of old women are breathing on the back of her head because she is not kneeling. The old man beside her cannot kneel. He makes an effort with one arthritic knee. She has seen a crippled dog looking longingly at the base of a pole before. Unable to lift its leg. The impression is the same. She has folded her hands in respect and bowed her head for everything. And all that it wants her to do but can't. The church is warm. The end of her nose has gotten warm again. And her fingertips. She hopes the service will go on and on so she can gather body heat and save it up for the long night.

The two girls in front of her go forward after a long pause in sounds. Other people are filing forward too. They will receive a wafer on their tongues. When the sisters return she hears them talking about buying a new pair of shoes. Young men have gone forward too. She would not have believed it. That they could believe in wafers while they are young and men.

When mass is over she watches all the Catholics leave their church. They are in a hurry. And one woman is laughing. A few have stayed behind on their knees. She wants to tell someone what she has seen. After the church is empty, except for the people kneeling far away by themselves with bowed heads, she goes to the candles because she has nowhere else to go and the small individual flames are friendly. She looks at the statue again and then she kneels because she has never kneeled, and she lights a candle because she has never lighted a candle. And she says the name of a Catholic she once knew because there is nothing else to say.

It is a night of doing what she has not done before. In case there is something to it. And then she goes out into the night, empty of feeling.

The cold surrounds her and nips in wherever it can. She thinks of two places to go: a place to get warmth and a place to get food. Two essentials. She will go to the Thrift shop and buy a sweater and then to Joe's Cafe to eat.

Short Mexicans bump past her by the sweaters section,

as they buy pajamas with feet for their babies. She chooses a second-hand sweater. It is wool. She is freezing. It costs thirty-five cents. And there is no place to put it on. It is not the kind to pull over her head or button up. She will have to wear it under the shirt she wears now.

Joe's looks formidable. She cannot insert herself into everyone's raucous good times. They are all having such fun inside. She has never been there, but peers in the window as she passes. There will be another place. She has heard of another place.

There is one open door in the next block. It is the Adult bookstore. She can feel warmth as she passes. She has become a temperature-directed creature. She stops, hesitates and then steps inside. A short man is pacing up and down as if he is a guard. His arms are folded across his chest. She turns and reads a sign: *All Movies 25 Cents*. The man paces out of sight around a partition and she darts into the nearest booth. There is a large screen before her. And a slot for a quarter. And privacy. She is off the street. She looks for a quarter in her purse, and finds one. She is suddenly discriminating. Perhaps she has chosen the wrong one. She peers around her partition to the one across the aisle and reads its title. Then she gets up and looks at the title outside her booth.

The manager kept passing by my booth and glancing in through the crack of the curtain. I wondered if he thought I was here for the pornography, and maybe wanted sex and he'd be available. I waited until he rounded a corner, and dashed from the place, now back on the street after midnight.

Everything was closed, no lights. The main street in this small town, dead. The only place I knew that'd be open in this part of town was an old hotel, the Faulding, where I'd seen vagrants hanging around during the day and sleeping on the sidewalk at night. It was just a block away. It was the only place out of the night, now that I was out of my house and on foot.

I knew Alex was snug in our bed, the children in theirs, and I was a piece of meat to these vagabond men, eyeing me as I stepped toward the only light. The man behind the counter bordered by two plants dead in their pots, looked like a criminal. I asked how much a room was. He seemed entertained, an unlikely customer. Smoke poured from his mouth as he said $15. OK, I paid.

He led me up the stairs. I thought of *Psycho*, the Bates Motel, and lay in the hotel bed seven miles from my house, from my husband, from my home.  Mother, wife, defiant female. A woman with hurt feelings from the insults of her husband. No money in her purse after paying for a bed to pretend independence. All night I woke to sounds, seeing myself stabbed, raped, and killed.

In the morning, I took the bus home. Al was too busy to look up from fiddling with some gadget, and the kids were at school. Only the tiny dog jumped as high as my head and ran around in circles to celebrate my return. She was the barometer to the family cohesion.

# The Picnic 1

With a normal couple. It has been so long. All the people we know have been divorced. The Joneses are happily married. I am uneasy. What if our real views come through. What if they discover we are not normal or happily married. The first thing I do is remove my mustache. I do not want to have a mustache around them. They may read something into it. I use the depilator that has been in the medicine cabinet for thirteen years. I leave it on for twenty minutes. When I rinse it off and feel my upper lip the mustache is still there, but curly. There is no time to drive to the drug store. The chicken is baking in the oven. Carrot cake cooling under tinfoil. Basket packed full of paper plates, plastic forks, root beer, wine, and celery sticks. Alex and I climb into the car.

They are ahead of us, idling their engine along the curb at the entrance to the park. Two happy heads. In the front seat, side by side, wondering which site to choose. We gesture, not particular. We follow them. They creep along waiting for a sign. Through our car windows, they nod us into a nice spot by the volleyball court. Ralph Jones, the normal husband is a handsome man. He turns bright pink as we all get out and make sounds of greeting and acceptance over the spot. He smiles deep and averts his eyes. Shy. But we know his reputation: upright, decent, an engineer with several inventions accepted by GM. His own tennis court. I look for a clue into their happiness, while Heda, the normal, happily married wife talks incessantly in a matter-of-fact tone. She is unassuming, homely, overweight, smiles continuously. Exposes orange mineral deposits on her teeth. I am after their secret.

Our sons are best friends. They have instigated the picnic. They are like twins: blond, blue-eyed, tall, thin, playful. They roll on the grass like puppies and then scamper off into the oak woods. We, the parents, are left alone to become acquainted.

I touch my curly mustache, stroking it for reassurance. And pour four glasses of wine. We stand and talk passionately at eachother for awhile to open up. Gradually the men draw apart from the women and go into their masculine stance, golden arms folded, feet spread, chins lowered to shorten their vocal chords and deepen their voices. We women take to the quilt thrown on the grass, aiming downward with our heaviest parts. We talk animatedly about where we have been in our lives up to this very moment, as couples. We part the blinds on our pasts and give eachother a peek. She wants me to know that she was an only child, with a possessive, efficient mother. A mother who would not let her touch the house, who let her read her way through childhood as they were both dragged across the country by a nomadic father, a lithographer who moved from city to city every three months. She sits upright on a large ample bottom and tells me that she had too much as a child, had to hide most of her Christmas presents so her friends wouldn't resent her. She is still her mother's daughter in a pink sweatshirt, basic black nylon slacks, baby fat, corroded-toothed. I wonder why she should qualify for happiness.

We sip from plastic cups and she tells me that Ralph comes from poverty, a Scotch-Irish family of ten kids, was next to the youngest, was isolated on a farm in Iowa until he joined the army, was shocked by what he saw men do in the army, had a severe father who wielded a belt and kept him in line, was as virginal as she was when they were married. This information whets my appetite for the already blushing husband. I glance at the blond and pink Ralph who has had such a hard life and who is standing now next to my own husband. I study his chiseled Scotch-Irish profile. Try to find his deep-set blue eyes. Wonder why such a handsome man married this plain and homely woman. A virgin on his wedding night. Was he too afraid to handle beauty that night too? Did he not mind being all thumbs with homeliness?

Heda was fifth in her class. She graduated with honors. A brilliant woman who went into motherhood hesitantly. Who couldn't breast-feed because of her intellect. Whose babies were born with congenital problems of one thing or another. Babies who vomited up her chemical resistant, maternally reluctant milk. A woman who had learned to believe in books so thoroughly, so habitually turned to them for information, that she did not trust her body or the infants that came from it. Who did not know what to do when she couldn't see it in print.

I change positions because one leg is going to sleep. I shift and squint into her eyes as she continues her story. I half expect her to suddenly come out with the exact reason why they have not messed up their lives like everyone else. Why they are still going along as if nothing is the matter. I want her to tell me that she knows it is a shame Ralph has never had a beautiful woman. Has always remained loyal to her and convinced himself that he was happy, confusing it with doing the right thing.

They struggled for fifteen years. Ralph going after a Ph.D. the whole time, and working on the side. They lived in chicken sheds, in tents, in tiny apartments. They converted a barn once. Before finally breaking into the easy life. Now Ralph had a good job, the children were healthy, they had a spacious home. She confessed that she had been near a collapse after the struggle was over. The doctor told her it was a reaction to former challenges being removed, called relief. She said she had never been a mother type, had never wanted to stay home, play in the kitchen. Had gained weight. In dealing in food the way a banker deals in money, she grew fat. Had embezzled food, tucking it away inside her mouth, dreaming of the job she would get someday again, outside the house as executive secretary for a small branch of a large company.

The men pour themselves more wine. Ralph is not a drinker, but he keeps a low profile and sips at his cup, not drawing attention to himself. Holding on tight to a life away from his childhood poverty. I try to detect what holds him so tight. Why it is he can go on and on and never snap.

In defense of Ralph I tell Heda what I know about poverty as seen through my own childhood. I know she will tell Ralph later. I communicate with him through her. Then I tell her about the affluence of my husband's childhood. I make her side with him, understanding him. I arrange us in sets of likes. He and Heda. Ralph and me. We begin to laugh. There has been so much information about our pasts thrown in. We are struck by the humor of us all being alike but different. We laugh at the differences. The similarities. Ah, life. It is funny. We laugh and laugh. We gesture at the air, to brush it away with out favorite hands. Scooping it towards us, pushing it away. How strange life is. Ha, ha, ha. How simple. How complicated. How interesting the equations are. The men look down where we sit laughing. They begin to smile, stretching their sunburned lips tight over their teeth, over their women having so much fun together. What a great idea for the boys to plan a picnic. What a great picnic it has turned out to be. I want to take Ralph by the hand and let him know how unhappy he is without knowing it. How much happier he could be if he only knew. I want to walk with him through the woods, to slip away while everyone is laughing.

# The Least She Could Do

She tried to explain how it was with her. "Everything's so complicated. Nothing is easy. I can't just do something just like that. There's so much more to it," she whined.

"Like when the babies were little and I'd tuck them in, I'd have to tuck the blanket all around them, make them cozy and push it in tightly here and there equally on both sides for a kind of balance." She did not see him as she spoke. She looked at his face and saw understanding and compassion instead.

"And then your sister Nancy came and covered them one night and she simply laid the blanket over them flat, and that was it. Just pulled it up and covered them. It was that simple for her; but I can't do it. There's a lot of emotional stuff with everything I do. Everything. It's all got to be balanced. It's got to mean something to make me feel safe. I can't just pull the blanket up and let it be, I've got to tuck it around and push here and there and get everything just right."

He looked at her with eyes that tried to be kind.

The criticism was gone; He did not want to say "just shape up," this time. She saw his kindness and did not want him to be that kind. It carried a responsibility for her. When he refused to accept her, she was free. Now his kindness unnerved her. She would have to like him and liking him meant she should be good to him.

She was crying now, and painting herself helpless. "See, I'm neurotic. Hopeless, It's all too hard just being alive and trying to do anything at all. It's all too complicated."

He lay them down on the floor and held her so that she could not twist away. He did not know what else to do. He kissed her cheek and tried to find her mouth but she strained her neck to keep it away from him. "I love you," he said.

"For sure," she said, believing it and not believing it,

knowing all husbands loved all wives and it meant nothing at all; It was like the baby blanket. It couldn't be just his word on her ears. There had to be a lot more. It had to be just right. He had to be a certain way. She had to be sure, to feel that it was warranted. She did not feel lovable; she did not love herself yet and she could not let him love her; she resisted and tried to push him off.

He held her and spoke of sex in her ear. He told her what he would like to do and what he wanted her to do, and she wanted to laugh, that it was all that simple after all. Just open up and take him in and she would be safe. And it really was that simple. Just be good to a man and he would see to it that you were safe. Just be receptive, and as long as you listened to him and acted seriously about him and brought out the good in him and caused him to feel powerful, ample, functional, important, he would take care of you.

He was pushing his hips into hers and saying, "Take it. Caress it. Let me have you...." And he went on with words she appreciated because he felt something at all and she was glad one of them felt something. But she was not stimulated. She slipped off one pant leg and her shoes and opened his buttons and he sighed, and then she threw her leg over him and moved awhile, taking out a breast from the top of her bra, pulling her T-shirt up and pressing the nipple in his mouth.

He said, "Oh, yes. Let me have your beautiful breasts." And, surprisingly, they did look good this time.

He said, "Are you ready? I'm ready," and before he finished speaking, he groaned with a distorted face, and she was glad he was happy. It was the least she could do.

*I have cut off my hair and have not eaten for three days.
I wear clothes I do not care about. I feel indifferent, as
I ride along in the truck. going on errands with Alex.
A caravan of marchers are by the side of the road,
wearing bright colors, exposing sections of bare flesh,
smiling, waving, being happy because they are marching
for some cause. They see me ride by as a passenger in a
truck. It is the way they will ever know me, a woman,
an ordinary woman, someone's wife, a tired female
going by. They do not know that I was not always going
by in a truck like this. That I have hiked along the
road before with uncut hair, sunburned face and brand
new flesh exposed in places to the sun. In an instant I
remember all the passions I have ever had for things that
are gone now. And I am confused about the way I did
not know myself during those times. The times when I
had been swept away.*

*My face in the window of the truck will always be "that
kind of a lady" going by, in their young lives. From
out of their passion they see an ordinary lady who is
trapped by her beliefs in her small fantasies. A lady who
is afraid of all the things they are not afraid of: of sex,
of marchers, of strangers, of odd-looking clothes, of
being along the side of the road. I am a lady who can be
found in any of the houses in any of the neighborhoods
they have passed. A lady with ordinary things on her
mind.*

*The truck door is made to slam. It does not close if it is
closed softly. Alex slams it when he gets out to go into
a store. And I wonder how many times a door can be
slammed before it breaks.*

# A Chance

At six-thirty AM I awoke to the sound of a curse. Alex has just cracked his bare toe against the fireplace while on his way to find the paperwork for his stocks. They are his first stocks and his first active interest in the market. And his first gamble for the future. Now that he does not care.

He comes back to bed saying, "Shit, that's why I'm on the bottom playing with junk, shit."

I am still on my side of the bed trying to sleep until seven-thirty. I offer, "What's wrong?"

"Have you seen the paperwork for my stocks? I want to give the broker a call and I can't remember his name, and the phone number is on the paper, shit."

I try to think, feeling afraid that it may be my fault, but knowing that I didn't see them. I try to visualize them. Papers. Nothing comes. I drift back to sleep. He gets up, stomps here and there still looking.

Finally he's back in the room again asking me to make him some coffee and to bring it out to the garage room. It is an apartment he uses for his office but because it used to be a garage we cannot call it anything else. As soon as he requests coffee I want to give it to him. I am not bothered. I am glad he needs me again. And I know I will get up and do it.

After ten minutes I am able to rouse myself out of bed. He has put water on and it is boiling. I pour our cups, and because a friend taught me once the pleasure of drinking coffee as soon as you get up, I sit on the piano bench next to his desk and sip my cup and watch Alex call Los Angeles. He connects up with his man. He knew the name of the firm all along.

I say, "Why didn't you do this at first. Let the paperwork blow away. Use the phone."

"This costs a fortune," he says.

"It's only money," I say. I want to curl up on the bench and get the thirty minutes sleep I lost. Instead, I watch Alex lean back, as he relaxes, talking to the only person who can help him anymore.

*Another dream: A stuffed animal was given to me. I left it on the beach. A giant purple dinosaur, soft and fluffy and loved by me. The tide came in and I remembered I had forgotten it, and rushed back to see it floating out to sea. A purple dinosaur floating way out there. And then it began to move in. It was washed up on the beach. I feared that it was ruined. But when I squeezed it out it was the same as before, only smaller and more have-able.*

# Out There

Marty was scaring herself again, reading the want ads and apartment rentals. They had been not really fighting, but soured on eachother for some time again. Life ahead looked like a stretch of barren land when a phase like this hit them. It was an emotional blight. They could not open their mouths to eachother without the words withering their hearts into dried stubble. She spent about an hour reading alternatives in her little corner chair and getting a glimpse of herself in a new life *out there*, as a dental assistant., or a hostess at Holiday Inn, or a trainee at Applied Magnetics. She saw herself leading people to dentist chairs and snapping on sterile paper bibs or showing them to dining tables and handing out menus or working with tweezers and minute electronic parts, assembling them under magnifying glass, and she knew how she'd be inside. She'd be a gigantic awkward water creature on dry land flipping feebly with tiny appendages, trying to move her tonnage back where it could glide smoothly.

Marty could not do anything except teach grammar school and there was no work for an older teacher who qualified for a salary in the second column of the pay scale. Only new first year teachers were being hired because they were cheap.

Old teachers hung onto their jobs with chiton-tight grips of tenures. Marty had traipsed home from the classroom years before to raise a family. She did not know it was home to stay.

Marty always underwent a chilling on the inside when she read about the possibilities of escaping her present life and flitting out into an unfamiliar future. She always imagined a faceless male appearing at a window of her new apartment ready to kill her. A bad man who had watched her efforts at freedom with extra-sensory vision and saw into her dilemma and knew of her helplessness against his evil plans.

Punishment was always in the form of a man. Maybe it was guilt that made her envision this form of punishment. Guilt over the forbidden wish to break away instead of staying and being a living sacrifice. Guilt that she should think of herself and want to attempt a life of her own rather than endure a slow death next to her husband in the long tedious plan they had made years before.

She put the paper down and basked in the relief that she was still *here* and not *out there* yet. Her home held her safe in its familiarity and the sourness faded a little from the man who had said hateful things to her over the years. What were hateful things after all compared to the *unknown*.

She swung back into the routine of pressing a mound of ground beef into a skillet until it was crumbled into small enough pieces for tacos. Probably her thousandth pan of tacos over the years. But what was a thousand tacos against a barren taco-less kitchenette in some dilapidated apartment building that she had yet to find?

Money. If she could get enough money, she could go away from all the *old* into all the *new*. She could avoid drooping in the doorway of employment bureaus with spaniel eyes begging for a scrap of job. She could avoid viewing the cheapest apartments and seeing the scum of past tenants dripping from and stuck to the sinks and toilets. She could avoid the smell of musty rugs and walls. She could avoid going from her old life into an older life. What was her fresh little home, even if it had become a prison, against the old staleness *out there* of the only thing she would be able to afford.

She thought of running an ad of her own in the want ads as she busted up beef in the skillet. It would say: *Wanted: New Situation.* And then she couldn't go on. Hope was always in the form of a man. It was like learning to swim. You jump in and the motions are learned after you are in the water. You jump in and somebody catches you and holds you from sinking until you've mastered the strokes and kicks. She had stood in a pool for six weeks once and urged her tiny tots, playfully named the Tadpoles by YMCA., to jump, "Come on, jump, Mommy will catch you." And they did and she did and they

186

learned to swim better than she ever could. Her mother had never stood in a pool and promised to catch her. She learned to swim in the ocean at sixteen, battered by the waves. She never learned to dive head first. Now the newspaper urged her and her instinct urged her and the world of *out there* urged her to jump in. But she balanced on the solid form of her old life and could not jump. She teetered, hesitated, held back and would not jump for fear that it wasn't true. Nothing would catch her. She would sink. She did not trust anymore. "They" were not reliable. "They," her resources. She knew how she could get after jumping. How she could close everything out and move around in the mysterious weird underwater world of her emotions and come near drowning. The most important movement of all, that of positive responses to the currents around her, she had lost. Her movements had become thrashings of anger and fear. Quick talk, laughter, bullshit, a happiness were what would keep her buoyed. And so she would sink unless she learned how to believe in those things, after growing solemn and cynical in a hide-out over the years.

She went about crumbling meat and wondering if she could ever make a leap.

Her heart leapt at a sudden thought that someone might be sneaking up behind her to give her a push.

# The Fort

Step Right Up. Try your hand. Why not. We do it at the circus. And isn't this a circus. Whether I'm skilled or not I'm throwing the ball. Will *they* call me *bad*. Is that worse than not being called at all?

*They* say to tell it as it is. Start from where you are. So I will. I'm here. In this little house we've worked our asses off on for thirteen years. Alex and me. It's our place and even though we never really accepted it as *our place*, never gave up believing there was *a greater place* out there, up ahead (some abstract location) we put everything we could into making this place as good as we could make it, because we had children *here* and they needed to have a real place. To be. In real bedrooms, eat at real tables, sit in real chairs, Be in a living room that existed. Or so we thought. To have all the stuff in their lives that their friends had. So we have tried to be like all these other people around us so *they* wouldn't be staring and making us feel funny. But we felt funny anyway;

So, I'm here. In this little house. And I love the little house, except for it not being a big house; which would impress everyone. I would like that. It would make being easier if some *big house* spoke for me, and people stepped back, to let me pass. But I like the little house because it is what I am and it is not too much for me. I am comfortable in it. A big house would draw me into itself and absorb me and I could not be *so* simple, So, I'm here. In a house I both love and hate. A place suited to me; but does not give me an advantage over anyone else. And it's fall.

I am waiting for my husband—not waiting. I never wait, But I know he is coming and I know when he steps in, I will go out. Not in body, but I won't be here. I can't be here when he's here. He will want to know what I've been up to, what I've done and I know he is asking if I have done anything I shouldn't have done. He wants to know because he has taken it upon himself to protect me from myself, which is really protecting himself. I never know exactly what he means. He never asks it that way. He says, "Any news?" And when I tell him what I've been doing and what has been going on because I am compelled to tell him, I am afraid to keep anything to myself, to have it alone, he gets angry over the thing I liked doing the most, and he is pleased most with the thing I like least, in fact, had to force myself to do.

I don't know if this means that whenever I am the way I want to be he disapproves because I am what he really dislikes, or if I'm being a certain way so he will not like me and I will be able to have something of my own, even though I am afraid to have it all by myself without his knowing. I eat a half a loaf of French bread thinking about it, pulling off hunks, cutting chunks of butter almost as thick as the bread and pressing the two together.

I love French bread. There is something about it that I need. I pad my insides where I feel empty with the large, solid, soft white spongy pieces of bread and swallow cups and cups of thick whole milk, It is all very greasy and goes down easily. Butter fat. Bread. I finally cannot eat another bite although I have not eaten enough. I can never eat enough, I want eating to be endless. But I am afraid to be fat. Some women are brave and can be fat. But I cannot. So I do not let myself overeat. The bread and butter and milk, which seem like over-indulgence, and is, for the moment, will not be because I will not eat for the rest of the day. I will abstain until the big wad I have swallowed works itself down and out, similar to the eating habit of snakes.

So I am here. Stuffing bread in my mouth because I am here.

And I guess I am afraid of something and I believe having a lot of bread in me will protect me. Or maybe I don't think that. Maybe I am trying to guess why I do it. And my husband is due home, at which time I will leave because that is the way it works.

I don't know where I go. But I go. Maybe there is an attic place inside me where I hide until I hear the click of the door as it closes, the next time he goes to work. Maybe I creep down from there to peer and see if he is gone. And when he is, I breeze around, turning on the radio, opening all the windows and doors that have screens and make it my house, no longer his house, even though I can see his shoes under the chair and pants flung over the chair and I pick them up. But *they* say to tell it like it is, and I keep getting off (in the old sense of the word) and I have to start from where I'm at. I'm here. And the only reason I know I am here, is because I'm not anywhere else. If I'm nowhere else I must be here. It is called deductive reasoning based on observation. I am not where I want to be. And I want to be somewhere. And it isn't here. That is the whole point. The reason I want to "tell it like it is," is because I want to be away from here. Away from all I know about being here. I want something else.

When everyone went off to school and Alex went off to work I was left here by myself, and it was as if they were waving goodbye on their way down a trail toward a whole other land, and I was left to "hold down the fort" so they would have a place to come back to some day, to remember and to visit, and I'd die alone in defense of it, so when they came back they'd see me dead, and they'd be sad but they would never say, "Wasn't it too bad that she never got out of the fort?" They would understand that I died where I was *supposed* to die and the sad part to them was the dying, not the still being in the fort when I died. So they all waved goodbye and gave wet kisses with pink young lips, even Alex. He has a young mouth too, even though he is forty. He's never lost a tooth and his mouth is as sweet as a child's. Even though it spits fire. It's his inheritance. A German mouth. They hold up. And off they went. And left me behind. To eat bread. To be afraid. To fast after gorging. To look out through the windows. At the world. To feel as if my hairline grows down to my eyebrows. As if I am the dullest and dumbest of them all and cannot go off and wave to someone else.

There is a sadness in being waved goodbye to. It leaves me here. Especially in the fall.

# The Interview

I go out to be interviewed for a job. All the cinching together of my body. And fixing of my face and hair so when they look they will see somebody they want to hire.

It is a job in bicycle safety. There is a government grant for research on why kids are still getting killed. They even pay to train you. I have always wanted to be paid and trained at the same time. I paid hundreds for an education once.

I have only one outfit that is presentable in public for formal occasions, I have worn it for three years. I am getting tired of wearing it every time there is someone important to see me. The sweater has three blackbirds flying across the chest in front of a yellow moon. I bought it just before Halloween and it cost more than I usually pay for sweaters. But, I liked the picture and pictures were the latest thing. It came with a matching skirt which I never wear because the hem is just below the knee and I can't get used to exposing muscular calves and nothing else. It looks matronly. So, I wear the sweater with a colorless pair of double knit pants which are my best ones even though I got them on sale at a discount store. They hang well and make me look thin.

They make me look as if I have no hips. I believe a hipless appearance will help me get a job. When I slip into three-inch cork soles, the pants come down just right over the shoe tops.

All the time I am getting ready, about twenty minutes, I am thinking about how young everyone has gotten to be anymore who work behind desks and hold positions of authority, and how old they used to be when I got my first teaching job. I was a young teacher right out of college and all the other teachers were old. Then, Alex didn't want me to work. Didn't allow me to go out of the home for ten years. When I went back part time as a substitute, everyone was young and I was old. Now it was my turn to know more as the older woman.

My past was supposed to add up to something in terms of experience. And something else. As I prepare to be seen now, there is an urge to cover up my face with a paper sack, pull it down so they cannot see me *now* as compared to *then*. I want to hide what has become of me since my youth. Talking through a sack would keep them from seeing the difference. My voice is still the same as then, and my body could fool them in the sweater with the birds. Young people are afraid of old people.

I think of the men I've seen behind desks, all of twenty-seven or -eight, and how one, in particular, kept digging one thumb nail into the other thumb nail until the muscles of his forearms stood out tense, while talking to me, because I made him nervous. I was ten years his senior and that authoritative image that had always presided over him during his impressionable years. There's a school teacher look to me. Harassed around the eyes, high nose, skinny neck, bony fingers, tailored blouse. He knew that I deserved his desk and his position more than he. That I could not take the word of a young man who was still trying to lower his voice to get respect.

All the different men I had encountered for various reasons in the last few years were young. Where had all the old men gone? And me, in the same outfit, giving the same impression, wanting to make a joke of it by telling them to spit out their gum, wash their hands and face and show me their nails, take out their books and turn to page... and do the work.

As I drive the fifteen miles to the conference room at the district office, I glance in the mirror and squint my eyes in an attempt to see myself through the young assistant supervisor's eyes. He will be waiting. What will he see. Who will he see. Have I been home too long. Will it show? Will I look like the fry cook, laundress, and domestic all dressed up in funny clothes. Will I look like the household skills I have been doing all these years? What will he ask me? What will I tell him? How can I tell him about myself in twenty minutes? How will I look when he puts me down in black and white? Will I look better on paper than in person?

I suddenly wish not to be visible. Only audible. And then I

don't want to be audible. If I must be visible I want to possess something easy to see. Gigantic breasts so they will speak for me. Or piles of blonde hair falling over my shoulders to make his eyes go funny. Something. Anything. To help. As I get closer to his scrutiny, I wish there was a way I could be, that didn't need seeing or hearing.

I arrive in the parking lot at the same time one of my favorite songs comes on the radio. I use it to drown out the vice superintendent who has come to rest in my brain like a termite, boring tiny holes through my self-image. I enter the Spanish style building with its highly polished tiled floor, long-legging on cork soles with the birds on my chest, and step crooked on the grout and lunge forward toward the operator who is centrally located before her switchboard. I recover my balance and ask her where the bathroom is at the same time. There is a dark woman in a blue dress sitting as still as a statue in the posture of someone waiting for an interview. I am early. I do not want to sit still and silent in the chair beside her and wait for my turn, so I go into the bathroom and look in the mirror to see once more what *they* will see when they look at me.

When I come out I see that the dark woman is not a woman at all. She is a girl, a young lady. I am the woman. It is an adjustment my vision has to make every time I come out in public. I am no longer in the mainstream. I am sloughed off to the side as any old cell is against the walls of a circulatory system. I have to remember that I am older now. Maybe old. I have to see through what I used to think I was and reeducate myself. She is younger. I am older. She, young; I, old. It is hard to get used to.

An older man is coming toward us. No, he is a man about my age. He comes through glass doors and asks if one of us is her. He uses her name. She responds. She comes to life and goes away with him, back through the glass doors. I take hope. He was not young. Maybe I will have a chance. But, she is dark, ethnic, young, of the minority. She is everything that is being hired. I am ordinary. I am common. I am in the middle of everything. Of class, age, color, and description.

**193**

I wait. I read. I try not to see the way the office personnel have been creative and ecological-minded in folding old printed material like fans and accordions and placing them around the pots of plastic flowers on the magazine tables for decoration. I try not to hear the operator as she repeats herself over and over, pulling and punching the switchboard, becoming as automatic and mechanical as her equipment, knowing if she puts care into it she will burn herself out by the end of the day. The dark young applicant comes out through the glass doors into the waiting room, moves across the floor like a manikin on wheels, head held high, not showing signs that I occupy the chair she left twenty minutes before. I ask her if it hurts. She smiles. I smile, pretending we are at the doctor's. She disappears into the parking lot. Then, he comes toward me, asking my name. I nod. Yes, that is me. That name. We shake hands and I remember not to present a dish rag. I offer a firm grip. The touch is brief.

His hand is cold and wet. The hand of a man trapped in a building under paper. He opens the glass doors and directs me toward brown doors entitled Conference Room in white letters. Inside there is another man. He awaits the arrival of the next applicant. It is me. I am part of their plan. I think what fun this could be if we were here for fun instead of bicycle safety. He gives me his name and offers his hand. I repeat his name to get it right and forget it, thinking instead about how perfectly he is cast for the role his is playing. So typical a man to be waiting behind a door called Conference Room in a plain suit, plain hair, plain eyes, plain shoes, plain personality.

Ordinary like me. As I sit down at the long conference table, I feel lucky to have found my own kind. I am thinking that perhaps they are tired of interviewing children and will be glad to get their teeth into a mature woman.

They begin the interview. I am suppose to understand everything they say. I fight to concentrate, embarrassed that my perfumed hand lotion can be detected so well. It tells on me. I want to laugh. I have been home so long with random thought and spontaneous action that this sudden need to pay attention and be present and presentable has made me giddy.

We are so serious. About bicycles. I want us to go back to being a woman and two men, not an applicant and interviewers. I want my femaleness to count. I do not like it to be ignored as if it isn't there. They look at me as if at upholstery. When they have said their piece, it is my turn. They listen attentively without looking at me, playing with the smoothness of the table under their fingers. We are embarrassed by our roles and know better yet don't stop. They are getting paid and I want to get paid. I try to account for myself in the eyes of the school district.

While I talk, I cannot think of any reason why I should be hired over anyone else, except for enthusiasm. That is what I can offer their program. It comes to me as my best qualification as I speak. I picture the young dark woman in the blue dress and wonder what she told them. Did she have a history of being safe on a bike? So soon from her childhood bicycles herself. When I stop talking, the silence hurts my ears. It is suddenly very hot in the room. I wish I had said an extraordinary thing. I can see that they can see there is no reason to hire me over anyone else. Nothing stands out.

If they noticed the birds on my chest they did not show it. They remained untouched by my whole presence as if my voice came through a vent, from a vent, from someone standing outside the door. I am an applicant. It is an interview. There is nothing else to it.

When I stand to leave, they stand. I beat them to the door. It is over. I have been evaluated inside their heads and they remain silent. Courtesy is the only thing they show. Rudeness would be more honest. As I exit through the glass doors into the waiting room, I see a new applicant in my chair. She is an older woman, no, about my age. I adjust my vision. In a gesture of good will to a fellow applicant, I hold my arm as if I have just had a shot. We laugh, and I go out into the parking lot.

# Requirements

We want to love again. Eachother, if possible, or anyone. Just to feel love again. Alex dreams of holding a girl tenderly. He wakes up saddened and tells me about it. He believes the time for falling in love and loving a sweet, gentle woman has passed for him. That he is too busy handling me, the woman he is responsible for. The woman he is married to.

I ask him who the woman is in his dreams, wanting to believe it is me when we met. He tells me he doesn't know. It is no one he knows. A vision. That it could be me, in my good moments. That it is an impression of a woman. Of a sweet and gentle woman who lets him love her. A woman who brings out the feelings of love in him. He tells me how his heart ached during the dream, loving her, holding her, being tender. It left him sad when he woke up and saw that it was only a dream, he confesses. That he knew he could not love like that. There was no one and there was no time. His voice is still sad as he tells me about his dream. He has had this dream before. And he has told me about it before. Each time I am threatened by this dream woman who can let herself be loved, who can bring out this tenderness in Alex.

We have been together too long. I do not say it. We have shown eachother too much harshness. Have seen eachother's faces contorted with anger. We have too long demanded tenderness from eachother and got anger back. Have waited for the other to be tender first. Have accused the other of not being able to be tender. Have shouted, "YOU'RE INCAPABLE OF TENDERNESS."

I dream of being held by a faceless man. My dreams are of a man desiring me. Of wanting to hold me and be tender with me. Sometimes after these dreams, Alex's of tenderness, mine of desire, we grow sad together and hold eachother and talk about what we have done to eachother. About what has happened to us. Sometimes, as we comfort eachother, Alex grows tender and holds me.

Before falling asleep the next night after that morning of sharing our dreams, after our work is done, Alex watches a war movie. It is another one about a bridge. He thinks he is watching a movie about courage, fortitude, and other virtues. I am not a man. I can see only that the movie is about *one man out-doing another, hairy chests, armpits, and after I toss the big hand grenade I will go get a girl with big tits and impress her with my big dick and the next day I will win the war single-handedly*. Most of the scenes are of guns and bombs going off. There are about two lines of dialogue which go like this, "Hold you-h fi-ah." Alex is tantalized while I turn my back to him, and try to drown out the sound with a pillow, knowing there is no way I can understand war movies, so therefore, there is no way I can understand Alex. I mutter, "The peace that passeth understanding," from years ago in Sunday school from under my pillow beneath the noise of the TV.

Alex and I join the Unitarian Society for a church because a friend asks us to. It means nothing except good coffee during hospitality hour after the lecture, which is not intended to be a sermon. "Used-to-ness," I say to the little guy at Unitarian one morning who looks like Don Knotts and holds his cup of coffee in the crook of his index finger and has come up to me to chat.

# Fathers Die

Alex went on with unloading the gas tank from the back of the truck. He did not put anger behind the force he usually used to move a tank full of gas which was bigger and heavier than he. Ordinarily, he cursed and said, "Get in there, you bastard, come on."

But this time, because his sister had just phoned and told him their father had been killed in a car accident, he grew red pushing and heaving and did not say anything. And when the gas tank was unloaded and placed on the stand, he stood looking at it for a long time.

There was gentleness in the way he stood. The force was gone from his body. And action. He hung his left arm and smoked with his right arm and did not move for a while.

When he walked away there was an elegance in his step. Acceptance looked good on him. It gave him tenderness and silence. And calmed him. It took things out of his hands and lessened his responsibility. It made him a passerby. It put him at peace. He thought, that is the way life is. Fathers die. They all die eventually. There is nothing to be done about it. Nothing is required of me except this. To take it. To let it come into my mind and stay. And to know it. That is all we can do about death - to know about it. To acknowledge it.

There was relief; a boneless relief as he ate dinner and watched the news. A softness. A listening. "What else do you want to tell me, Life? I'm listening. Go ahead."

# At the Park

*You never see a raft full of women coming in
out of the sea. Gloria Steinem.*

Nuns come by denying the flesh, ignoring their breasts which
are jutting up with sensory nipples craving *touch*. The drum-
mer of a rock band is so young I do not let his soul beat stir my
groin. I silently rehearse a lecture for John about homosexual-
ity. I will say to him, "Why don't you go into the kitchen of
a nice restaurant and tell the cook you want to make love to
him because you liked the way he cooked." The viewpoint
excites me. He will see his folly and why he should not love
everyone who comes along. As I pass the nuns I understand
why they are nuns, because *I do not stand out in the crowd*. I
have blended into the herd. No outstanding coat of silk or
antlers of great beauty are mine. None of nature's eyes search
me over, fascinated by extraordinariness. I am *them*. All these
people *out there*. Neither male nor female exclaim as I pass. Or
draw in their breaths.

I do not want to leave the park until I make some impression on *the people*. Where I am should matter. A record of *me*
should be imprinted in the minds behind the eyes. No one
should be able to run over me and past me with their eyes
without stopping to study. As they would a thing of interest.
But it does not happen, so I continue to wander.

A young Mexican boy is given the heavy responsibility
of carrying the orange sodas for his family picnic. His som-
ber cheeks and careful step tell of his concern to live up to
it. The nuns are gawking and pointing at trees, keeping their
minds occupied with clean subjects. A couple, feeding the
birds, make subtle hate comments to eachother. Insinuations
that the other does not know how to feed birds. The man is
a dark beast type who has wasted himself on *being good*. His

**199**

satyr head is full of *husband* ideas and fantasies. His balls and calves have atrophied. He is walking around with arms and chest that have shrunk so not to be in the way of the *desk*. To fit into an *office*. I wonder about the way he is built. Did paperwork sap *that* up too so that only his eyes and several lobes in his brain and his pencil-holding fingertips move with energy, containing circulation.

I watch them as they move toward the wooded part of the park with their bread crumbs and angry words. And the way he contradicts the black hair jutting from his satyr forearms and cheeks. A gelded stallion.

A scientist goes by. His preoccupation excites me to distract him. But I do not know him. The facts and figures inside his head entice me. Jan comes up with corn on the cob in her braces. The braces are holding her teeth *in* because she is thirty-five and has a disease of the gums. She tries to talk without showing her teeth. She is too intellectual to think fast. I am too emotional to think slow. We make a rapid encounter and then go away from eachother whispering to ourselves about *what we should've said instead.*

Some religious kids are standing in a row singing about the power in the blood. Their pimples and faded tans and over-shampooed hair go as exteriors. I want to *test* them to show them that religion is not that easy in case they should continue with it and find out that it is.

A woman with a French accent and no children believes in a child's ability to be cruel to a lizard because it gives her a place as *protector* of children. But she looks away.

The park buzzes with bodies. Like a large cradle. Sets of eyes viewing other sets of eyes. And *Life* liking to hold itself. Touching and fondling, smelling and nuzzling and exploring the known. *Age* liking to hold it's antimatter *Youth*. And *Youth* liking to wallow in the lap of its antithesis *Age*. Children on top of adults. Adults under young children, supporting their bodies. The imbalance of *can't have anymore*, or *yet*, knowing itself by its opposite. A clean and old man telling a young boy who is playing in the dirt, "You're dirty."

But Indian shorts on a Jewess. They are her invention out

of old cloth from home. A Japanese girl with a shiny new camera dangling from her smooth golden shoulders. Everyone's arms are crooked for holding beer cans upright in their hands. An oblivious toddler investigates without restraint. We all let her do what she wants, her eyes turning to observe, showing their whites in case she gets under our hooves. We allow her freedom as long as we know she will be capable of knowing all that we know someday. We regard her as intelligent even though she does unintelligent things. She is like Columbus. In search of spice, led by her taste buds she is discovering new lands.

*Marty and Alex holding unmanicured hands and walking behind people along Cabrillo Blvd. at the art show, viewing, not the art, but the cracked and dry heels of women in front of them. Women who are attempting to have beautiful faces. And Marty saying "How ugly these feet are...."*

# The Right Place

From eight-thirty on, her ears automatically listen for his car. "Moon River" plays. It should be a memory song for them. They saw the movie before they were married, but they did not save *memories* then. They were looking ahead. Only ahead. They did not say, *We'll remember this later.* They did things because they were in their present. But they counted more on the future, knowing it would be the *right place.* Up there they would, could, be safe enough, established enough, to say, *Ah, this is good. Let's make a note of it in our hearts and remember it later.* But they never did. No sentimentalities. So she established them all by herself. And she tells him, *Listen, this is my favorite song....* He looks sad, as if it's unfair, and more than that, a crime against him. But she had to bathe occasionally in sentimentality.

The new lamp is pretty so she leaves it on. She does not use its light. She uses its beauty to lighten her spirit as she waits. After a long time there is the sound of his car.

The moment. The very exact moment they see eachother again after he is *home.* After thirty-six hours. The first look. They each fear it. It is never right. They do not look forward to seeing over and over again and knowing it is true that *There he is* or *There she is. The one to whom they belong. And who belongs to them.* Even though they do not want to part. He looks to assure himself that his holdings are intact. And if she is not grief-stricken, he knows all goes well and remains the same. He knows what to expect. She looks to see the same thing. No holes in his body, no wounds. No accidents. He is a whole plug to fit back into the opening through which he left. He is *back.* Snug. They are complete. Finished. The same story, until some other time when one of them will not be able to see the other. Either he will disappear first or she first. It is the way two people end. Not at the same time. First one and then the other. The one who goes first goes witnessed. The second one goes alone. Alone because no one else seeing counts, except *the other one.*

After Alex drives up and we have our first look after thirty-six hours, after we make a mental note of status quo, and after the comfort of knowing we are persevering, relief will come. I will turn out the lamp, turn off the radio, no longer listen for the sound of his arrival, and we will proceed with the work that waits for us to do together to maintain our home. Relief will reign.

# *In the Distance We Saw Gold*

The gold of the setting sun caught our eye on the Padaro Lane ride. We stood on the overpass to watch the sun set since the tall trees blocked our view from the roadside. Cars shot underneath us, making quick violent sounds, one after another. A steady stream going north and south along Highway 101. We did not notice the cars and inhaled the exhaust, breathing deeply, believing it was good wholesome air because we were outdoors and up high. And because it was the ending of a day, therefore endings should be good. The air of endings. The sound of endings, and the view of endings.

We leaned against the concrete railing, balancing our bicycles with opposite hands while holding eachother around the waists with our other hands. Alex said, "There's beauty in that," and sighed through his nose.

I said, "It's too thick. There are no striations. It's too much a big blur for beauty."

Alex said, "Yes, there's beauty to be seen in it. In all sunsets," determined to see magnificence, reassuring himself that it was somewhere.

I glanced at Alex to see what he was getting at. I said, "There are no sharpnesses. It's not severe enough." Alex was silent, not paying attention to what I said. I had babbled on too much for as long as we had known eachother. It was past him now. It didn't matter. I had something going with myself, he figured, that he couldn't be a part of. In the beginning, he tried to make sense out of what I said, and it got him in trouble. He learned to stay out of it. And I learned to let him have some illusions.

I said, "It's nice to stand here and watch a sunset anyway."

We blinked a few times and sniffed and mopped our faces in oppression mannerisms, doing what a man and woman do with their faces when they stay in one place too long without anticipation of a reward at the end of a day, or at the end of their lives. Nothing to look forward to while they toiled on together living their daily lives. The gold of the sunset reflected in their blue eyes.

Alex said, "They can say what they want about the evils of being rich, but I'll tell you there's nothing to beat it. Even for the stupid who don't bother to develop themselves. Even they are better for it. Nothing can touch you." It was a subject that come up when they looked over a long expanse of land.

Alex's words sent me into a vision I had of the rich. I said, "All through my childhood I would see some big long dark shiny car with one-way windows so you couldn't see in but they could see out. It would drive by and pass me and people inside would be dark-haired city people wearing dark clothes and looking straight ahead, not looking at me. Not needing to look around for anything. They were going somewhere, and I always felt left out when they went by. My shins felt bony and nicked. And my knees felt knobby. And I would remember my hangnails and begin to pick at them and bite them again."

Alex smiled and I laughed. We could hear ourselves through someone else's ears.

I reddened and mopped my hot face with my cold hands. I sniffed and wrinkled my brow, and Alex joined me in these facial expressions that stemmed from demonstrating our outsideness together. I could hear his whiskers scraping against the calluses on his palms, as he mopped his perplexed face. We sniffed in competition for awhile in the cool evening air and I wiped my nose on my sleeve.

We looked in the direction of the sunset but did not see it now. We saw ourselves being our own gardeners, cooks, handymen, and cleaning women. Alex saw himself as his own maintenance man wearing a wad of keys on his belt while he maintained our home because he "would be drained if I started paying for services." I wanted to prop my hands and feet up to let the blood run back down out of them so when the time came that I could afford a beautiful naked evening dress and go to a ball, I could pass for "rich." Otherwise, the bulging veins would give me away as someone's scrub woman. As my own.

The sun disappeared and the blur of gold faded as we remained shivering together above the freeway. Alex bent and kissed me on the cheek. I wished we could wait until we were rich before we kissed so it would not be a poor man kissing a poor woman. There was something pathetic in it. Something of consolation. When the rich kissed the rich it wasn't consolation. They planted their lips not to comfort one another, but for some other reason. Not out of weakness. Out of strength. I had never been kissed by a rich man. Alex had never kissed a rich woman.

After all the gold was gone from the sunset and the grayness began to clabber up into curds and we got on our bicycles and pedalled on down the road together toward our house which we could have been happy with because it was the best one we had ever had, if a long black car hadn't passed us going to the rich neighborhood a few miles beyond ours.

# The Hawks Watched Her

She didn't know why she lied about it. It wouldn't have mattered one way or the other. She had been jogging while he rode a bicycle alongside her. And she had led them along a seven-mile route of foothill road, sweating and viewing the sea. Uphill their speed slowed to lethargic movements. He had to get off the bike and walk, breathing heavily, And then they raced down the long southward slope and he kept braking his tires to stay even with her.

It was somewhere along the downhill side that she saw them. The hawks. And pointed, keeping her pace, and said, "Look… Look at the hawks… They're always here… They watch me go by every day… There's usually two of them…"

He looked at one hawk circling above a rounded low hill top. His eyes were bored, preoccupied with other things. His own thoughts. But she kept saying it as if there was some notoriety in it, "They always land on that telephone pole… Watch… And then they watch me go by… There are two of them… They're here every day at this time when I go by… And they sit and watch me… Aren't they beautiful…"

He did not seem to hear her. He did not say anything. She exclaimed some more over their beauty. She wanted him to know of their exquisite beauty and that such beautiful creatures were her discovery and that they took notice of her the way she took notice of them. And that they took time out for her. They landed and watched her.

She had seen them maybe once before together and probably never separately. In fact it was the day before and they had landed on the telephone pole and closed their broad wings and pulled at something in their claws, looking down as she ran along the road beneath them. She had tried to see them more clearly as she ran, to see their faces, but she took time only to marvel for a moment and then she was gone from them. And did not think of them again.

Now there was only one. He said, "Maybe someone shot the other one. Wouldn't that be too bad if some kid popped it off for fun... I miss those owls.... Remember those owls that used to land on the garage... I still think someone shot them." His creased brow looked up at the single circling hawk; as he concentrated on its possible extinction. And she was sorry she had told him that the hawks were always there. And she did not know why she lied. And about the way they watched her every day. As if there was some glory in it. As if it should mean something about her importance, understand why it meant so much to her to be watched by a hawk. Or by a couple of hawks. And why she had tried to get it across to her husband, about this wonderful communication she had going with these two wonderful creatures that didn't include him. That every evening along a foothill road, two hawks circled and landed over her presence, while he was at home watching the evening news and polluting himself with beer and cigarettes, and shortsightedness.

She felt dirtied by her need to prove such things to him. And to try to make him jealous and envious. That she had come to that. To be noticed; By *any* eyes. Even birds.

He wasn't impressed. He hadn't noticed her urgency in telling him about the hawks. He sailed along on his bicycle while she thumped along the ground with a swift downhill gait. After they passed the hawks his eyes went to a rancher's water pump; placed in such a way on a hillside that it interested him. And she was left alone with her lie. But it wasn't the first time she had tried to look good to him by rearranging the facts. Before they were married, she told him about winning a body contest and about winning a poetry contest and about being singled out one time by a psychology teacher for having the best definition for psychology. About the great love boys and then men had felt for her at one time or another, About having been beautiful once. Before he met her. So she was safe. He would never know if she told the truth or not.

And then it gradually dawned on her that he didn't care. That he didn't believe in her or believe her. That he reduced the contests to "cattle shows" and "high school English departments," and the boys and men to "greasy oilies." As they rounded the bend and headed northward toward home, she did not like her lie much or the hawks much. She did not care if someone would shoot them now.

They sat talking with the difference of their ages between them. His past was his childhood. Hers was young adulthood. That was one difficulty. She could draw from her past as a valid reference. He had to draw only from so many recollections of babysitters, men of prey, and television programs.

Walking onto the beach with her eye twitching because there is so much happening. Wearing almost nothing meaning nothing anymore. Sunburn lines are part of her body, not unlike a distant voodoo marking on a female across the world. All summer she has been carrying her clothes around in her car, and sometimes in spite of threats to her comfort she attempts to believe, "Where I put my clothes, I stay." No one wants her to work for them. The want ads laugh in her face. As she reads the requirements she doesn't qualify for. She steps into the ocean water and the smell of onions on her breath reminds her of better food than she has eaten. She has only eaten an onion. There was no meat. No sauces. No gravy. No protein juices from slaughtered animal flesh. A breaker hits the back of her head and soaks the hair she wanted to keep dry. Young men think she is interested in them. Old men know she is not. And men her age look for women they call girls, younger than she is. She tries to write a résumé…a work definition of herself, knee deep in salt water. All the women on the beach believe they are nymphomaniacs. If the ifs were juggled around. And every wife is proud that a homosexual once liked her husband. It is proof that he is a real person.

# Husband

They think we are from the City. That we are inspectors that have come to check up on what they are doing inside their warehouse business. Alex's short haircut, clean-shaven face, slacks and cotton sport shirt are suspicious, We have driven up in our white City employee-type station wagon. They have all glanced over at us from their various posts. Young men and women in odd matching garments, dirty long uncombed hair, too thin, bad-skinned, hungry, cold, hopeful that they "make it" in the glass-making business. Some, down on their knees doing something in front of a machine with a greasy rag in their hands, others milling about across the blacktop yard, on their way to getting a part to fit into a pile of junk they have assembled at a waist-high work table. The doors of a hand-painted van are open and piles of stuff are spilling out.

We walk into the old warehouse shop and a young man struts up to Alex, chin high, fierce, fists tense. He is short and it bothered him that he has to look up to meet this man who is barging into his private shop. He stops Alex with a penetrating eye and physically blocks his path. After Alex introduces himself and me the wife, and tells the young man he is a friend of one of the partners and just wants to look around to see how glass is melted and forges are built, the penetrating eyes study Alex, still suspicious, trying to read between the lines. He steps aside, and Alex strolls in casually, assuring him he is no one who cares about anything they may or may not be trying to pull off. I follow Alex as he wanders into the depths of the warehouse and stands gazing at the machinery and the tables laden with freshly baked glassware. Wherever Alex goes I go. We hear a steady roar coming from an outside patio opposite the entrance, and move toward it. The young man darts here and there but returns sporadically to stroll beside Alex and catch the questions.

The roar comes from three fire brick forges that glow red hot around the loosely fitting front blocks. The warmth radiates across the entire patio and I turn to warm my back and cool my eyes, standing beside Alex who is stooping and bending to get a good look at these ovens. Several scraggly girls have come to hang around the patio in their cotton rag clothes and study us from their peripheral vantage points. One uses a cat for an excuse. It sleeps in an overstuffed chair which sits outside. She leans her bony thighs against the ragged stuffing and probes around the cat's ears with long delicate fingers, glancing now and then toward the furnaces but never at us. Several more scrawny girls come out of nowhere, as if a silent alert has been sent out by telepathy. They pass by in the darkness of the warehouse, taking us in, and then they are gone, to show up again somewhere else. Always busy, but round-eyed. My matching blouse and pants, the coordinates I chose that morning, my freshly brushed hair, painted lips, shoes, suddenly go grotesque among these waifs who drift past with mirth in their eyes, to study me, this kind of woman they have heard about and probably had as a mother, but lost contact with. I stand isolated among them, an endangered species. Their curiosity separates us. They laugh at me without moving their mouths or making a sound. They have an understanding about women like me. A stereotype. I am all the things they have given up; my beliefs are their jokes. I am glad for the roar of the furnaces. One at a time young men show up, dirty, thin, homely. Everyone is homely, as if they come from one large family. No one has tried to conceal their homeliness. They all have the same bad skin, pale, dull, marked with flaws, dry spots, freckles, moles, unwanted hairs and wanted hair in abundance. Only the short fierce man is gifted with regular features that line up in a way that is pleasing to the eye. Being "boss" is part of his appeal. He radiates energy like his furnaces.

One girl comes to stand beside me and compare the heights of our shoulders. She is taller, she is proud of her skinnyness. She stretches her frail torso as long as she can get it and pretends to warm her back the way I am. She looks into my face and a smile creeps around her mouth. Warming ourselves. It is a funny game she has not thought to play before. She wears an undershirt that hugs flat "tits" and stops the game of "bras-siere" entirely. No shoes, and tight denim pants. She is proud of the way the denim seam fits right into the crevice of her ass and separates the flesh between her legs. She keeps stretching with her feet in a wide stance so that her ribs and hips jut out. Alex is behind us twisting and maneuvering his head in order to see every aspect of the roaring gas ovens. The girl tells me that she and the guy she came up from Orange County with her friend are going into the glass-making business with this guy and she gestures with her head at the young man who is explaining and pointing out the features of the furnaces to Alex. I glance at them and see Alex nodding and nodding to show he understands the principle. Pride has come to replace suspicion in the eyes of the young man. I tell the girl that my husband wants to get into a business of his own some day and is always interested in seeing other new businesses and how they are set up. As I talk, she watches the way I talk instead of listening to what I say. She is interested in me as a mechanical thing, my style, the way I function. There is only one word she has caught: *husband*. It dates me, waves a flag. Blares out. She wants to play with my concept of myself, like a toy. So she tells me again how she and her "husband" have come up from Orange County to go into the glass business. *Husband* becomes the key. It goes with my clothes, car, hair, face, and the imaginary ticky-tack house I must live in. She says that her "husband" has not had to borrow any money to get started in business. That he had investors to get him going. She says. that she and her "husband" like it up here because there was no future in Orange County.

Alex is satisfied with all that he has learned about the forges. He shakes hands with the young man who stiffens masterfully. We amble out the way we came. The young people fade away. Curiosity satisfied. Comparisons made. Threats removed. They turn away and find work to do as we drive away. A husband and a wife team. I look at Alex, my husband, beside me, and wonder what I *should* have called him.

# *From a Distance*

I apply for a job at the library. The City sends me. Last week the City gave me orals. They heard me speak by asking me hypothetical questions. What would you do if you had this job as Clerk and someone came in and said such and such …? I left flushed over the novelty of it. So they sent me to the library to follow through for the position. There were three women again, at a long table in a conference room. I wore a skirt and sweater to look typical.

A friend said he'd think I was a librarian alright, and no one would ever guess I was really wild.

I said, "What do you mean, don't librarians fuck, or what?"

"Your hair," he said, and smiled.

The three librarians on the panel talked me out of the job. The pay was too low. I couldn't have this summer off. I finally backed down. They said, "A bright person like yourself should be Assistant Librarian."

I left wondering, "Bright? What did I say?" I rent a library typewriter and type up a legal form afterward. It is an electric typewriter and cost a quarter an hour. I figure it is cheaper than gas. If I drove home to type and back, it would cost more. A little boy whose mother is typing, too, finds a quarter on one typing table next to mine. He holds it up guilty and honest in one gesture, hoping to keep it. I say it is mine.

I really believe it is because I have left my purse alone and looked to see a clock in the periodical room. Then I discover my quarter on the other side of the typewriter. I feel too corrupt to give it back to the little boy. Later he is crying because his mother is finished typing and he wants to stay longer (probably hoping to find more money). I type up my form knowing I have cheated a child and there is no forgiveness.

Not getting the library job, even temporarily to give me

a few bucks for summer makes me devious. Suddenly life becomes an endless grey wall, an institution. I go for a four mile run and it simply hammers on me like so much drudgery with no exhilaration.

Later I am standing at a red light on the main street with three letters in my hand. Business letters. People are sauntering up and down the street. It's about eighty degrees and a slight wind is whipping hair back from foreheads. In the throng of people across the street waiting for the light to change stands a young couple. The girl is in white jeans and a white pullover, T-shirt. She wears purple cowboy boots and her hair is pulled back in a side-sweep. They are smart and lazy and when the light changes they stroll toward me and I recognize it is my own daughter. I draw back to the curb before they see me and wait, leaning against a jewelry store, looking and looking at her. Then they see me.

Up close she says, "Hi." Independent, as if I am just someone she knows.

I answer "Hi," taking her cue and keeping distance, too.

And as they pass by I step in beside them and she asks, polite, impersonal, "What are you doing today?"

I say, "Going to the library," casually, as if I am speaking to an acquaintance in passing.

She says, "Well, have fun, bye...."

And they stroll on while I fall back to cross the street toward the library. I glance at my daughter as she walks away. I see her easy stride beside her young man. I see she is a companion to him, a buddy, perhaps a lover: and I see she is confident. She is grown up. She has passed me on the street, and sent pangs through my chest. I am stabbed in the heart by the passing of time, of losing my place. I will go home after the library, away from her. I am on the outside of her life.

She dropped by on Mother's Day with a tulip in a pot and said, "Hi, well, I've got to go now, here...okay, see ya...." She allows herself to be hugged and kissed on the cheek by me. I felt awkward.

I have never been a hugger, except for puppies and tiny kids. She stretched her neck and leaned away. I didn't want to crush her bra against mine, so pressed my shoulder against her shoulder. It was a strained effort at warmth. And then she left. I looked at the tulip.

It was in bud. It would bloom in a matter of days and I could watch the whole process. A quiet intense performance of blossoming into full maturity. Is that what she had given me? A kind and gentle demonstration of herself. Was she saying all over again, "I've grown up. I'm separate from you. Can't you understand that and stop trying to still be my mother."

We had had terrible words in the last time together as mother and daughter, as she pried my tentacles loose from her young adulthood. As I tried to suck her back into childhood she yelled, "When does a child grow, Mother?"

I yelled back, "Only when you can support yourself."

And she said, "Well, you've never grown up then, have you?" and stomped out. It was true. I lived as a wife, piddling at part-time jobs to fritter away the time and money on odd-ball things. She saw this and knew I also did not know how to be out in the world and make my own way.

I watch her walk away from me now, as if I am just any-one. I see she is strong and healthy and sure of herself and sure of her life working out. I see her strong runner's legs in white denim. I see her erect, proud head and shoulders. I remember how intentional I was in creating this health and strength in her and how she'd complain once in awhile that I would never let her eat junk the way other mother's did their children. As a baby she loved blackberries more than any sweet; and I drooled over her appetite for them. She made them look incredibly delicious, the red juice dripping off her baby chin, and her tiny hands taking more and more, and her green eye dancing with taste.

As she disappears in the crowd it becomes a kind of time-less, endless day with the sunshine and traffic stretched out and on and on and people strolling. Like a picture of Paris where "there will always be lovers going by." It is this forever-ness I feel she is a part of. Those times of afternoons of being young which seem endless until then and, unnoticed, it is gone.

On the drive home after not getting a job, going for a run, seeing my daughter, reading in the library, crossing the street, I see a Mexican family having a birthday party in their backyard. I drive by and crane my neck to see it. It is a bumpity backyard with unmowed grass outside an unpainted house with a back door stained from years of greasy hands, remnants of paint already peeled off, wood rotting on the warped back porch steps. A table is laden in the yard with bright pink cake on a bright pink and white tablecloth of paper from Hallmark with matching plates and cups. Little boys in striped T-shirts are punching each other in fun, wrestling and rolling in the grass. Some adults stand around talking. Aunts, uncles, married sisters and brothers? Little girls run underfoot in their communion dresses and patent leather shoes. Big red hens walk around, interested in all the unexpected activity, pecking at the ground under the table, in anticipation of crumbs.

I drive down Bath Street, looking for two palm trees I used to know that used to grow in a yard. It is a yard of a house where I ate a chicken dinner once when I was very hungry and I cannot find the house. The palm trees are gone. I search the lawns for evidence of their stumps. I have not thought of that house in twenty years. Suddenly I want to see it one last time.

At home I click on the TV. I see a film about ZsaZsa Gabor. She has a whole roomful of clothes. It is Howard Hughes' old mansion. She says it is the smallest place she has ever lived. The camera crew must have been advised not to come too close to her face because all through the film I long for a close-up and never get one. My eyes have been trained by television to go right into the eyes of the subject, and I find myself missing this usual tactic of filming. I am so used to getting to see the light in the retinas of the eyes of actors and to examine every pore of the face. I grow bored with this detail, and annoyed having to view Zsa Zsa from a distance....

# The Dog

… likes me more than anyone else. It is a burden to try to do his devotion justice. In the evening he lies in the corner and watches me. He sighs and his eyes blink and cast glances in my direction waiting for a cue, my every wish. I go to the kitchen and he moves with me and takes his corner where I will be within view, unaware of who I am, which century he is in, that there are more savage people than I and more civilized, that all floors are not self-polish tile.

I throw a piece of fat on the floor. He knows appetite not history. He knows about my anger. He quivers when my voice is too loud. But he is not afraid of things that will tear his throat. I put on shoes. His tail wags. We go outside to run. He knows my frailty although he has never seen me wounded. He makes sure the way is safe, running up ahead and coming back, knowing the skin on my neck is thin. I lie down on the ground to rest, to look at the sky. He cries and licks my face, afraid I will never get up again. He warns passersby not to come near. I insult him with praise.

"Good boy" is like saying Good sunset; Good ocean, Good tree. Good world for being the way I want it. I am god. I make him mine. With obedience. He dotes on my whims, is a fool over my affection. Is afraid of my disapproval even though I am so weak that he must protect me from other dogs.

(PS: Is he afraid of his strength, that he might make a mistake and kill me, the frailty, that he needs. Like Alex?)

# Last Night

Alex and I went to Thrifty Drug Store to buy throat medicine. Our son lay around coughing and asking for cough syrup, refusing honey and lemon, and saying, "Get the good kind, not the kind you usually get that doesn't work." I have caught up with everything around the house and ask Alex to come along so we can browse and have fun, the way I used to do with other people. People in my family and I would go through a store and have fun making jokes about the merchandise. I miss that. It occurs to me that I haven't laughed at all the things on the shelves with someone for a long time. Too long.

Alex is happy to go along. He sits in the car when I park in front of Thrifty as if he plans to wait while I run in. I say, "Come on, come with me." He is surprised, "Alright, didn't know you wanted me to." He dawdles, does not walk right alongside me. I am eager to go down all the aisles with him, but he doesn't even know it. Once in the store I go through the turning gate and move right on to the first shelves. Alex does not follow. He is nowhere in sight when I turn to point something out. I stand on tiptoe and look for a trace of his blond hair above the shelves. Oh, he's over in the magazines. I cannot get back out the one-way gate, so call, annoyed, "Alex, come on, hurry…" He dawdles, It begins to get on my nerves. I peer around an aisle and my eyes seek the contents of the magazine he holds open, suspicious. It is a girlie magazine? No, I see generators and engine parts.

Relieved. Good old Alex. His mind always on machines. Thank God. I couldn't take it now. I couldn't take him lusting after female flesh after all that's happened. I could have at other times. In fact, expected him to, and he never did. It was amazing to me that he never did. Now, I'm too tired. Have no fight left. I'm not fleshy the way I was. I couldn't make sense of it. When I was fleshy and believed in the flesh and was able to fight fleshy fights I could understand it. Now, it'd be odd. Strange that Alex was looking for *that*.

A female body. How absurd. Our life is so much more important and serious than that now. He almost lost his life. Our kids went into rebellion. It's a life and death issue now.

It would be uncanny for our life to be on such a simple matter anymore, as the male/female.

He finally ambles over, slow to catch on. Not used to tagging after a woman, me.

I say, "Let's look at everything. Hey, it's been a long time since I did anything to my eyelashes." I approach the cosmetic counter and touch some sale mascaras in a dish. Alex is beside me, eyes blank not really seeing the mascara. Still picturing those motor parts, perhaps not yet into what it is I am after. I move us along to all the small appliances we used to want so much. Browsing long ago we used to long to have all kinds of things. We used to feel left out. Alex, sighs, isn't it funny, all this? I don't want any of it anymore...

I guess we went through that stage. Funny how that passes... I say, "How about a blender?"

"Okay," he says, taking me seriously, "if you want one, here's one..." It's one of the best models. He believes in buying sturdy machines. No tiny toy that will break. I say, "No, I don't want to blend anything anymore. There was a time I did, though. Isn't that incredible." I truly am amazed, remembering thinking in terms once, of making blended drinks, like smoothies, or blending ingredients for a meatloaf He says, "Here's something." It is a juice extractor. "Oh, God," I say. "It makes me depressed just to imagine squeezing the juice out of everything." I pick up a little hand beater and touch it to his hair. "Hey, here's how you can comb your hair every morning, ha, ha." He lets it pass. Hasn't begun joking yet. Finally, though, it takes. He picks up the smallest coffee pot, in a row of super, multi-buttoned coffee makers and percolators, and tugs at the little lid, "Here's something. You can make one cup of coffee in the morning, ha, ha ... If you can get the lid off." I watch as he digs his thumb nail between lid and pot. I say, "Hey, it's one way to get coffee grounds all over your kitchen," and gesture how the lid will come off unexpectedly and swish the pot, flinging in one direction, lid in the other. That does it. Big laughs. It feels so good. Slapstick: we see the imaginary kitchen wall. "You should give that to your mother," I laugh, getting dangerously close to bad material for humor. He laughs too, this time... picturing his mother's spotless white walls.

We pick up the irons next. I say I only want the least expensive. I hate irons. I point to the $13.99 box. "You want a box or an iron?" he joins in the quick quips. I laugh.

The display irons are on top while the boxes I point to are on the bottom shelf "This one, or this one?" he picks up the two best. "None," I say adamant. "I don't plan to replace that one I have. It'll last until the kids are gone, after that I'll never iron again." "It'll last through about ten more droppings," he laughs, suppressing the actual sound. I see his neck working with mirth. He is getting giddy. It's his way of being happy, having fun, to get silly. I keep it going: my way is to get more and more sarcastic. Together we move down and around the toy aisle.

"You want any toys?" he asks in his near to bursting with laughter voice. "Not tonight," I sneer, smiling big, trying to think of some snide remark, glad we're finally having fun, pointing to a masked space man. We finally find something to really guffaw about in an out of control "belly burst," as Alex has been known to call it, with some negative connotation. It's a little 39-cent space gun. Alex picks up the plastic sealed bubble and peers in at the miniature space pistol. He laughs so hard, tears squeeze out of the corners of his eyes. I laugh too, gasping for breath. My stomach muscles hurt. The design. The clumsy idea of a design. Alex says, "It looks like a nose, ha, ha... just think someone is making a million dollars on that, ha, ha..." and ends with some sadness. He adds, "That's my problem... I wanted to give the public something useful. A submarine ... How stupid could I get. Something they could use. Look at this piece of plastic. That's what makes the money. Junk, trinkets." His mouth turns down, remembering

221

the submarine he never finished, still sitting in the backyard. He never finished it because he lost faith. It became a joke to friends, family and neighbors. Ha, ha, who are you to build a submarine? He never actually said he would never finish it. He just began to do other things, build onto the house, things that got social approval.

Recognizable things. Things that made sense to other people. "I could never sit down and design a senseless thing like that. That's my problem," he says.

We gaze down the sports aisle. I change the subject. "Hey, look at the keel, creels, whatever they're called. From Korea. I'm going to get one for a purse. Only 69 cents."

"You need a fishing pole, don't you?" he asks, coming out of his mood. His voice gets easy and carefree again. "No, but you do," I encourage.

"You have to need one, so we can go down this aisle to see them," he says, and warms me with his desire to look at the poles. "Oh, yes I *do* want a fishing pole." And we shuffle along passed all sporting goods. The fishing poles are at the end of the aisle.

Before we get to them I point to a row of jock straps. *Supporter* is printed across the front. "Hey, do you need to be supported?"

"Yeah," he laughs in a chuckle.

"Hey, look at all these men jumping rope, clutching clutchers, wearing sweat belts around their guts... see what some men are doing." I chide, picking up all the packages in turn with pictures demonstrating the use of the item to show him.

He looks, "My God," he says. It's a whole world out there, we are led to believe, of men getting stronger, and stronger. "How about these?" and he picks up one big shoe-skate out of a display pair. He turns it and reads inside, "Size eleven." Then, "These could fit me, by golly," incredulous that a pair of roller skates have been designed to fit him. He laughs, "I think I'll get them."

"Hey, let's do. Let's each get a pair and skate up and down all the streets where we've done nothing but work before." I mean it. I see us living a whole new lifestyle. I turn the price tag and read aloud, "Forty-six dollars... God, well..." Then catch the joy of it again. "Hey you know we could. We could all go skating all the time." I am believing it. "It'd tie us together again. Unite us. It'd be fun..." Alex is smiling big over the idea of it, too, perhaps picturing himself and our son whose sixteen wrapped around a street light pole in a heap of arms and legs laughing and trying to get up It's a very happy picture of the family after all that's happened, all the not being of one mind since they grew up. All the arguing, slamming doors, and threats to run away from home. It'd be a way to be close again. To be a family. We linger over the skates, considering and then we're onto the fishing reels. Alex turns the handle of a fishing reel very slowly, watching exactly how the stainless steel bar guides the line into a neat wrap. Evenly and smooth. No mess. It is an expensive reel. I find the sale poles at the end of the aisle, wrapped in cellophane. "Here's the whole thing for only $10.95, pole, reel, and even hooks... Hey, why don't you and Adam go fishing?... you could, you know. You *really* could. Take the dinghy, row out and fish by the mile buoy." I see father and son sitting there with a lunch I've packed, eating sandwiches, talking, laughing, being together. Catching a fish. Faces peering down at it on the bottom of the little boat, blond heads in the sunshine, figuring out what to do. He, still the father, with his soft cheeked son. Both blue-eyed and curly-haired, vying for what should be done... cut the line loose, or unhook the hook. "No, Dad, this way," "No, son, this way," "Here, let me" ... "No, I'll do it," and it being no big thing. And their minds together on how Mom will really be happy. "She loves fish," they'll agree... "and so do the cats," they'll add. Their pride over such a simple thing: but meaning everything now, at this late time for them. No extravagant trips to Europe, or projects like building a spaceship together. Only this simple act: catching a fish. It brings to my mind the rhyme I used to sing to my son: something about Daddy catch a little fishy, boy is a man, Mama fry it in the pan...I can't even remember the words now. The sweetness of it hurts. They *never* went fishing. It was always work for Alex. He was too busy, and they were different personalities. The son likes friends. Alex was a loner. And a worker. We linger over the poles. Our jokes subside. It is a possibility.

Finally we look for throat medicines. We read labels. It takes a while to find them and we grow wearing imagining everyone having so many ailments that these remedies are a thriving business. Allergies, bowels, sleeping potions, heat rubs, prophylactics, desensitizers for men (really for women), eyes, nose, ears, babies, ah, throats. We choose Hold and also take a bottle of syrup to stop the cough. On our way toward the check stand we pass through cleaning fluids. "Drano," I say, and Alex grows anxious. "Not really," I calm him. I take a can from the shelf, "just in case." "Hey, here's that stuff that smells so good, it turns to white foam." I take a bottle of that, too. "And this," as I pick up a can of lemon smelling floor wax, "and this," stacking a box of Bounce on top of the armload.

Alex cannot keep up. He stands beside me, watching this sudden enthusiasm over all the sweet smelling cleaning fluids. I go up close to one shelf and say, "Hey, look." It is rug sweetener. I am sure that is what we need to help us. "After all those animals on the rug, you simply sprinkle this on and it takes away all the smell … " Alex remains passive, being beside me. Allowing for my excitement. Not really with me. I say, "If things smelled better. You know. I've never believed in nice smells before. Like the laundry. You know. But maybe if I made everything smell sweet around there…" I am thinking of all the stink I've allowed to accumulate … a strong urge to freshen up my life flows in me.

We make our way toward the check stand and I say, "Oh, I love bamboo shades, look…" Alex glances at the shades that are always six feet long and our windows are eight feet. We check all the sweet smelling cleansers and the throat medicine and then exit to the ice cream counter. I look at Alex. He looks at the ice cream. He feigns denial.

"No, you won't buy me one," trying for the humor we had, but we don't laugh. There is a very short and thin and old man watching the ice cream lady scoop up his cone.

He wears a workman outfit, khaki pants and a plaid flannel

shirt. He is very clean. These are his after-work clothes. He is cleaned up. I am thinking, "If suddenly he didn't get that cone, if suddenly there was an earthquake of if the police dragged him away for being a transient, if something interfered with his getting an ice cream right now, he'd care.

He would really care with his whole self. He wants a little pleasure. Just a taste of sweet once in a while. He wants that ice cream cone. I see his withered face watching through the glass as the girl digs deeper for a scoop, and he anticipates the taste.

*THE END: Seeing everyone's worries in their faces as they near the end. Seeing everyone's various stages of disrepair in the front of everyone. Being frightened of their faces. Old women peering at french fries through Medi-Cal lenses from out of cataract eyes, worried that they may not be able to get them past their false teeth and down their throats. Worried about choking, making a scene. Dying in Thrifty. On the floor. Spoiling their hair-do, breaking their glasses, swallowing their teeth, losing their earrings, getting everything mixed up. Not being able to separate anything any more. Forgetting eating, what should be eaten and adorning themselves with what should be eaten. Not understanding the differences anymore, without hard concentration. Like babies, but pinching their brows in concern. Clutching bony hands. Old ritual rings still encircling fingers that have forgotten where they are and what to do. They hold eachother like lost people in a woods at night. Seeking warmth, familiarity.*

# Fifteen Years

*SAVED: I dream of strangers. A faceless man, someone I do not know, who will come along someday and save me. Then I know: The reason I've thought I'd be saved by a stranger is because I'll be saved by the strange new part of myself if I'm saved at all.*

# At the African Club

They sat at a little place called the African Club in Feldkirch, Austria. It is on the ground floor of Hotel Hetch which the tourist office says was a guesthouse of a duke built by a king in the 14th century. There is a sidewalk entrance to the African Club but they have come down the spiral staircase in the center of the hotel and entered from the lobby. She and Alex. They could hear the music from their room on the third floor. The air throbbed with the distant sound of bass, viola and drums, while they tried to nap after dinner. It lured them awake. Somewhere, someone was having fun, it said.

It had been a long day, maybe 150 miles, finishing up Germany and starting on Austria. They were half way through their vacation with four more countries to go. It was a whirl-wind trip, stuffed into a rent-a-car with their three long-legged Jr. High kids. At the end of 30 days, they would have done four thousand miles. That was the way they did things. Maximum effort. Alex loved the challenge of getting them across nine countries in thirty days. He had rented a red Simca. That was one side of the trip. The other side they had promised them-selves was nightlife—after the kids were in bed.

They sat in leather chairs, sipped drinks from a leather-topped table and viewed the other guests. Chatter, glasses, costumes, atmosphere. Alex said, "There are places like this all over the world. People in bars just like us, doing just this. And here we are in Austria."

She remembered the way a friend would say "Woopee" and twirl her finger in the air. Seeing her hands made it hard to comprehend that they were here, in Austria, far away from home. It was like being anywhere else. There was no feel to it except for a kind of vague knowing of it. We're here? The same old hands, fresh from twelve years at the sink. Just having fin-ished a day of passing out cheese, bread, sausage, cucumber and apple juice to everyone in the car. For 40 miles, while everyone else was seeing lakes with mirror finishes, mountains that rose up out of nowhere like giant buffalo heads, she was seeing bread, cheese, and sausage in her lap. It was just like at home, but without the convenience of home. After a day of that, how could an evening at the African Club change things? She sighed, sipped, wished for something, suddenly to be the glamorous, flamboyant woman about the world. It was the brochures. The woman on the brochures. Oh, those advertisers knew what they were doing. Lure the little housewife across the world, promise her intrigue. The model was always an obviously well-cared for woman, with long limbs. One long white arm on the arm of a gentleman wearing tweed, and she getting interested glances from equally attractive gentlemen in more tweed. And her look, the look of a well-bred flirt. The best of both worlds. Security and intrigue. And here she sat, only secure, beside Alex, who, surprisingly seemed quite content. He gauged his contentment on her happiness. He thought she was happy. He had brought her all the way over here, that she had wanted to go to Europe. Then she had urged him out of bed to follow her to the African Club. He had pleased her. And now he was pleased with himself. He was that kind of a man. He got pleasure making her happy. He probably never would have come to Europe on his own or to the African Club. He liked other things. To build. He would probably be puttering around in his shop, fitting pieces of things together if it hadn't been for her.

Now they were somewhere. And she was not happy. *Where were all the continental men? All the intrigue?* She looked at the backs of the men lined up along the bar. Stylish shirts too tight along their waists. Even the young men were going to pot, bald, thick. She studied the nails of a man who had his arm around the waist of a woman. They were bitten to the quick. She looked away. She looked at Alex sitting beside her, smoking, sipping a sidecar with good hair and teeth, thin as when they had first met. He was the best-looking man in the place. But he was her husband.

Again her hands struck her as not the white long-fingered

smooth-skinned hands of the vacationing lone female on the brochure. She felt homely, domestic, short-fingered, too close to her kitchen, too soon out of her house, still able to visualize the lime green tile of her sinkboard. There was no transformation to being "abroad."

She got up to find a mirror. She had to see that she was not homely, not short-fingered, not what she felt like at the moment. She headed for the ladies room: *Damen*. It was through the lobby, at the far end of the room. On the way, she passed the entrance of the hotel, stopped, peeked out through the paned windows, and saw that it was a clear, crisp night. She stepped out and stood on the cobblestone walk and gazed about, trying to get something out of it: *I'm here.* Narrow stone buildings lined the narrow stone streets. Shop after shop. She wondered, *Could I live here? Could I never go back? Could I make it on my own without a husband or children? Could I never be a part of that whole thing back home again? Could I be without an identity? Without a place?* The thought lured her, as she pictured herself in straight skirts and sweaters, and going to work in one of the little shops, being that strange woman from America cloaked in mystery to these citizens.

She did not know how long she had been standing there dreaming when she became aware that someone was watching her. She turned and was startled by a man in black. *Was he wearing a cloak?* He stood motionless. And he did not take his eyes off her. She moved toward the entrance, and slightly nodded in his direction and smiled. The smile of a woman who wants not to look frightened, who wants to greet a man in his most decent place. He neither nodded nor smiled, but kept a penetrating eye on her eyes as she passed through the door and into the lobby. In the bathroom mirror she saw that her cheeks were red. She pressed her cool hands on her face. *Who was that?* was blazing through her head. *Who was that man? Who is he?* She felt seduced. The face she saw in the mirror was not that of the little American housewife on vacation. Her eyes had taken on the look of the woman in the brochure. It frightened her. She felt glamorous, striding across the lobby, glancing toward the entrance, almost afraid to see the black cloak, wide shoulders, strong nose and chin, and the dark piercing eyes . She shivered. He was gone. Had he been only a phantom in her imagination.

She returned to her husband with her heart pounding, still repeating over and over the unspoken question, *Who is he?* A part of her, the wife part, said, "I think I just saw the Continental Man," and was sorry. The woman part regretted the indiscretion, the disloyalty to her lover. She was undressed by his eyes, and made love to in that brief encounter. Beside Alex now, she felt in the throes of an illicit love affair. She disliked the little wife for wanting to tell on him. To laugh with the husband over the lover. And she wondered about this man who caused loyalty in her.

She said, "Do you think, if something happened, I mean if we could not go home again, could we become people of the world?" Alex looked at her. She said, "I mean could we ever be wild again?"

He was used to her. He knew what she meant. He said, "I suppose it'd be only a matter of adjustment. Change your situation, and people change. Sure." What she wanted to hear was, "You've never been tamed. You're a wild undomesticated creature. A world's creature. Not a house creature." But he didn't say it.

She was sipping her drink with her long fingers when she spotted again the dark figure. This time he was at the far end of the bar and was watching her. How long had he been there. Her face grew warm again. She looked down at her glass. She could not look up. She thought back over the past few minutes and wondered what she had been doing. Had she made housewife faces, laughed, sat like a mouse. What did she look like to him. How did he see her. She became too self-conscious. Could feel his eyes bore through the dim bar light. She wanted to blow out the candle on their table. Time hung, stilled.

She didn't know what she and Alex talked about for the rest of the evening. She was only aware of being watched by a mysterious stranger who had the power to seduce her from across the room. And then he was coming toward her and passing by their table on the way out. Those dark eyes looked into hers until he passed through the doors and disappeared into the night. Her cheeks burned. He wasn't wearing a cloak after all.

# The Transformation

A few sneers from him and she is transformed into a depraved hag. In an instant. There is a transferal of visions, an invisible witch doctor method in which he wills her to see his version of herself. And she has no resistance.

It begins with his way of scoffing at her presence and with her belief in his powers to know certain things. To be *right*.

She is left being a huge, grotesque, and even physically crippled creature at the stove or at the sink or at the table, wash basin, in bed, or in the yard. Wherever she is and whenever he goes into a fit of hating she becomes made into an ugly absurdity. An awkwardness.

Her mother walked with a limp, and when this hate comes hissing, through his teeth toward her she becomes her mother. A heavy form, hobbling and swaying over her own feet. The formless memory of her limping mother solidifying in her mind like a lump of pathos or sadness or inescapability or finally blatant punishment. Punishment for not being what she *should have been.*

Now she is made to hobble around her home while he opens and shuts doors and spits out vehement epithets. And even though she knows it is self-hatred he spews, she grows into a monstrous beast, limping from room to room doing daily things that cannot be left undone. Her nose raises high in an attempt to thrust off the weight of insult, and her chin juts furthermost outward of her cringing posture in its effort to preserve dignity.

Their being together has become critical. It is too important. They have begun to look upon eachother as witnesses to some unbelievable crime that is being committed against themselves by an invisible killer. They have begun to cling like two inmates, both hating and needing the sight of the other. The other's presence being evidence of perseverance. And at the same time the presence of the other being evidence of endurance, or confinement, that they are still here, that neither one has escaped yet.

He needs to have her moving about the house, making the little sounds a woman who belongs to a man makes in her course of serving him. Puffing pillow sounds, preparing food sounds, cleaning floors, pans, clothes sounds. The sounds that assure him that he is being cared for. And at the same time, sounds that strike his ear as sounds of a trap. No-adventure sounds, no-danger, no-challenge, no-freedom sounds. At these times when sound changes from the cheery tones of a refuge to the deadly clink and clanking of a lock on a cage, he rises up and curses her, curses domesticity, curses food, furniture, shirts and shelter. And she is jolted out of routine movement by the flow of adrenalin. The chemical feeds into her bloodstream and causes her knees to bump into one another with new known strength. Her elbows and wrists and neck, all the hinged places in her, play and reel and ache with imbalance, preparing her for something she cannot call by name. Her mouth opens, face contorts, throat tightens and loud sounds come out. The sounds, that he cannot bear to hear. That make him wince but do not interfere with the effect of his voodoo on her. She swells up many times her original size and the expansion causes her to bump into herself. To stub her toe on the rug. To slobber, to stagger, to swagger. A teetering, fanged, be-clawed thing performing an act of self-defense, warding off accusation. Froth is part of it.

Froth is expelled from both their mouths, They are wild, mad, rabid dogs, snarling, sick, weakened with maladies, their spiritual bodies riddled with fear that smells of death. The message that he wants to get across to her, that she must accept before the anger can subside is that of her absence of worth. He must exorcise his own self-doubt and cast it into her and watch her wrestle and writhe as she fights with it. He wants her to believe that she is ugly, lazy, selfish, and not wise. That she is ignorant, foolish and indiscriminate. That she would sleep with anyone. That she cannot cook, clean, and even cannot care for children. That she is nothing. He forces it into her. And *nothing* replaces the *something* she thought she was and she is empty. At last she shrinks and shrivels to a size smaller than she was before the anger made her expand. And the sight of her wretchedness and smallness feeds him. When he sees that she is crouched on decrepit hind-legs with withered forearms that are useless against his powers, he recoils and goes away, closing the bedroom door behind him, leaving her in silence and stillness, except for her pounding heart. The miniscule organ in her chest has registered everything.

The tiny muscle has received the message through its ventricles and auricles, squeezing and spurting it, pumping it into all parts of her. With contractions, mute and internal, bloody and consistent and precise, it has transformed her.

*CONFUSION: A butcher went to work every day for twenty years. He wanted to do other things, but instead stuck to what he thought he ought to do. The right thing. He chopped meat all day long and at night he came home and made love to his wife, who also resembled a cow. He knew exactly how she would come apart at the joints, so embedded was the routine of butchering animal flesh. Her limbs and the beef, pork and chicken and lamb were all the same finally. He looked for meaning in his work. He soon made love to the side of beef, and came home and chopped up his wife. When they asked him why he did it, he was embarrassed and apologetic.*

*He said, "I didn't mean to. I forgot where I was. I thought I was at work when I was at home, and vice versa. I'm sorry."*

# *Transformation 2*

He could love her again, if she gave up everything she had
become, living with him, and went around the way she went
around when he met her on campus fifteen years before.
Scared, quiet and sarcastic. She did not know anything. She
was afraid to speak, to say anything for sure. She was afraid
of everything. She walked with her nose in the air, shoulders,
back, feet straight ahead, stomach sucked in. In an attempt
to cover fear with pride and aloofness, a pride she didn't feel.
He could not get enough of her unsureness. He asked her
out every day for three months just to see the way she looked
down and turned red and said her father wouldn't let her. He
was a fool, for the trap she set. He got caught in her shyness,
the pathetic doubt. The quiet sadness, the sarcastic remarks,
the fear. He fell for it, and they were married. No longer alone,
taking cues from him on what to think, what to say, what
to do, her self-doubt sifted into insistence and hardened. She
insisted on being doubtful. She was no longer apologetic, she
rose up with an aggression that repelled him. At night, in bed,
asleep, next to her, fifteen years later, he has begun to dream
of holding a passive, quiet, frail and frightened girl. It is the
girl she had been. A dream girl who threatens her now that
she has become so tough.

# One Time

One time Alex took me for a plane ride. He rented a little four
seater from Apollo and it was the first time I believed he could
fly. He had been working for the Airline five years and his job
was always abstract to me. Sometimes I would picture what
he did. I'd see him sitting in his pilot's seat at the controls and
pulling levers and pushing switches and buttons and reading
instruments on the panel, and the plane would race along and
rise into the sky ... But it was never real to me ... his flying.
Then one day he wanted to fly me to the desert. To Las Vegas.
I wasn't sure what to wear. I saw myself stepping out of the
plane in Las Vegas dressed up in a nice sporty skirt and blouse
and high heeled sandals; but at the same time I saw us crashed
on the desert, and walking along, stumbling over rocks, crawling on my knees from the rubble, and decided I should dress
for the crash. I wore pants and tie-on shoes, and then changed
back to the skirt the last minute. And heels. I thought, "I'll
take the pants and good shoes along, and change if I survive."
I pictured how my red skirt would look being tossed on the
ground next to the ruined plane, while I dressed in khakis to
crawl along the desert, all hurt and broken, thirsty and dirty
and twisted.

We didn't crash. My feet in delicate white strapped-on
sandals felt vulnerable as we rose into the air, slipping sidewise, unlike a car, Alex gained altitude. It was amazing: seeing how he knew how to fly. Loving him after that was different. I was humbled. I believed he deserved any attention
I could give. I would always make love to his ability to fly
after that. He circled the little plane around and around before
attempting to make the mountains. He said that's how small
planes with inexperienced pilots crash: they head straight for
the mountains and think they can gain altitude and find, too
late, that there is no air lift after all, as they approach. Then

they go into a panic and try to pull out of it and the engine stalls and that's it. They fall from the sky like a rock ... As he tells me this, and because I'm in such a vulnerable position (I must believe he knows what he's doing) I worship his intelligence, as our little plane clears the mountain tops with ease. I gaze down horror-stricken. I will always be good from now on, for this: for my not having married one of those inexperienced pilots. For not crashing.

He tries to explain the VOR chart. It is a round chart with a moveable part which directs a red line across air courses. I listen and look and try to understand how he knows exactly where we'll be at a certain time, and which direction everything is. He says, "Now you set it for the Palm Springs station."

I say, "I don't know how."

He explains again ... I feel hopelessly stupid. It won't be for another ten years that I'll have the urge to learn to fly ... when I break out of a certain oppression and want to be everything and know everything. And then we'll be divorced.

I watched Alex's blond boyish head as he flew. A short German nose, curly toddler's hair ... the blond curls his mother made him water down straight. His beautiful golden neck ... a smooth strong true one.

There are such air pockets. We drop and are caught, drop and catch.

I tell Alex I will have to throw up. He is wearing his Hawaiian shirt.

He has not counted on my air sickness. He says, "Here, use this," and takes off his shirt just in time. I bury my mouth. He banks, one wing up, and the pressure on my head is so physical, as if there is a giant magnet and my brain is solid iron. It pulls me over to one side. I try to see the ground, to find a point of reference. Nothing ... I look at Alex in his white undershirt. We have leveled out; He is clear-eyed, pink as a baby, and fresh as a new cadet. He is 35 and looks 19.

His whole family has sky-blue eyes and translucent flesh and those golden halos, as if they have just come from heaven.

I say, "What would happen if I'd stick my head out the window to throw up?" He doesn't hear me. He is enjoying piloting, setting the VOR chart for the next point in time and space. I want to ask all the questions that will feed my sense of fear. I want to know about decapitation from the force of wind, how far a body part has been found from the crash site, anything to frighten me and keep me making promises and respecting everything. I say, "What if you just flew by sight?"

He says, "You can do that on a clear day, but if you don't have instrument rating, you're in trouble in clouds..." Again a pang in my groin over his power of flight, his knowledge... I could make love this second to his skill and understanding of instrument flying.

Later, as we near our destination and he talks on the radio and says, "Roger...ot, ot, six," and all the code talk, blood floods my cheeks and I am his, completely.

In Las Vegas I alight in white heels and light tailored blouse. There is such a glare on the concrete in that heat where we tie up our little plane (like an animal that might get away overnight), I put on my dark glasses. Like a celebrity I am stared at as we make our way to rent a car. It is because I am walking in an uncertain way because of my new respect for Alex.

# The Enemy

So I am here and Alex is coming back after being away. But I have been here all along, I have not been away. I have only tried going away by eating too much bread, appeasing the thing that wants to go away. And by doing many other things because I am not dull.

I only appear to be dull to those who pass by and see the shadow of me through my open windows, moving on the inside of my house. I have books stacked by my corner chair where I read by the glass doors. I have a cupboard full of fabric remnants, remnants from all the sewing I used to do. Remnants I make into items of art, dolls, murals, collage that I sell at the Sunshine shop. I have pressed flowers behind glass encased in strips of lead, I have pressed flowers under the bed, in the *Bible*, in the *History of Man* book, between newspapers with bricks on top for more arrangements, to be put behind glass that I have not gotten to yet. I have a frozen pheasant in the freezer, feathers and all, waiting until I finish a taxidermy class so I can mount it. I have a stack of children's stories in my filing cabinet, old ones, current ones, stories I have written for children all along. For years. And I have envelopes of photographs I want to do something with. Enlargements I made in the darkroom. And ideas for more in my head, And ideas for articles to write. Lots of ideas. And lots of stuff around the house.

It is not that I sit around and dwell on the fact that I want to be somewhere else. I do not moan. I keep busy. I have caught on to what women are doing today, not caught on, but already knew and was doing it. Keeping my mind off dishes and diapers and detergents. I have always done something else. "Stimulation" being the key word for women today. I have stimulated my mind with projects, causes, books. And I have stimulated my body with my own hand. It's true.

Alex is due home. And I have already gotten something for myself. I have practiced monosex. I have been a monosexual for as long as homosexuals and heterosexuals and bisexuals have screamed and hollered for recognition. And I have never thought of trying to get recognition for it. I do not need laws to be passed so I can go to a monosexual bar and express myself in public. I simply lie across the bed and give myself something.

Is it love, or sex, or just touching? Does my body need a kindly hand? A hand it cannot find anywhere else? Is it that no one likes my body in the way that it needs to be liked? That Alex (as well as other men) see it as a thing to be had, taken, to get? A thing that will perform for him like a trained dog? I don't know if that is true, but I prefer to be alone.

So before Alex comes home with his penis, with his anger, with his sweet hot fire mouth, with his frustration, his need to love and to be loved, to be successful, to be more than acceptable, I touch myself until it is all the touching I need. Even though I do not like the feel of my own body, I touch myself. It never feels the way I want it to feel. To my hand I am like any pile of meat anywhere, wet, soft, changing shape at will. An amoeba, Flesh that is only flesh and not super flesh. I would like to be super flesh, like in the pictures. It is what advertising has done. Or is it. Why do I want to be super flesh?

I like being able to take care of myself. I can accept my body and take pleasure. It is the privacy that gives me the most pleasure. That I am not hassled by another whole person being there, wanting things. Distracting me, making me self-conscious.

*They* say women are turning to other women because women understand each other. But I cannot understand that. A woman would be the same as a man, another whole personality there to contend with. All her problems, her desires, requirements being in the way. I would still be self-conscious, even though the word is out: *Tell your partner what you like*. It will excite him. I cannot tell him. I want it to happen by itself. If I tell him, then I no longer want it. Exposing what I want scares it away. If he does not already know, then he will never know.

But I have told him. Because he wanted to know. So Alex knows. It's been thirteen years that he's known. He is clever that way. He has not been one of those men to jump on and jump off, although at times I wish he had been, so I would not have had to get involved. If he had taken his pleasure in spite of me, I may have been able to fake something and out of that pretend I was someone else. But he wanted me to be there. Really be *there* and participate. He wanted a sex partner, not an object.

And I was used to being an object. So I fought self-consciousness and became more self-conscious in the fight. He insisted that I go all the way to the peak of the pleasure he could cause, and because it took so much doing on his part, I grew to dislike myself. Or I always disliked myself and he made me see it. To dislike my inadequacy. I hated being exposed. I hated being "inadequate."

That is probably the whole point in writing this. *Inadequacy*. My inadequacy. And the word "overcome," one's inadequacies. To learn to have *normal*, healthy, positive responses to normal healthy situations. That's what I cannot do. That's why I eat bread, press flowers, take pictures, practice monosex, to try to get away. From "wrong" responses. Or is that true?

But I can't talk about it. How can I tell it. How can I tell where I am now without going back to where I've been. I would have to tell what I had to do to get through childhood (Is it what everyone had to do?).

And I do not know how to say it. I would like to be delicate even though it is not a delicate subject. The coarsest things have to be said in the most delicate way. It is what we are taught. It is what science has put into our mouths. We do not have to say *shit*. We can say feces, as a subject, or eliminate, as a verb. But I do not know how to say the thing I want to say. I will not say it in terms of *sucked off*. But I am not sure if I ever learned another language for it. A language in between slang and clinical. I do not want to be clinical and talk about *cunnilingus*. Or to be religious and use *sodomy* and *fornication*. I do not judge it.

I cannot say it until the words come. I do not have a language yet. A personal language to tell what happened. It was not as simple as words that speak only of physical acts. It was the non-physical part I do not have a language for. That is not to say I did not have a non-verbal language for it. I cried, I got mad, I got scared, mean, sad. I used words as sticks to strike with. But I never developed a language.

*They* say to tell it like it is. Start from where you are. I'm here. Alex is coming home. He is due in a moment. Every sense in me awaits. Ears, eyes, sixth. Because I must be ready to sprint. He is the enemy. Bambi's mother was right. *Do not trust them. They are men.* Or did she say *man*? Does that include me? Is that who I sprint away from. Myself? as only Alex can reveal it to me.

*The awkwardness. Alex's feet under the blanket*
*by her face in the morning. And his disapproval.*
*Bumping their heads on the roof of the car when*
*they sit up after sleeping. Creeping over rocks to the*
*green water of Lake Mead to bathe and get a coat of*
*powdery alkaline on themselves. And his anger over*
*last night. Shaking the car at the gas station to get*
*the air bubbles out so more gas will fit in. The heat.*
*Swollen feet. And his irritability that she is the way*
*she is. Going to see an old girlfriend and nothing*
*being done with her life yet to show her old girlfriend.*
*Eyes stinging from tears in the bathroom over being*
*caught this way, the way she is. Standing in a*
*store's dressing room four hundred miles from home*
*without any pants on, still trying to be what she isn't.*
*Buying a pair of pants that will make it happen.*
*and wanting to be honorable at least. But knowing*
*she doesn't have that and that would have been easy*
*to have. Or should have been. Wanting to interpret*
*everything, every person by the way they affect her.*
*And at the end, sitting in flesh in front of her father,*
*so even he sees she is no longer his daughter but any*
*aging woman, while he hides the triumphant feeling*
*he gets over a child who always thought he was old.*
*She sees her nostrils in the drinking fountain when*
*she bends to drink. A stainless steel reflection.*

# Naked

It was the way she cleaned the toilet. It was over that. He said, "You sprinkle cleanser and leave it." She said, "It doesn't take a chisel and hammer." He said, "With this water it takes more than cleanser." She said, "I swish the brush around." He said, "It takes more than that." She said, "I don't go out and buy all those special cleansers." He said, "It doesn't take those cleansers... It takes elbow grease." She said, "Your mother doesn't keep a hospital sterility with elbow grease. Have you ever looked under her bathroom sink?" He said, "She spends what she earns on what she wants and uses or wastes it according to that." She said, "I do too. Or are you saying cleanser is all I get, even though it's all I want anyway."

She leaned on her elbows across the table from him at a cafe. He cocked his eyebrows to see who was overhearing their argument. They were "having coffee out" that morning, for a break from the usual routine. He had told her to either order a sweet roll to eat or pour lots of sugar in her coffee to keep her sweetened up. She did neither.

"All that's officially required is what a hired maid would do. Go in, sprinkle cleanser as an abrasive, and swish the brush around. It's a whole different kind of job to request that I get down on my knees and scrape the sediment off the porcelain with a sharp instrument." If he had been a fox, his ears would have moved to catch any hint of being overheard. He cocked his eyebrows this way and that, knowing he had done it again, walked right into a public place with her big mouth and bad mood.

Back home again, he went his way, out to his shop, and she went hers. She got out of the house and headed for the hill. There were certain things he believed about her that made her pity herself. She believed they weren't true. And she pitied the way she was inside his head. He viewed her as a pathetic child who was never taught to do anything right. Who refused out of ignorance to be taught. Which left her on the outside of people. And being on the outside hurt her. That was the tragedy. That she didn't know that it was her strange performance which made people reject her. Yet she wouldn't change. Like cleaning the toilet. He had told her how to do it properly, effectively. So that it was clean. But she kept doing it in a way that was not effective. He felt sorry for her dilemma. She was a trapped creature. Trapped by bad habits and stubbornness. Or ignorance? And she needed the very people she snapped at. "Bite the hand that fed her," was one of his favorite expressions. Like a coyote in a cage. And he the sole keeper of her fate. He could let her go to run hungry and get shot at, or keep her, throw in tidbits and scoff at her mock viciousness.

The way she showed up in his thoughts, and the way his heart went out to her in her predicament, and the way he placed himself as her master, made her feel helpless. And helpless turned to anger.

Crowded, as if crouched inside the cage inside his mind, she made her way to the top of the hill behind her house. A two-mile hike. Sagebrush scraping her pant-legs. Heat exuding from the sage-scented ground. She picked her way along the trail she had hiked over the years. Hiked pregnant at times, and hiked with lovers at other times. She had made love under the giant oak tree at the top of the hill, had rubbed the imprint of acorns and twigs on her bare bottom.

She finds her way to the lookout point this time. It is a sandstone rock standing higher than her head, from which she can see horizon to horizon. It's as if she is perched on top of the world when she climbs up, using an old Indian scooped-out hole as a handhold. She studies the grasses around the rock for a while. Once she saw a rattlesnake moving through the grass. There was something Godlike about letting it move and just watching it and not trying to kill it the way everyone she had ever been with had done when they saw a rattlesnake. To just let it be.

She listens for sounds. In being alert and half frightened of whatever must live in the bushes, the anger over his not liking the way she does the toilet subsides. In its place comes a pleading. She begins to shake her head slowly from side to side. For what? What is she sorry for, or afraid of. *Why does a pleading start. Please, please, please, what?* She gazes and lets the *please* cry out until it stops. She gazes at the ocean, the neighborhood, the towns off in a distance, the highway, the railroad. All the territory where she has been passing her time.

The rustling of birds in the brittle dead leaves under the oak trees brings small shots of alarm to her heart and impulses of alertness. Finally she gives up listening and adjusts to being alone, allowing for the hill to be alive with movement. A few strange mountain flies buzz around. She grows dull and strangely sensual. No one. There is no one up here. No one knows she is here. There is no one who knows where she is. No one can see her. This sensation. Being beyond human vision makes her want to be naked. Slowly, glancing around once, she begins unbuttoning her blouse. She parts it, unhooks her bra, releases the tension of the straps, and enjoys the feel of the slight tug of weight of her breasts. This looseness creates a longing in her groin.

She leans back, naked on top of the world and closes her eyes and lets the breeze play with her body. Nipples that never feel the stir of air respond. All over, every hair is gently pressed eastward. The delicate follicles create goose bumps that stand out. She envisions a snake suddenly striking her most vulnerable places. She places one finger on her tongue and touches the moisture to each nipple. The warm air currents turn icy cold for an instant passing over those two spots. At the same time she opens her legs and feels the warmth of the sun there. It is like the warmth of a man's mouth. She arches upward toward the sky and gives up all her resistances in the only way her body can. She gives in. Gives up. Her body releases itself. At the point of release she is receptive to everything. The sky, the ocean, the air, the rustling, snakes, the smell of sage. It is a painful pleasure of letting go of all the holding on, insisting in, defending against. And then it is over and she grows immediately aware of her nakedness and embarrassed by it. She dresses in quick gestures, acting as if she had never been undressed. And then she sits looking around. She sighs and grows bored with the rock and the view. As she climbs down she is wondering—What if they all knew? What if everyone knew what she just did? What if, when she descended into the street, everyone had filled out a questionnaire about each woman in the neighborhood to find out the one most likely to go to the top of the hill to make love to herself and they all marked her name?

She pads along the powdered dirt path, reading scats along the way. Coyotes, foxes. Poor things have a meager diet of hairy, bony, almost meatless rodents. The grey fur is excreted undigested. Bits of bone, skull, claw. The vision of her own life below becomes voluptuous by contrast. It is full of stuff, so full that an issue as paltry as toilets can ensue like so much residue off the top of a fat, engorged, full-bodied life. She plans to get his chisel from his shop as soon as she gets back, and carefully chip the deposits from the bottom of the toilet loose. She can do it now.

Having something away from him, away from everyone—for herself, to own and *have*—a secret, gives strength.

# Latest Thought

I tell Alex my latest thought "Sea anemones can't spit." There is something significant about it. It means all there is to mean about not being able to un-do something. As my voice drones on, I hear dead silence and know he is asleep. I am left alone, sitting on the edge of the bed talking to myself about myself. So I get up and go away still talking out loud. ""Why do they sell sleeping pills. Nothing puts a man to sleep faster than the prattle of his wife's voice."

Later I weep on the phone to the sound of *his* voice telling me I am selfish. He has sung his usual single-word song to me: "ME ME ME ME ME ME ME…," to make his point. He has told me that I am a know-it-slob and liar. Those are not his words, but it is what he means. He says things in other ways. He thinks I have not given him enough attention. It is always after a two-day silence and then I call to talk about myself that makes him hateful. I am always surprised that he does not care to hear it. That he wants to talk about himself instead. We each vie for first place in the friendship.

The last time we had a night together, he took his cigarettes and keys and left me in the car and went in to take "a piss," as he called it, but did not come back. So I went in, desensitized, under the guise of using his phone. I sat in his chair and said quiet things to him about wanting to go away. He lay on the bed smoking and it was the first time he decided to call a halt to his bad moods. He said, "I wish I had never met you. I wish there was never a you…. Never had been you. But the alternative is no good now. So…," and he took me off the chair and insisted that I be next to him.

I got his point. It had come to that. Having me was only one degree better than not having me. It was the first time he did not leave it up to me, whether to stay or not. He had always wanted to watch to see what I would do before…to leave it up to chance. Now he took me. It was an act of will. A statement. An opposite of passivity. He did not want to be lonely. I was padding.

As we lay there, he told me that he once asked a girl if she loved him more than God. It was the only girl he came close to marrying once, because she fit his boyhood ideal. A Catholic girl who would never "sin." She said, "No," that she loved God more. He called her a plain-clothes nun. And did not like her anymore. And after kissing, he saw her makeup all around his mouth!

I asked him if he thought I loved him more than God. He said "Yes." And I was glad because it was all one. God. Him. Life. I told him I could not love anyone if I did not love everyone. And God. He smiled. He was pleased. But it was too late. We had already gone through our friendship. We had stayed in the first stage, the stage of preliminaries for three years. Because I was married we could not go on to anything more. And it had gotten us down.

I used to go bored instantly when my father fainted. And I went dull then, on the bed beside him when our emotions were intense.

Later, when we relaxed, he wanted to pretend we were brother and sister. So we did. We slept side by side. And it was the closeness he needed.

I woke first and watched him sleep. He was a boy away from home, scared of the hard-core love games. Wanting what he and his sister had felt when they lived at home. I wanted to give him the kind of love he needed. But he made it so hard to do. He thought I was a liar. Because there was no future in it.

# Because They Were So Jolly

They sat, there in their bedroom naked, he in a chair, she on the bed with their bodies dangling between them, free to do whatever they pleased. They were of the belief that nothing was wrong. Even though her mother had frowned upon "playing with yourself" and shamed her at an early age, and he had a widowed mother who had not partaken of sex for thirty years, they sat together in their bedroom, curtains drawn, and were free to do whatsoever pleased them. They could think of nothing much to do. They had simple tastes. Tying eachother up, whipping or wearing certain undergarments or boots meant nothing to them except as pictures in books, as a curiosity, to see into the needs of other people. They had even laughed over some of these pictures at the absurdity of some of these needs, the paraphernalia and contortions of the human body. Yet they had no interest in performing these acts themselves.

They sat nude, she swinging one foot aimlessly and he smoking and sipping cream sherry, and their eyes looking sometimes with interest and sometimes with used-to-ness and sometimes with laughter at eachother and at their own predicament: Here they were. Without clothing. Flesh bared, open to whatever popped into their minds, and nothing really popped into their minds.

Finally he said, "I'm going to shave you. Lie back." She laughed as he fumbled in his overnight case for his electric razor.

"No," she protested, giggling but lying back and protecting herself with her hands.

"Lie still," he taught, "Shhhhh...."

She calmed and let him shave her, jumping only once when the razor nicked her gooseflesh skin. "Shhhh...," he coached.

Then it was done and she took a shower to rinse away the whiskers. She looked at herself in the bathroom mirror, standing on the tub on tip toe to see into the high medicine chest mirror and she did not like what she saw.

She warned him, hollering through the wall, "I look horrible," and then she entered, slightly proud to have let him shave her, thinking it was not really that bad, just different, even kind of funny looking, He was still poised in his chair and ready to see her when she came in. He laughed a small high tickled sound as if he had just shaved the cat and it amused him by looking so comical.

"You, laugh," she accused, holding back laughing herself but slightly embarrassed.

"No," he denied, although he had just laughed.

"Yes, you do, you think I look funny. You made a fool of me. Here I am shaved and you aren't. I'm a fool and you are laughing."

He laughed some more because of the way she knew her situation so well and was on to him. And then she began to laugh. They both laughed. She laughed with him because she knew that he had not planned for it to look funny or strange or new or so pale. Or picked like a chicken. She knew that he had planned to be aroused, not amused. So they laughed together and rolled around on the bed laughing. And they had a better time than usual because they were so jolly.

# *Coming Apart*

SHOULDERS. A SCENE:

Sitting in the movie last night at the Montessori auditorium on a fold-up chair. Newly bathed, runned, tanned, in new cotton pants. A new, brand new nice feeling. Healthy, strong, and still gaining distance away from death. I could sprint to safety in a second if the building caught fire. Yet sitting there I cannot get my back and shoulders straight enough. I twist and turn and itch. It is no simple thing to sit. I must sit in such a way that if accumulation of that posture gathered (and it does) I believe it will not result in a distortion of my tissue and form. Sitting is a fight for two hours. An active battle with time and gravity... I cannot relax and hunch. I grow tense staying erect. So I play with the angle of my structure through the whole film and wonder how everyone around me can sit so still for so long and appear to hang just right from their skeletons. All of us full of bones.

A SCENE:

They are kissing their children goodnight. Books are stacked on each bedside table. They turn off lights, make their way to their bedroom. He is undressing first and stands in his shorts rummaging through a stack of *Science* magazines, placing one near the bedside lamp. She undresses down to her underwear, puts on one of his undershirts, and begins doing sit-ups on the narrow strip of floor beside her side of the bed where, on a sewing machine table, sits a 5-inch TV, which she turns to the Dick Cavett show. It is always on by the time she is here, doing this. About 11 PM. He reads on his stomach and she goes through her routine of exercises. By the time Johnny Carson is half over, he is asleep on his face, magazine still before him, and she gets in the shower to rinse off the sweat from the whole day. She sweats a lot. Even in cold weather. Before she turns out the light she looks at her husband. His blond curly hair is back. She is back. Everything is surprisingly back....

A SCENE:

They are holding eachother in the middle of their house in the middle of the day. A paperback book lies on the counter with page 68 folded down. It is the page where the little orphan girl (a true diary) is holding her pet pig's bleeding head because the foster farm family have just slaughtered it. It is a hot day. A heavy days The house is stuffy even though all the windows are open. As they hold eachother, their sobs can be heard by two little black dogs who stand around waiting to be fed. It is a small house. A house they have lived in for 16 years. It sits north and south so the sunshine does not filter into the dark front part of the rooms where they stand. He is in tan corduroys and a cotton shirt. Silver is just beginning to appear at the sides of his blond hair. There is a fresh scar coming out of his eyebrow to the middle of his forehead. They are both slender people. She has brown hair and shows tired lines in her face. Both of them have blue eyes and strong arms. They are rearranging positions so she can see his face. His mouth turns down and his eyes are truly red and dripping tears. She pulls back and rubs her face and turns the book over, sitting down on a stool. She says, "Oh, why is it so sad to us?" He is shaking his head, stands there looking at her, and when new tears fill his eyes, he looks at nothing and lets them fall. She goes to him again. He says, "It's that I may not go on … the kids will be alone … I won't be here to help them…" His voice cracks and he can't go on. She finishes, "and we found our meaning in them … what will we be without them?"

ANOTHER SCENE:

She is running. Sweat is dripping out of her scalp into her eyes, ears, between her breasts, off her elbows from the creases in her arms. Her chest heaves and she opens her mouth like a fish, open, close, open, close, to get more air, expanding her chest. It is a steep grade alongside the foothill road. He is riding a bike, slower and slower, pushing until his calves sting, and finally getting off and walking the bike.

He cuts across a dry grass field and meets her as she is heading downhill, half a mile on. The sun has just set and the sky over the ocean is ablaze with orange streaks. They overlook the whole countryside, their neighborhood, nestled beneath them, the Pacific Ocean, beyond, and the 101 highway breathing its traffic sound off in the distance. It is all downhill now, and flat ground back home. They talk as she runs and he pedals. "I worry about the kids. How are they going to make it in the world? Those simple things, dangers, what can we do?" She feels warm tears replace the harshness she has lived. He looks at her and she can see that he too has tears.

# A Small Payment
## (like Patty Hearst)

She sees herself kidnapped and forced *away* from all that she has known. Away from husband, kids, house, job, three meals, her own car, the bathroom routine, the diaphragm, the regular sounds. She hears tough, or at least strange men's voices, unreasonable commands, ideas, words. She has to do what she was not ever supposed to do before. (She gets to be bad.) Anything but pain comes to her mind's eye. She cannot bear the thought of pain, does not want to imagine being hurt, especially permanently hurt. She sees scenery going by and feels herself speeding away in a get-away car. She is getting away without lifting a finger. Without being blamed. Without guilt. She is tossed roughly into a corner somewhere where she has never been before. On a couch in a place where nothing relates. She cannot give it a name. It is not Oxnard or at Mama's, or over in Las Vegas, or at the show, or in the library, drug store, Safeway. She cannot put her finger on it and it comes to her as an isolated place from all the other places she has ever been. She is treated unkindly which leaves her free from obligation. It frees her and she can be what she is. She is scared. She has no leverage. She cannot get away with the old tricks. Yet. They don't apply. She cannot say no. Cannot go off and be mad, pout, have a mild fit. She faces her abductors and smiles and shakes her head in mock despair. She is more excited than she has ever been. Even if she does not get out alive. Even if she can never return. She has done *all that* before, in a house, in a store, in a library.

It is the first time she is real. With people who do not care, who do not want her, but only to use her as a tool. To get what they want. She gets wildly observant, taking them in, witnessing up close other misfits. Innocent idealists who believe they can do exactly as they please. It pleases her to watch them, these men who have taken her over to the other side of the law. She pretends to side with them, to understand what it is they are after, to parrot ideas, to believe in their goal. It is not much different than what she has been doing her whole life. Up to now. They are impressed, crushing suspicion. She gets in close. They like her. Everyone has a better time than they thought they would, while she never forgets that it is a skill. She survives. No one ever sends any money. Because there is no money. They have taken the wrong woman.

They let her go with the confidence that she will be cool, will not hold grudges, has not resented being taken, will not tell. She looked too much like a school teacher. They could not kill her. They could not slay a childhood image. They open the door of their black get-away car and let her out on some dingy street. She bids them farewell with a look of care in her eyes, compassion. She is magnanimous. She was able to be *anywhere* without losing her head. Without attachments. She never sees them again.

And when she goes home, she looks happy. And everyone believes she had a good time. They are all mad. They look for blood or mud, or relief on her. She says they were not bad. She says she liked them and wished them no harm. That they did not harm her. Her husband wants to know details. He wants to see if she is the same. She goes back to making spaghetti and cheese at the stove. He sees her there just like before, except she looks different, as if it's okay to be there now. As if she has been somewhere else. He is upset. He doesn't want her to have gotten more than he gets. No one wants her to have gotten to do what they didn't get to do. They are all slightly annoyed with her. Everyone is irritated. She hums a little and thinks of the way it went... She is relaxed. The way she got to have something she really wanted and did not owe anyone for it. No explanation or apologies. She feels a bruise on one cheekbone. It is small payment.

# A Light Moment

They survey their new bedroom and tell eachother how they will decorate it. He says, "I wish there was a wrap-around curtain rod and it'd go from here over to..." and he doesn't say the next "here" until he has arrived over to it. And then he takes an imaginary pole and tells her, "Then, instead of pull strings, we'll have a bar and just go around like this," and he walks around the three-walled window, pulling closed the imaginary drapes with a non-existent pole.

She says, "I don't know what kind of curtains should go over the windows there above the bed. I'll ask your mother. She'd know, or have some idea. There are so many. They could be soft and light, or knitted and hangy."

He says, "Let's put Venetian blinds on them." She looks at him to see if he is serious. His face crinkles up and she laughs and joins in his game, "Yes, Venetian blinds on the two side windows and a... a... pull shade on the middle window and then I'll hand paint some designs on the shade; It'll be *beautiful!*" And on and on into the absurd they go, devising all the things they have secretly thought of doing just to get the job done, but never daring to try, until they are laughing with tears in their eyes.

They are laughing until they cry because it will be a long tedious time before they have finished installing the rods and drapes and little mechanisms that must go over the windows.

*She was making love to a mentally retarded man in a hospital in order to revive his belief in things. It was sad. She was fighting revulsion. And she lost her voice. She could not speak. Her throat was hoarse.*

*There's a waiting girl inside her. In a green field with poppies and daisies and a light warm breeze. She has brown hair and a smile, this waiting girl, because it is coming. But she does not know what it is.*

*A heavy truck goes down the field with its tires chirping under the load. She believes at first they are cries of seagulls. The television brings into her house a desperate trek of men going through snow. Someone is always near. All the bedrooms are moist. Like places where frogs live. All the children are moist like frogs. Their hands and breaths smell of the swamp. A primitive smell. Another sound comes. It is the sound of distant earth or snow crashing down, tons of weight. An avalanche. But she sees it is the close sound of corn flakes being poured. And in the midst of this room she wants* the form. *A set thing to do so* it will be done, *and she will have a sense of* completion *for at least one evening.*

*She wallows in nebulousness and obscurity instead, feeling either too big or too small.*

# *Without Choice*

Inside of my house I cannot tell where I stop and things around me begin. There is no longer a distinction between the things I have seen over and over again and me.

We have grown together and marked eachother and adapted so that separated we exist out of context. When I see the things inside my house I think of myself and I believe they are what I am.

Paper flowers in a brown handmade clay pot on a teak Pier One table from Denmark, Walnuts in a yellow basket from Omweg's, orange mats and a wooden bowl full of Harry's oranges from Porterville on Carolyn's yellow metal utility table on wheels. A fondue pot from Thrifty. And a painting from Aliso School by The Kids. Brass candle holders from Sarah, a holder for knickknacks from Mama. Gords, an ant farm, Mrs. Naefs' thirty-five dollar antique desk; Never Cry Wolf from Don, who calls it Never Cry Wuff, because he has a speech difficulty caused by a misshapen lip that he hides from sight behind a black moustache. It is about wolves and I have become a wolf, reading it.

Hot lemonade is beside the book, because I am hoarse. And Alex is returning somewhere in the sky from Newark or Kennedy airport, and before he left I asked if Newark was New York. And it gave him more on me.

Monks cloth, in off-white and unbleached white is at the windows. And Mr. Watson and Mr. Morales are dead, and Mr. Wilmeth is dying of a row of heart attacks, and the three are with me inside of my house because I cannot get them out of my mind. It is as if they are dying in my presence and pointing and saying, "See, see how it is."

There is rain, flat against the window like a one dimension stage window, The room becomes one dimensional. It is a flat painting of my existence.

Indian beads on a wire, strung by Warren from a birthday craft from Aunt Adrianne connect me to themselves as if they are an extension of my eye. Vision becomes a physical tentacle that touches the beads as they hang on their wire. The atmosphere is pressing against my face. It is thick and real and solid and holds me as an ingredient, jelled within itself.

Stains by Zeke, the black lab, are on the rug where he has lain around and scratched, and there are stains from me, from spilling furniture polish, as I wipe the things in the room and in my psyche. A little white Volkswagen waits out in front. It is from Sarah six years before, and its nose is now sidewise because I bumped into the side of an old woman from Van Nuys. Her car. And we both got out and were abrupt with eachother and then I apologized and went away with a bump on my head which hurt only if I pressed it; She had dashed out into my path. And the apology for bumping her looks at me from the twisted nose of my car as it sits outside, waiting for another ride.

Hot water for more and more tea with lemon, endlessly, is in a pot on the stove. And I will pour it through my body as I am being poured through some greater body.

# The Separation

I ate all the food I was served and then ordered coffee and leaned on my elbows on the table and gazed at the people as I sipped from the cup. Alex went back for seconds and the three little children went back for seconds, and after awhile they attempted to go back for thirds and fourths as if smorgasbord was a game. Alex ordered coffee and lit up a cigarette and said, "It's amazing isn't it."

I darted a look at him, but thought, *Yes, it is, that we're still together.*

"It's amazing to think that a place like this could keep going, don't you think?"

"It's logical to me. Why not?" I said with my head turned away from him, giving him a profile.

"When the Copper Coffee Pot is robbing their customers?" he asked.

*God*, I thought, *Here I am ready to leave and he speaks academically about the restaurant business. It's like him... Concentrate on the external world if the inside one gets too mucked. His mother's lesson to him: Don't bog down in emotion, son. Turn off your heart and listen to the news. Keep your mind occupied and it won't dwell on vulgar things....*

He sat tall, blond and small headed; blowing smoke, holding the cigarette with a foreshortened hand, and not looking directly at me with his light blue eyes. The black pupils of his eyes had always reminded me of a rooster's speck-seeing eye. The way he turned them onto a person when he was looking for a speck.

# *Style*

They drove over to the valley to look at a horse. When they got there they found themselves looking at a ranch woman who knew everything there was to know about horses. Through the boards of the corral fence, as they leaned like cowpokes in the heat, she told them about the appaloosa she had for sale, how she had broken it, trained it, introduced bits, progressing from chewable bits to the hard bar it wore now at four years old. As she talked, they peered through the fence at her self-confidence, her ability, her success, at her whole life style, and saw all the things they weren't. They knew nothing about anything they had. Even though they kept two horses in a field behind the house they could not talk for more than one minute on anything they knew about the horse except what they had noticed by having it around. When the woman mounted the appaloosa and took it through its performance in the ring, they grew sick inside, thinking of their two pampered and spoiled horses at home, one horse had even been brought inside the house and fed carrots out of the refrigerator once. For fun.

They had laughed and laughed and wondered what the world was coming to. It was a big joke. The horse before their eyes now was a ranch horse. A horse used to round up the cattle. It was a work horse. Its flanks and rump were nicked and scarred even though it was still young. Its eyes were surprisingly intelligent and aware of where all the human hands, fluttering around it, were. When they gestured to brush the flies from their own eyes, the horse tossed its head. It was cautious as it stood in halter as they talked. It did not expect soft kisses on its muzzle.

As they talked to this woman in cowboy boots and a mickey mouse T-shirt who knew so much about horses and had this gelded appaloosa under control by her side, they grew uneasy. The whole idea of kindness to animals which was cradled so carefully inside their brains, nurtured so tenderly day to day, began to look like sheer folly. They were left leaning on their elbows in the sun like a couple of buffoons. The woman's quick glances from the privacy of her own beliefs, at them, after they would make a comment about what they wanted in a horse, told them she knew what clowns they were. How far away their premise was in owning a horse, from hers, Her straightforward honest face and talk was absent of doubt. She knew what she knew and it served her.

Her words, "the ranch, work, obedience, getting the cattle rounded up, how fast can this appy come out of that chute and rope a cow," struck them like blows. They were made ashamed of the way they had come to live: A soft arab mare with gentle eyes and delicate legs. A buckskin gelding so willful he would not let a bottle of fly spray be pointed in his direction without taking off with his tail held high. Both useless consumers. It occurred to them how their animals had become like them.

When, they drove away from the ranch, from the good common sense, they had just heard, from the hearty woman, from the half-scared obedient ranch horse, they were depressed. How far they had come from what they knew to be right. How did they get so far away from people like this woman. What had happened to them to cause them to be living their ridiculous life style.

They began to argue, First the cats had to go. He made a fist and beat hard on the steering wheel to emphasize how important it was to get rid of the cats. His frustration caused him to swerve in order to miss a sign.

"We can't go on letting those cats mess up our life...." He was referring to the cat hair and dried blood on everything. One cat had an allergy to the sun. The tips of her ears had scabs which she scratched, and splattered blood all over the front of the house. Another cat was deaf, another brought its food to the door step to eat, where they tracked it up and down the walk. Still another, the old altered male, sprayed a male scent on everything he passed. It had been a constant irritation to them, but he had given in to her pleadings over the years. She would clean up after them. *Don't take them away.*

The ranch life, as he envisioned it, gave force to his argument. "You can see that that woman is all practicality. She wouldn't put up with a bunch of animals destroying her ranch house. She's been around animals all her life and knows how to control them. She doesn't let them run her life. If the animal doesn't serve a purpose..." and he made a clean sweep in the air with a flat palm... "she gets rid of it." He meant *kill* it.

Her ears were plugged with emotion and also from descending downhill. They careened around curves as she gathered her words and threw them at him like stones. She was filled with the ranch woman's abilities in contrast to her own ineffectiveness and did not need to be accused of keeping cats for the sole purpose of encouraging them to destroy their home. Self-reproach flowed inside her already. She had never read about horse care, had never accumulated the necessary information to keep a horse, had never even learned to ride. Contempt over her large capacity for ignorance filled her, along with the usual resistance to his idea of getting rid of their four cats. He wanted, not only her permission, but her approval. He wanted her to see his point. To get rid of her sentimentality and replace it with practicality. She felt her way through the argument, trying to understand why they had gotten such a mess going in the first place. How she had become a hybrid person next to this ranch woman. Why her attitude was "pets," not "animals." She had read something recently and the latest coinage of their predicament excited her.

"We're situational neurotics," she said, knowing the ranch woman would frown on analyzing a thing this way. She would either do something about something or not do something. There would be no time to figure and consider and feel out *why* or whether it was right. She continued, "That means if we changed our situation, like getting rid of the cats, our frustration would disappear and we could change. Some people cannot change, even if the situation changes..."

He said; "It's all that blood and fur, all those flies, all that kibble..."

She said, "Why do we keep animals the way we do in America today... why do we want to treat them like people?... is it because we feel sorry that they are animals and not human. Is that why we give them their rights, let them into the house, feed them the same food we eat, see to their every need and comfort?" She remembered. feeling strange one day while watching the horse roll on the ground to coat his back with dirt and protect himself from the heat and insects. It struck her odd at that particular moment and she could not accept the difference between herself in the house with cold cream and the horse outside with flies. She was amazed, sorry, scared that they were so alike and so different.

He said., "Back on the farm, animals are useful. They earn their keep..."

She said, "There's something to be said for having an animal for aesthetics. A spiritual reason. An experiment in perversion. An awareness of another creature for what it is. Function isn't everything. The cats make me feel good... sometimes..."

"Only one of them hunts," he said,... "Or it used to before it got fat and lazy. Now all it does is bring the gopher to the front porch and leave gopher guts all over the mat..."

"Primitive people sleep with their animals..."

"That's practicality, not sentimentality. They eat them the next day too..."

"Peasants let them into their houses in the winter..."

"Not out of love...The old cow would freeze in the night and they wouldn't get to milk her if they left her out in the snow...."

"Egyptians. loved cats...."

"They had slaves to take care or them, too..."

They countered eachother's comments for twenty miles until they were back home again where the four cats were waiting for them, perched around the yard, the dog lay on his belly on the door mat. Inside, three rats in three different cages gnawed and chewed and generally consumed and destroyed whatever entered their wood chip nests. A hamster slept by day in the bathroom in a cage and ran in a wheel all night. Bags of cat and dog kibble, horse pellets, and boxes of rodent mix were tucked away wherever they would fit, out of sight.

"Pleasure," she said, as she got out of the car.

"Pleasure isn't enough," he said, "Animals have to serve some purpose." He was distorted around the eyes and mouth. His face was worked up to look like a painting of Judas in anguish after selling his soul for foolishness...

"Then *kill* them," she shouted, "and see if we are like that woman." The cats raced into the house with high pitched meows. They were hungry. "After they're gone, after we have gotten rid of all the useless, furry hungry things in our lives, after all the fur and shit is gone, all the time and considerations is passed, after silence and absence, then what? Will we be any different? Will we become sensible ranch people? I know that I will be exactly the same with or without the cats."

"That's the tragedy," he said, almost in a whisper, looking at her as if she too, was an animal that had gotten away with too much, never trained to obey or perform properly, kept not for a useful purpose, but as an act of kindness and decency. All that rhetoric pouring out of her mouth like so much shit that had to be cleaned up day and night. He sighed while she opened a package of pork melts for the cats.

# The Math Major

I wanted to go home. Here we were again eating out, not any different from the lonely singles hanging around night life. Lonely doubles. Married. Going on eighteen years. It wasn't that we hadn't developed interests. I watched Alex eat. He never concealed hunger. Neither did I. I had already swallowed my steak, baked potato, beans, salad, and french bread with a lot of butter and sour cream. Now I sat back and stared ahead at the people, or glanced at Alex. Once I decided to really watch him. I looked at his eager chewing, his eyes that saw only taste. I pressed my sore finger on my glass of ice water. And took a drink. He was okay. He had a right to be the way he was. To chew hungrily. But I wanted to be somewhere else. Gone. Without being in hearing distance or sight.

A big group of night-clubbers come in and take a table near us. Three couples. I am estimating: old, fat, slicked-up. Still trying hard. Pathetic, but okay. Why not. Why fade away and die? It's okay. The hags and old farts. I view the women's soft clingy dresses, gathered at the guts, loosely, with tie strings. I take note of their men. Polyester plaid slacks, navy blue jackets, ties with stripes. Stoops, pots. But even so the one with the white hair takes my attention. It's funny how high his pot belly is. More a barrel chest. No belly. He's probably younger than I am. Just a bloat up above and those long skinny legs dangling down. He's still firm-bodied. Not as old as he looks. Kind of youngish, actually. This old man, to have a high solid gut. And he's familiar. That face disguised behind old age. Squinty Hemingway eyes, cheek bones. A wide sunburnt face. I begin to watch him more closely. *I know him!* It occurs to me that I dated him twenty years ago. It's Bill Boggs!

I, at once, review the woman he's with. Her soft belly hidden under mauve double knit jersey. Expensive. Hides a multitude of sin. He used to talk about liking to use his straight A mathematical brain on pulling off the perfect crime. He was a practical joker, too. It all begins to come back. I wore a pink satin dress. We went to a movie I suppressed gas all evening, until my stomach crashed and fell. It was a dress I had sewn a long curving green satin stem onto from shoulder to hem, and pinned three bursting pink roses, spacing them. He liked breasts. Big boobs fascinated him. My sister had huge ones. I didn't. Not like hers. He used to stare at her when he came over. She was a freshman in high school, I a freshman at college. He was a junior at the university. A math major. I had heard that he had become a nuclear physicist.

As I watched him guffaw at his table I was reminded of a used car salesman. Slicked up on a night out. A wad of bills in his pocket. I look at his wife's old buoyed up boobs. Her dark hair and mediterranean features. Some society woman? So he married a cute little thing. With legs like toothpicks beneath that hem, pillaring up to all that post-birth-giving softness that never snapped back. She's all those girls he followed around on the beach. I cannot take my eyes off of her and then off Bill. Seeing myself back then. And why he didn't choose me. I thought I was in love with him. It was the first time I had ever said, "I love you." And the last. He never asked me out again. I had "loved" him because he was exactly what I had always wanted in a "boy," He, mainly, was a contemporary of my brilliant brothers. He and they were in the same classes, making the same grades. He would joke about their brains and honesty. They were in earnest....

They had no money; they got by on their brains. He had money. He just happened to be brilliant on top of it. He got a kick out of poor boys being as smart as he was. He always came over to visit them and joke around. He asked me out because I was there. I liked the way he joked, his brains, his Hemingway face. His long skinny legs. I didn't like it when he said he'd like to pull off the perfect crime. It made him shallow to me. My brothers were doing serious things with their brains. It's as if his mathematical mind was wasted on him. He had no *pain*. No searching. No straining forward. He eased into college and cruised by and sailed into nuclear physics. He never could understand why I was shy and moody. He didn't care. He wanted a good-time girl. This wife is a good-time girl. She tucks a hankie in his coat pocket, now, flash and splash style. And everyone around the table is focused on it, on Bill. The main personality. They get a big kick when Bill feigns sneezing Dopey fashion and blowing his nose, then cleaning his ears, and even lifting one leg, about to wipe his ass. Yeah. It's got to be Bill. That's his kind of humor.

Alex is ready to go. After such a big meal, he is sleepy, has been nodding off on his side of the table. He looks at me, as I watch Bill. "Ready," he asks. "No," I say. "I want to stay longer." The musicians have come in and set up, plugging in their guitars and piano. "I want to dance," I tell Alex.

"What?" He is confused. "I thought you said you were bored. Tired?"

I lean forward to tell him that I have discovered someone I used to know. Alex strains his ears. The place is noisy and I am force to shout it too loudly. "At that table over there... I think that's Bill B... remember just before you started taking me out... the math major...?" He rears back in a knowing nod and glances over. Then he frowns. He looks right into my eyes, wide awake. I smile, feeling silly. And whisper again, "I just want to watch him awhile. I'm fascinated. It's amazing. That old guy with white hair. I want to stay." Alex slumps down. He grimaces to show disapproval. I ignore him. I haven't been this interested in anything for a long time. I am not bored. The music plays. Bill and his table get up to dance. It's Bill. I'm positive. That's the way he would dance. Lazy. A joke on the woman. He stands in one place and she does all the work. His little dark-haired soft-bodied wife is all over the floor, sweating and staggering, while he pivots on one foot and positions her here and there with an extended hand. A big wide smile across his face. The court jester.

When they have exhausted themselves I tell Alex that I want to dance. I am feeling very thin. Very brown-haired. Very triumphant. The men at Bill's table have been glancing at me. I am imagining that I am attractive. Bill has even turned around, wheeling, in mid-mirth and focused right on my face, stopped laughing and momentarily registers me in his scotch and water brain. Was it my face that struck him or recognition of the past.

Alex holds me in his arms, wrapping them all the way around, I am so slim. I am a little lithe slip of a thing as we step around the small slick dance floor. And strong-legged. I am so strong and healthy. I can see Bill looking up at us from his table.

Alex laughs, "You're stiff as a board," he says with chuckles, knowing what I am doing. I am rendered foolish. *Of course I am not looking so good. He is sorry he married her instead of me. I am not showing anyone,* is at the back of my mind, but still I prance and step around in front of their table. Even his wife is gazing upon me. My legs are not supple. Alex cinches a new hold on my rigid posture. My perfect slenderness I am showing off to Bill B. Alex is slightly humored and annoyed at the same time. Mostly sleepy. A big meal. A drink or two. "Let's go home," he says again.

I persist, "No."

He teases, "Go, Baby, go." I squeal in protest. Muffling it against his shoulder.

We laugh. We feign being in love. Being happy. He shows Bill, too.

Bill the big math major. I have mentioned it over the years. Alex had never met him. It was a threat. Now he sees the white hair, the slick shark manner, the slapstick, the pot-belly, the salesman loud talk and laugh. The soft wife. The crony friends. "You're lucky you married me," he whispers in my ear. I agree, but do not like ruining an image from the past in Alex's eyes. "Is that him?" being a blatant surprise in eyes. "You thought that was great?"

At home that night, after Alex is in bed, I go to the telephone book and look up Bill's address. Montecito. Of course. I knew it.

# The Picnic 2

We spent so much at the store. It cost about thirty-eight dollars apiece and we dumped it all out on the grass on a blanket and squatted around, our crotches pressed right up under our (and eachother's) noses, and selected these unhealthy items. And ate them. Just because we wanted to "have a picnic." It sounded good. We must have had old-fashioned pictures in our minds. Of deviled eggs, potato salad with sliced eggs and paprika on top, little hand-made goodies, and a big chocolate, thick-frostinged cake, which everyone would have said was a shame to cut because it was so pretty. We planned the picnic with some ideas from the past, or from novels in mind, but in fact it was a grimy affair: all the ingredients on the ground. All of us on the ground. Knees popping and breasts drooping and faces hanging, and the men standing above us, refusing to sit on the ground, and holding heavy store-bought salad and hot dogs on lightweight paper plates. Alex finally saying, "They make these plates thinner every year," and testing the corrugated paper between forefinger and thumb. While I kept watching Suzi. Trying to get in on her affair. To be a part of it. She was all excited now. So different from before. Her eyes a wild, crazy California blue, and all that creamy make-up I imagined getting all over the pillow later in his apartment.

Creamy-skinned and desperate-eyed and her mouth so pooched and puckered and silvered. She was all sex. All forty year old sex and how it's done while you have a family picnic. She was all discrimination and secret-packed, and wearing no bra. New fullness at the breasts, but even though, her nipples jutting up, and the lower curve swinging heavy without support. We had laughed before (before her affair, when she was still innocent-eyed, mother and wifey-eyed) about our nipples. "In these T-shirts, ha, ha, you've got to go like this, and get them both pointing in the same direction, ha, ha." Two soggy-breasted mothers with pre-adolescent kids laughing loudest at themselves. Not being at fault. Laughing at nature. Nature did it—not me, was the joke. The nature of the breast after awhile. Oh, these plump days, and now, ha, ha.... but now Suzi is plump again and well pumped up with sex. Her lover must be a lover indeed, to make her look so good.

As I eat chicken and turkey and beef franks, and pale store-bought cream-filled cookies (Ah, how sickening in hindsight) and smear mayonnaise and mustard across white puffy buns (white death), I keep looking toward Suzi to "tell me, tell me what's going on with you.... what's it like." But our husbands soar above us, perching plates upon their volleyball-exercised fingertips, owning us, supervising, keeping watch, pressing down with tennis shoes. Rex behind Suzi, Alex behind me. They fork in bites of manufactured food with tiny plastic implements, sometimes missing their mouths and dropping marshmallows on the lawn, and making droll statements about their wives. Their wives, *we*, have become the focus of their attention for the first time. Ever since we stopped caring to please. As soon as we got interested in something else. Now the men can't leave us alone. They watch us, face in our direction, turn like shadows on the sundial. Curious. What will she do next.

Suzi called me twice last week and said, "Will you cover for me tonight?"

I said yes, yes, urgently, confused.

"OK," she said. "We're at a movie tonight, Okay?"

Yes, yes, I was all agreement. But I didn't know what she meant. "But we're not actually going?" I asked.

She ranted. "Oh, you're hopeless, impossible, ha, ha." Then again she tutors me. "If Bob calls later, or anyone, you and I went to a movie tonight, got it?"

"OK,!" I say, feeling not very good about it. She hangs up in a roar of laughter, like revving her engine, digging out, spinning her tires. I can see her squealing her sprattled Cadillac wheels all the way to Goleta, where I'm sure he is waiting: her lover. Some guy from the art department. I try to visualize him.

"He's young," she said.

*Of course,* I thought.

'Who needs an old lover. Not an old woman for sure. Old lovers are for the young women. They can take it. An old woman can't take anymore oldness. She's got enough of her own to deal with. It's a law of physics, a balance of nature."

And Suzi is so naïve. Believing her lover's youth is unusual. I want to say, *It's as common as the sun coming up. You're right on schedule: forty, a young man comes along, he makes you feel the staleness of your old marriage. Come on, didn't you know that already?*

She is so excited among the plastic utensils, soda pop, potato chips. And I am such a voyeur, while our teenage children call, "Come on Mom, let's play volleyball, stop talking, hurry up, Dad's waiting...."

# Fall?

She woke up with a headache and did not open the curtains when she got out of bed. The open, loose, on and on way about the outdoors crept around her shoulders and she kept it off with closed curtains and snuggled into a chair after making black coffee. The dream was still fresh in her mind, swimming around and coloring her thoughts. The dream had ended just like the day before had ended, incomplete, not finished and not polished, leaving her disappointed in the way she was. And that day had ended with nothing to do but to sleep off the way she was and cleanse herself of it so she would wake up and begin again on a new morning and be different. To be better. To be what she had not been able to be yet.

It was very simple what she wanted: simply to be what she was; and to stop clowning around and avoiding it, She laughed too much and smiled too much and got angry too much and got sad too much. All evasions. Nothing was ever that funny or that sad or that bad. It was all nervous, staccatoed reactions that rumbled her diaphragm and kept her appearing responsive when she was really not feeling responsive. She was really bored with most things, the staleness and the familiarity and the commonness of most things. She had not felt or done or thought anything new for so long that she could not remember when. She was used to everything. Even her attempt to gather new things had become old. And the small new things that she could gather, mostly ideas in books grew stale fast in her mind as soon as she let them in and made them hers. They became as homely as the rest of her thinking.

New ideas laid against her old brain like fresh little snowflakes with fine intricate patterns, each pattern unique and different from the last, and melted on the dry hot barren convolutions and evaporated. Yet she longed for newness in any form with a blind and mute probing. In the form of these books which were wasted on her, or in the form of new sights, sounds, things to do, see, feel. New people, new places, new ways to be, new anything, But there was no more newness; and had been no newnesses for a long time, Any new thing became suddenly as dissipated as the snowflake ideas against her dry arid inner self. She always knew what it would turn out to be or mean or what someone would say or do. To her. For her. And it was never much. She was left alone with the oldness of herself, and the headache in the morning and the no desire to let in the new day. A day that was waiting outside the curtains, but a day that would repeat another day and bring nothing to her, nothing of change, nothing to make her new.

The fright of living as a rancid thing with no fresh source flowing into her caused her eyes to crease down with annoyance. That such a thing could happen and did happen struck her as a violation. She had known people who were dull because of their private stagnations. They had moss clinging to the banks of their minds and hearts and souls and to every fiber of their bodies. And little pollywog things to say that slid and wriggled and oozed around in heavy sludge and fed off the moss. People who, before they spoke or acted, would say and do predictable things, because of the little swamps they cultured. And now she herself was becoming one of these soupy pools that fed off itself and spawned useless thoughts like creatures that go nowhere, are always wet, and ridden with gnarls and warts, and are metamorphizing into off-shades of greens and greys and browns. Never bold. Creatures that have voracious appetites for small readily haveable stuff that grows along the edges and never goes beyond those edges into fresh places or swift currents.

It worried her. Her head pounded. And all morning she let the new idea of not experiencing anything new torment her. She refused to accept any newness that would turn old, even the new sunshine that crawled along the lawn with tentacles, lighting up all the shadows of the night. She did not want to make it hers and see it grow dim.

In her fear of staleness she was drawn to the stale and old. She opened up the wicker trunk and lifted out album after album of old pictures and searched the faces of herself and of everyone back then. She wanted to see when it had happened. When had things started being old. She saw all the newness they had had once. New babies. New clothes. New smiles. New hair styles. New ideas. Big ideas. New big ideas All grinning senselessly. Holding their shoulders back, doing the whole act. Wearing all the costumes, And then she saw it. It was there in that one.

The red hot confidence she had had once that had sealed her mind closed like home-canned peaches. Summer confidence. Not knowing about where she would be now confidence. Not wanting anything except to preserve summer peaches confidence. Not believing summer would ever be over confidence. It had closed her. mind and she was infected with botulism. Mental botulism.

She was airtight and deadly because of the poison she carried. Poison to anyone else and poison to herself. The slime of the rot that was taking place would slowly eat itself up until there was nothing but a hollow dried crusty emptiness. And then a void.

She closed the books and figured she was still in the simple first stages of going sour. But she knew the spoilage would take her to the last stage and leave her unoccupied. She would be vacant. She pulled the curtains and squinted at the new rays of sun as they crept across her lawn.

The cleansing therapeutic rays of the sun's light.

It was Fall. The rays would be weaker than in the summer.

# Three Things that Have Happened Today and It's Only 9 AM

(1) Alex lies reading about the universe. I have just awakened and turn my face to see where he is. He lies on his stomach. We are still in bed under the covers. The goose-necked lamp is on, on the desk beside the bed and yellow light pours down on Alex's yellow hair.

Outside, beyond the window, the day is full of white bright sunshine. Beside me, in bed, all this warm golden glow is going on, and I let my hand touch it. I lay my palm on his soft curls, under the flood of electric light, and he turns to see me. Our faces seek one another wherever they are. I say, "What are you reading."

"A book," he smiles. Our voices come out soft and new because it is early and our energy lies in wait. Unaroused. "Of course," I say, " a book, but what book, I mean."

"*Science News*," he murmurs. "About the universe." A space of silence between us, and then he says, "We're so insignificant. So small. It makes me feel good."

Earlier, or did I dream it, he was awake before I, and leaned against me saying to love him, that he needed my love. He groaned about what was going to become of us. "I've got to get courage again. I've got to believe everything's going to be alright. The children, what will become of them. How will they get along... what will we do without them, now that they are growing up and about to leave...." I roll over under the warmth of the blankets. Newly awakened, I hold him. Was it a dream or did he say that as I slept. And now he is happy that we are a speck in space.

(2) The lateness of the morning, the longness of the bright blue sky. I missed the beginning again. The day began without me. I get up in a rush to make up for it. To catch it. I have calls to make. Business to attend. I go to the phone in the front room and see that my phone book has been left open and on one blank page, in pencil, is slashed out: "I hate my mother." I know it is the oldest daughter. She does that sort of thing when she's mad. Writes it somewhere. I raise my voice. Without anger. Just to catch any ears within hearing behind walls, in other rooms. "Who wrote this?"

"I did. You make me so mad sometimes." It is her. Once I found a note to God in her room. It was about how much she loved him when she was younger.

I say, "Well, erase it now. What if someone else goes through this book..."

Silence. Then, "Well, it's your fault. You make me so mad... you erase it."

(3) The other daughter appears. Her big blonde face is right up next to me looking in. We are face to face and she is saying, "Remember when I wanted you to get some fever blister medicine, that special kind that prevents fever blisters, and you didn't? Now look. A fever blister. Thanks a lot." I see a bluish welling on her bottom lip. "You've been driving all over, why didn't you get it yourself?" I am still undisturbed.

I go back to the bedroom to get dressed. I stand naked in front of the big mirror which has leaned against the bedroom wall for seventeen years. I pose like one of the muscle ladies on TV the night before. Alex saw them, too. I say, "Look." Alex looks. "I could probably take a few classes and get a certificate in body building. When the kids leave and you not yet disabled, I could work in an old age home and teach physical fitness. Like that lady on TV." I recount to Alex the one in the news. She had a little haircut. They all sat there in their wheelchairs and did exercises with their arms. "She'd call out instructions. They had to think, right, left, plus it was good for circulation... .Even when we're old, I could do that... Look." I pose again. Alex says, "You've stayed in good shape. He more than looks. He gazes. He gazes at how important I am making it. I turn and strike other muscle poses in jest. "I do look good, don't I?" I ripple my stomach muscles, flex my chest, tighten my leg muscles, and arms. "It's proportions. If you're laid out in good proportion." I suck in my stomach until my ribs stand alone. I turn. He views, studies from all angles. I watch the mirror, surprised. I grow more enthusiastic. "You know, it makes me feel good to look like this. You know? When I feel maybe nothing is going to work out, that everything's not going to be OK, all I have to do is to take off all my clothes and see that I'm okay. It makes me feel good. Do you see what I mean?" I look at Alex who is propped up on one elbow and still has his reading glasses on, holding one page of *Science News* in mid-turn. He nods.

"I mean, what if I took off my clothes and saw horrible things. Big gouges and scars. What if there were gross deformities? Oh, I couldn't take it. It makes me feel safe to see that I'm strong and normal. Naked. When I see how I am underneath everything else."

The daughters come in, in a rush. "Oh, sick," one says, as she glances at my nudity.

"Well, get out of my room if you can't stand to see it," I say.

"It's scary," says the other, "to see what I might look like someday, uh."

"Get out. It's my room. I can be naked in my own room…" I yell.

There is laughter. Tee, hee, tee, hee....

Alex laughs too. He says maybe I should put on my clothes.

"Not in my own room," I shout. "You don't know how good I look." I am yelling so my voice carries into the other rooms. And then I get dressed. I will look again later when I need to. When no one else is looking.

# *Every Day It Starts Again*

The coffee, the anger, all the animals and people. All the hunger. And later, in the evening, the run. And then an effort at fun. Maybe some wine. But it doesn't work. The wine won't take. I get a headache. I can't drink. I get sick. Throw up. The room spins. My body fights it. As if it says I can't go away. I have to stay. And face it. I'm forced to pay attention. To be present.

That is the worse part. There are no escapes. I used to be able to go out for coffee in the morning. I could waste half a day drinking coffee and avoiding myself. And half the night. Now I drink a cup and my head spins off. The top of it takes off. I get the shakes. And feel crazy. My mother said, "You have such a thin system now. You have no fat to absorb any poison."

For some reason it matters what my mother says. I like her to know. Alex is unable to understand my smallness and how little I can consume, and how much I am affected by it.

I keep wanting to know the meaning of it. The message. From my mute and present flesh. Why does it refuse impurities now, when before I could poison myself and it didn't care. It took it all in. Anything. Everyone blares out, "You're getting old. That's what happens. Your body can't take it, har, har." (The coarsest form of laughter here, worse than over dirty jokes.) As they, the same age or older, are abusing themselves and taking it, getting away with it.

Every morning I try again; there is no other way. I can't change to fruit juice. I think of the mourning cloak caterpillar. It is instinct to crawl in one direction. Once it starts there is no diverting it. It goes straight. Some come to a wall, keep going (but up now) and find an eave to hang from. A cocoon forms, and there is metamorphosis. Too many go straight into their deaths caused by things too big to understand, and there is no ability in them to turn right or left.

Yesterday I tried to break out. I said, "Let's get outta here," to Alex. We went downtown and saw all the people walking around. It made us feel better already. People dressed up going here and there. All the hustle and bustle brought life into us again. Then I thought I'd sneak in my poison. I ordered coffee.

Alex said, "I don't know how you do it." I was defensive; "It wasn't that much..." My head took off. We walked up and down and looked at everyone. And I was light-headed. Alex tried on clothes. He is at my mercy. I tell him if it looks good or bad. He sweats inside a tiny dressing room and comes out each time to my knitted brows. "No, that's not right?"

Nothing will ever be right. He is not The One anymore. Like coffee and wine. Even men. A man doesn't do it. How I hate to sit before a new man and have him say I am beautiful and he wants me and will give me things I want. Even things that I need. I always secretly hold back, "If you knew how little you mean to me now, you men."

When my cup of poison is empty I grow lonely. Left. I cannot reach out to my portion. Of comfort. That is the beginning: I go fill it again. Bring it steaming to my place. And I am safe for awhile. It is there. I draw from it. Even though my head is being pulled off to one side. until the top breaks loose and the contents are spilled out into a stream which flows toward the center of the room. A tugging current toward the skylights ... while all the hungry animals, especially that hungry dog circles the house, popping his frailty into every window, beckoning me: feed me, feed me, feed me....

I eat in front of the dog. I wolf down dead meat pressed between two pieces of bread. Carrion. I let the dog see my hunger. I make him watch my appetite and the way I appease it. Ravenous. Starving. "You are not the only one," I say to him this way. It's the way he believes I control the food, handle it, *have* it, and dole it out, that I get all I want. That I allow myself to have all I want.

The dog anticipates sharing. He waits. Stays alert. He is sure that I will share. Today I eat it all. And say, "Go Home."

I am confused about the future. How long can I feed a dog? When will it end? How will it end? The thought of throwing scraps to that waiting hunger, into the future, without an end in sight. A known end. I want someone to tell me, *It will last until Spring or next winter or Jan. 6th. And then it will end.*

I need to know when I will be finished with feeding this eager dog—out there and inside me.

*Eating cuticles and drinking coffee this morning. Because Alex towered over her in his big uniform (even with his hat on) and was angry.*

# The Gift

Mama gives me a stainless steel salad maker with a myriad of blades and a handle that goes around. She says, "You can make a whole salad in fifteen minutes and save your knuckles. All that cutting will give you arthritis some day." It is an expensive gadget, and sits on my sinkboard like a three-legged moon-walker, taking up room, glistening and reflecting. Brand new and shiny clean. Mama has always tried to get me to take care of myself. She has said over the seventeen year marriage I've had, "You're working too hard. You're wearing yourself out. Go out to dinner.

Enjoy life. The ladies I sit for pamper themselves. Hair dressers, health spas, out to brunch, lunch, dinner. They hire everything done. You've turned into a workhorse for Alex. Why doesn't he see that and take better care of you. Most husbands wouldn't let their wives do the jobs you do, all that weeding, mowing, helping him lift wheel barrows of cement, scrubbing. Why, most men are proud to hire window washers and save their wives' hands. Look at your poor hands. You can afford help." (Alex's mother has been heard saying the same thing, but in defense of Alex, against me.) Our mothers being the only ones to notice the signs of wear and tear on the flesh of their full-grown and married offspring, and to care.

The pride Mama took in my youth and beauty once. "Miss America" she called me from her socio-economic view point. It was her contribution to the American scene. "My Miss American Beauty Rose."

All that kind of flair. I was her first daughter, after two dark-eyed sons. And I was blue-eyed and fair skinned like my father.

Born with blonde ringlets. She'd kiss the little golden curls at the back of my pink baby neck back then, and wet them, with water and wrap them around her hard-worked, washboard, young-mother fingers... She saw me as a grown up lady one day, in fine clothes, good manners, my thoughts on elevated things. A wonderful man for a husband. A gentleman. Who treated me right. She moves the salad maker over to the counter and says, "Let me show you how easy it is to cut up cucumbers." I get a cucumber out and she fiddles around the cutter, adjusting blades. I do not look. Cannot look.

In fact, my vision blurs and I see only a crumb that is stuck to the stove. Very clearly I focus on this crumb and I feel sick, kind of wounded. A hard and stiff piece of oatmeal adhered to the side of the stove. For a moment my whole life is there. in that.

The gadget wears on me, appearing too complex, too involved. I say, "I like cutting things by hand. I don't want to make a salad in fifteen minutes. Really, Mama, even though it is a beautiful instrument and I thank you for the thought." She turns the handle and holds the cucumber and little slices begin to fall into a bowl she has placed at the opening. They are so thin they fold over and pile up in a heap of cucumber material. The pungent fresh sugarless odor of cucumber fills the kitchen air. Suddenly Mama cries out a little, stops turning and puts her finger in her mouth. It is the hand she adjusted the cucumber with. "You have to be careful to hold the shield down when you come to the end of the cucumber," she says; and I see she is bleeding at the end of her index finger. "Oh, Mama," I say. I hate to see my mother hurt.

I cannot bear it. She is so injurable that it makes me turn away.

She has brought me a bladed gift and is so proud of it and gets cut on it. It is too much. I don't want to know that. Cannot bear to acknowledge it. The cut is shallow, however, and she is soon past it and on to cutting up cabbage. She makes a whole slaw and then mixes up her jar of dressing, using sweet pickle juice and mayonnaise, adding garlic and onions. Onions are in almost everything she prepares. Onion sandwiches are her old standby remedy for any ailment. Onions and oranges were her cure for any of our childhood sicknesses (which were few, colds or flu) and I hated onions back then. "They sting," I protested.

"Okay, have a snotty nose, then," she'd say in her way of showing what my choice would result in. I am remembering that she didn't baby me then. There were no salad makers back then. She never hired anything done. She worked her beauty right out of herself. Her legs broke out in varicose veins, hands and arms got like a man's with muscle and vein. She worked for her home and family until she dropped in bed at night.

I tell her now, "You keep it, Mama. I won't use it that much. You know how I am about machines..." She looks disappointed.

Did she picture me gathering around with my family when she bought it, our eyes all glittering with curiosity and interest in this brand new invention, like a Norman Rockwell painting?

I try to show enthusiasm, but truly cannot get any for the cutter. I wish, instead that she hadn't spent the money, hadn't noticed I was getting worn out, and tried to help, needed help, didn't believe that a cutter would help me. Her solutions are always straightforward, even though this is the last thing I need. What I really need is everything else but a cutter. After all her effort, spending, care, this cutter will only be in the way. In MY way. What I need is for nothing to be in my way anymore. No more clutter. No more stuff I'll have to think about. I need lots of cleared space and only what I want to think about in it. The cutter sits there, taking up space and calling out to me to use it. Apply some thought to learning to turn all the blades and cut up vegetables. I don't want to make a fast salad.

I like to let my hands work and think about other things. It takes no thought to slice tomatoes, cry over peeling onions. It leaves my mind alone. My hands know what to do.

"You and Alex need to eat more salad. It'll save your health," she says. She is bobbing beneath me, my little helper mother. Her dark eyes dancing with joy, encouragement. Trying to get me to believe in the cutter. Teaching me how easy it is to live. I don't need to put out so much effort. My life could be easy instead.

I see it all there in her face. Her hope for my happiness. Just let her show me how. So I accept the salad maker. I smile and wipe at its beautiful expensive surfaces. "How much did it cost, Mama?" I ask to make her know I am aware of her large investment.

It makes her nervous. Now I can see that it cost more than she knew was sensible. That she went way out over what she could afford.

And I am standing there not wanting her to be out anything for my health. For it to cost her anything. She's already worked too hard for anything she's ever had. I coax her to tell me. She always tells me what things cost. She likes to show me that she can easily spend twenty or forty now, not like the olden days when that was a fortune. She is not telling me. Holds out, turns to the cutter and busies herself with it. "Mama, what did you pay for this thing?"

I raise my voice, sorry now; that she would get in debt over something like this. "Oh, Honey," she says... "Your health means more than money... save money and lose your life...."

"Just tell me," I persist. She is fussing around, trying to avoid the issue, afraid she'll be caught throwing money away, in someone else's eyes, finally she admits, "Plenty," looking down, "but I'm working now...the first payment isn't due until the first of the month."

"Oh, Mama... take it back, please. I really won't...." I taper off. She looks too downcast. Her gift falling through. "Your family will appreciate it."

I say, "Well, the kids will love using it. Rachael loves salad. We all do, And the kids like gadgets. They'll have fun. Thanks, Mama, really." I hug her. She is so short. With such a bosom. She smiles her sweet smile, The one when we praise her. She is so like a little girl. She feels pleased doing something about my life. She needs to believe she can help me. It makes her happy to think so.

# Conflict

She, unable to change a single thing, to chop at a plant, watches Alex slashing this way and that to rid themselves of vines. Of being choked. Her voice, pleading, threatening, *don't kill them.* Save their bougainvillea, save the double hibiscus, save the religious tree, with its drooping white flowers, save the mint, save the geraniums., and nasturtiums, save the loquat tree. Alex with shears, hunched over in fiend posture, looking for thin trunks, making clipping noises, branches and whole trees falling, piles of greenery lying on the ground. Fright and worry in her eyes about the crime he is committing against living things. What grows being sacred.

Their mothers in different towns living different lives. His, with bonsai trees in little pots along the windows, torturing them with strings and wires, weights and subsistence diets. Hers, with African violets chasing her out of the kitchen, blocking all the light of one window, sucking up water and Black Magic and demanding more. His, looking sternly at her Bonsai with a pruning clippers in her hand, contemplating no-nonsense and what she wants next, which contortion, which act of obedience she can instill. Hers, looking meekly, proudly at the abundance of African violet, wondering what it wants of her, asking it and giving it another helping, moving pots and pans out of its way.

Alex has cut down everything she has ever planted. He has wheeled their limbs away in the barrow to a mulch heap by the Sears grater. She fondles packets of seeds from the window, watching him, twitching with sorrow and anger.

# The Trip

She keeps reminding herself that she is not going on a trip for fun. That this trip is serious. A trip she might never come back from. She glances now and then at the bus driver and attributes kindliness to him, a new temporary male substitute taking her somewhere the way all men in her life have driven while she was the passenger. In her head is *a plan*: To get a car, a cheap car somewhere, and drive back and live in it. The ease with which the bus knows its way. It occurs to her that she is no longer covered by anything. She has no comprehensive coverage in case of sickness or death. She cheers silently. *Hooray. They can leave me in the street and let the flies buzz around.* Out the bus window she sees some Mexicans standing around the flame at Taco Bell the way the Indians stood two hundred years ago around their adobe ovens baking cornmeal bread. She is drunk with the only thing she has left: a sneer and her interpretation of what she sees.

She is going away as if she has enough time to make a change. As if time will not make its own changes for her, for them. For Alex and her. In time. They will change, trying not to change, and at last they will be gone. But, she rides the bus anyway, for five hundred miles, pretending it will make a change in her life. And later, when she is old, she will shudder at her recklessness, in not maintaining what she had before all the changes took place and destroyed it all anyway. She will ask herself why she didn't try to preserve this delicate thing that was only temporary at best.... The bus comes to an obscure depot and she gazes out the window at the dismal Greyhound facilities and sees the sputum and shit and puke on the sidewalks as symbols of her predicament. She knows the difference: that if she were in love and not running away, the same sidewalk would shine and all the ugliness would come to her as rich colors.

A yellow cock pecks by the side of the road. She gets a vision of herself preparing a meal for Alex and inviting him over to eat at her apartment. It keeps flashing on, the way it would go; all done on her own money because she lands a good job and draws maybe seven hundred a month. She sees him filing in, impressed. She is wearing a striped sweater. White and red-brown stripes, and has a bicycle parked and locked out by her front door. She looks well-kept. He is alarmed at how well she is doing without him.

A cat runs across the street in front of the bus and into the yard of a wood frame white house. It is like her childhood house. She could go inside it and know all about it. Every oddball shelf hammered up in corners of the bathroom and kitchen to hold junk. The woodwork smeared, painted over and smeared again. She looks at the little house and sees herself. It is so familiar. A thought comes to her about the house but drifts back before she can catch it, yet leaves its impression: shame. Shame brings guilt and guilt lets her know that she fears punishment for jumping on the bus and getting away. It plays on her for awhile and is finally allayed by imagining crashing and being killed in the snow on the ridge route. That will be her punishment. It would be suitable. She worries until the worry is replaced by the thought that the bus driver does not plan on being killed. He will take all precautions. He does not want to die. She watches the back of his head and it reassures her.

Her main concern before buying a ticket was to buy a tooth brush. She could not start a new life with false teeth. She must preserve her teeth above everything else. She reaches inside her purse to make sure that her tooth brush is still there. She wants to get up now and make her way to the back of the bus and into the small closet toilet and brush her teeth just to make sure that they are not beginning to rot out.

With the smell of exhaust and the motion of lunging, the bus pulls up at the end of its route for her bus driver. She had not planned on his being replaced. He glances at her and tells her that another bus will be along in awhile and to go in out of the wind. He points to a coffee shop across the street. She thanks him, absorbing his momentary concern, and makes her way without looking back, across the highway to the coffee shop. She believes in the evils of the world so strongly and fears its indifference and the way people can be "out on the road where no one can see what they do, where they do not have to account for themselves" that, as she enters the coffee shop and sees a waitress going down on her knees in a booth to wipe the table, she believes the woman is doing lascivious deeds to the cruel-looking customer waiting for his dinner.

She takes a stool along the crook of the counter where her back is to the wall, facing everyone. She faces a man who is eating the dinner special. He manipulates a large potato and gets it into his mouth, piece by piece. She is glad for him, that he has a big baked potato. She wants to cry over there being a hot healthy potato for him out here where no one cares if he gets one or not. The waitress brings her coffee and calls her Honey. A jukebox is playing and the waitress moves her lips to the song and does dance steps behind the counter as she writes out slips. A large black man gets up to pay his bill. He stands by the cash register and reaches in his pocket for money. There is a bunch of keys on his belt. She sees him going from door to door, being in charge of all those doors. The coffee tastes dull on her tongue. She wants to run back and plead: *Please let me back in, it's so ugly out here.* She catches reflections in the windows of all the real objects sitting around the cafe, and wonders if that is the way she thinks. The real things and then reflections of the real things.

She picks calluses from her palms. She has been picking at the calluses for two hundred miles. Calluses worn by working with Alex, using a shovel, a wheelbarrow. His last words, as she got away from his anger, were *You don't know what hard work is.*

She moves along in a pitch-black bus in a pitch-black night and she cannot picture Mojave on the map. It is as if she is nowhere.

You can't go home at thirty-five. It means your mother has failed. But she trudges in the snow after pushing toward *Mama* on the Greyhound all night. Her mother's house is a mile from the bus depot. It is snowing all the way. She is confused, flushed by the crispness of the falling snow, a little exhilarated by the walk, hoping her mother is home, wondering how she will thaw out her ears and nose and feet and hands if she is not home, but loving the threat of the cold. Freezing to death by her mother's house is better than dying in the yard with Alex. The snot on her face is in icicles when she knocks on her mother's door. As if by a miracle her mother appears. Big, warm, the same. Always the same. Her mother can't believe her eyes, but she knows without explanation, everything. She even laughs about it. Throws open her mouth and thinks it is comical that her daughter is covered with snow, in tennis shoes and cotton shirt, and is too frozen to laugh with her, with a mouth too stiff even to smile. They go into the kitchen where the oven and two burners are on to warm that part of the house, and where there is a little naked cornish game hen laying out ready to be dressed and baked. It is all so pretty and tidy and ready and good. Her mother's home is good. It makes sense.

She is fed hot coffee, ham and eggs, toast and honey, and garlic stew and scallops, leftovers from the refrigerator. She is not ravenous. She eats and feels hunger but she does not feel the greed for food that she usually feels. She fills her stomach with *Mama's* food, latching on to it like a big tit in the sky. Her mother hugs her once in awhile as she eats, whenever it occurs to her again that her daughter is really there with her, not that her being there is all that much, but because it doesn't happen every day and may never happen again in just the same way. Her mother is a philosopher at heart and has her way of making a ceremony over occurrences.

After the food her mother says, "You are worn out," and opens the door to the ice cold guest room, to warm it for her.

She dozes and wakes, dozes and wakes. And each time she wakes it takes a moment to realize where she is. She is inside a dream of where she is in her life, and finding herself in the spare room of her mother's house comes to her as a disappointment, even though it is a haven away from where she has been. It is not where she wants to be. Between the flannel sheets in her mother's guest bed was never her goal, even though her warm feet, remembering the snow in tennis shoes, rejoice. As she drifts into sleep again, she is a hairy beast lying against the ground and opening its mouth to let the spirit crawl out. The breathing of the animal, as the spirit goes out and looks here and there, leaving the animal form panting against the ground, is her breathing. It comes slower and slower. She is a very heavy beast that cannot move its head from the ground.

# The Ruin

One part of her not wanting to wake up and begin thinking about it again. To start knowing about the ruins. In sleep she is away from knowing. Drifting effortlessly into and out of situations. Everything happening easily in dreams. And the easiness ending with morning. With waking the automatic safety ends. She is awake for a long time before opening her eyes. Awake inside the darkness, remembering where she is. In an old house. Upstairs. In one small room with a walk-in closet and bathroom. It is a house she has been in before but under different circumstances five years ago. At that time she came as a guest to hear a candidate for U.S. Senate speak. What was his name? His wife looked like a man. They had the same coloring, pale faces and black and white in their dark matching clothing and haircuts. She thought then that the house was a elegant place. Early, rich Santa Barbara. Owned by a doctor and his wife. Both prominent people in a middle-class way. He was a doctor of psychology. She was a tall, dark, and handsome woman, really the man of the two. She remembers the man's alligator smile. A fair-skinned, fair-haired, blue-eyed man with a smile that said, "I'd like to eat you," to all the ladies. She had blushed and looked away that day when he smiled at her. She was intimidated by him, by the handsome wife, by the other well-dressed guests, and by the politician. She had never been to a campaign party before and her assumptions of its importance overwhelmed her. She kept being afraid, "that if they all knew how much I don't know about issues, I would be humiliated. And how little I know about anything. History, politics, even geography." She sipped a glass of beer that had been hand-pumped cleverly from some strange bagpipe-looking container. And sat next to Alex and looked askance all afternoon.

Now she was lying on a bare mattress in a room above

that patio garden. In a small rented room. The patio below was a ruin. Avocados rotting where they fell. Dead leaves covering what was left of the lawn and debris stored along the fence. The doctor and his wife were divorced. His wife rented out the rooms of the house. The place was shabby. And it smelled bad. It smelled dead.

She opened her eyes and saw that the sun was coming through the windows already. It had to be about nine. She hadn't slept that late for some time. All week she was up at seven waiting for the phone to ring to get her assignment to work. All week she jumped from school to school, teaching in place of absent teachers. This morning, before getting out of bed, she ran her hand over her hip bone and stomach to test how skinny she was now. The bones stood up sharp, jutting beyond her stomach. It was a curiosity. Her body. It had been about a week since she had eaten any real food. She had been living on coffee and cookies from the teachers' lounges. She thought of her stomach as someone she knew. Who would understand. Like a companion. She respected it as an equal.

She got up, brushed her teeth, splashed water in her face and stood staring out the bathroom window at a swimming pool below. A rotting lath and wire fence leaned around the pool. The grass was dry or worn away. Weeds grew everywhere. Pieces of wood lay off in one corner of the yard and had turned the color of soil. Grey. She remembered the doctor's sinister smile. He had been proud of his pool. Groups of people came and took off their clothes and jumped in. They had had wild parties after awhile. And then he wanted to keep one little girl around, in the bedroom with him and his wife. The wife objected. Five years later, she stood viewing how their plans had gone awry. And how hers had, too. The pool alone had withstood the passing of time, sitting sparkling, almost brand new in its freshness, in the middle of the ruin.

She had slept in her clothes on the bare combustion-resistant mattress in one corner of the room. She felt like a liar standing there looking at the pool. She felt as if it didn't have to be true what was happening to her. What had happened to them. That maybe she and they were all playing around.

Playing with ruin. With bare mattresses and old musty rooms, and visions of sad swimming pools. That she could call Alex and beg to come back. That the doctor's wife could call the doctor and start over again and this time make it work. Call off all the foolishness, all the breaking things up to a halt. That she could once again be that lady who went to the campaign party instead of a tenant, and the wife could be that tall elegant lady of the house, instead of a landlady.

To remind herself she could not go back she let her mind toy with the memory of it again. Her mind liked to go back to that particular episode and run through it again and again. It seemed a significant point in its existence, but she could not grasp the significance: She was being *choked*. She blacked out. Struggling. Then she was gone. And then she was there again. He was over her. His face was puffy and he was frothing with hate. He was making loud talk at her. He was mad about something, but she was far away. Surprised, confused, wondering what she was doing with him spewing in her face.

Vaguely remember that they had been having an argument. That he had said, "You don't know what that does to a man... when you do something like that." She smirked. That was the last thing she remembers doing, before he had her by the neck. She let him choke her at first because she didn't care. She knew it would do no good to fight. And then she couldn't breathe and she began to struggle. Then she was gone... When she came back she looked at the television screen, and was surprised that it was off. She had just been hearing loud master of ceremonies and seeing the bright lights of a prize show flash as it was just going off the air. Her throat was dry. She swallowed over and over, while he held her by the hair, keeping her face turned up to his. He was on the floor on his knees and she was hanging off the edge of the bed. Her neck was bent backward against the bed. He kept yelling about all the women in her family. Her grandmother, her mother, her sister, and her. She could feel the roots of her hair giving under the pressure of his hand. But, strangely, it was not her anymore who was there, whose neck he had been squeezing, or hair he was pulling. Or whose face he was shouting in. She closed her eyes and drifted with the confusion, until his fingers pressed her eyelids open with impatience. She felt herself ready to black out again. In a small voice she didn't recognize as her own she told him she was fainting.

He said, "Tell me you are going to be the way I want for once in all these years."

Her distant small voice said, "I will." And this time she knew that part of her was present to him again, because she felt cowardice move inside her. He shoved her head toward the floor with disgust.

She heard him sneer, "Yeah, of course you will." She lay there, afraid now. He had stopped yelling and was speaking as if to the world. A kind of stage rhetoric.

"The tragedy of the way you are has destroyed me. It does make me desire you to think of you taking pleasure with another man. God help me. It's perverted I know. This is what my life has come to... And I wanted it to be greater than this. All my energy has gone into this kind of thing. I can't take it anymore...."

She heard his voice crack. But tears stung her eyes. And then he was angry again.

"Your subconscious better get smart, girl. It better take over and save you. Let's see if it can act to survive."

She got up and took off her clothes.